The
Lazy
Boys

The Lazy Boys

a novel

Carl Shuker

Shoemaker & Hoard

To

Kathy Anderson

1976–1996

and

Liz Arrillaga

1974–2002

with love

Library of Congress Cataloging-in-Publication Data

Shuker, R. Carl, 1974–
The lazy boys : a novel / by R. Carl Shuker.
p. cm.
ISBN-13: 978-1-59376-123-3
ISBN-10: 1-59376-123-6
1. College students—New Zealand—Fiction. 2. Youth—New Zealand—Fiction.
3. Apathy—Fiction. 4. Nihilism—Fiction. I. Title.

PR9639.4.S56L39 2006
823'.92—dc22

2006012040

Book design and composition by Mark McGarry,
Texas Type & Book Works, Inc.
Set in Monotype Dante with Gangly display

Printed in the United States of America

Shoemaker & Hoard
An Imprint of Avalon Publishing Group, Inc.
1400 65th Street, Suite 250
Emeryville, CA 94608
Distributed by Publishers Group West

AVALON
publishing group incorporated

10 9 8 7 6 5 4 3 2 1

Well sit right down my wicked son and let me tell you a story
About the boy who fell from glory and how he was a wicked son.

—The Pixies, "The Holiday Song"

. . . down they fell
Driv'n headlong from the pitch of Heaven, down
into this deep.

—Milton, *Paradise Lost*

What's my name.

—The Clash

The
Lazy
Boys

It's a beautiful and shining autumn day in Christchurch today, Richey, and I am sorry to be the one to tell you that Anna Patton suicided the day before last at her home in Ilam. It has come as a terrible shock to her family and to Bronny and us. Her cancer had come back and grew up through her just like an old blackberry. The funeral is scheduled for April 9, at Riccarton House in Deans Bush, at 9 A.M.

Yours sincerely,

Man, it was fucking funny ay? Well first me and the boys, Easty and Tin, were getting into a few of the homebrews in my room and it was just disgusting man, all murky and syrupy and shit but we were still getting it down us, and then you know Henry, big guy from Salmond, he was the head boy at our high school, and he'd told Nick about this Salmond Hall party they'd organized down in the Polytech ballroom and so we decided we weren't exactly crashing it cos Henry had basically invited us and he's got a bit of pull round Salmond so I've heard, and so we decided to cruise down and have a wee look, scope out a few moisties, you know, see if we can score some free piss, and so we walk down there, it's just down the road from Unicol and we take a couple of riggers of the homebrew just in case we don't get in or it's B.Y.O. or whatever and there's this fucking great big queue, like about a hundred people all down the road, but since we had some piss we decided we may as well wait and just drink in the queue, and we gave away a few drinks to some chicks Tinny knew, yeah I know, like poor unsuspecting souls, and they like spat it out it was so disgusting, one of them said it tasted like it had ash in it but it's not that bad and so we had to wait about half an hour in this queue but none of us even noticed, we must have been fucking out of it even then, the homebrew's about 10 percent or something, we're thinking of getting it tested, but we finally like after like about half an hour waiting in this queue and

Tinny's doing some serious spadework on this Salmond chick and Easty set fire to his own hair, it was fucking funny man, with a lighter, awesome, but we finally get to the front of the queue and Henry's on the door, and he's a fucking big bastard and he's wearing this like he's cut a fucking soccer ball in half and painted it pink and got it on his head and he's got on this pink dressing gown and these great big furry slippers, like animal ones you know, fucking Wile E. Coyote or something, and they're the balls and he's like trying to look like a dick and it's like okay mate so it turns out it's actually a theme party, and the theme is P and he's going as a penis and Tinny just gives him this look, it was so fucking funny man, I wish I could do it for you, just like this contemptuous look, and but anyway it turns out that everyone in the queue is like dressed up in something to do with the letter P and we were so fucking wasted we didn't even notice and but he lets us in sweet as and he tells us Mark's sneaked in the Mother of All Bongs but he calls it the MOAB and he calls it a funnel and they're doing bongs in the toilets and there's fucking kegs galore, millions of people, heaps of chicks, and we like stagger in and find Mark in the toilets and you had to do an entrance bong of a jug to get into his toilet and it was easy after the homebrew normal beer's just like water and so we've got this toilet all to ourselves and we just keep doing bongs, like after the first one we're only doing half-jugs but it was still pretty full on though, and there's like piss all over the floor, piss on the walls, piss all over us and the floor's slippery as and this big like piss and water fight ends up starting cos I slip over on the floor right, my foot just slipped out from under me, I was really pissed too, as well as the floor being real slippery, and anyway I slipped over and like smacked my back on the step of the urinal, didn't even feel it at the time but I've got this fucking massive bruise there now, yeah and what happened was I stuck my hand out to catch myself and it just like slid down that like stainless steel backing bit of the urinal and I just kept falling and smacked my back and my hand just like slid down into this fucking gross blocked up urinal, all people's piss and those soaps and beer and cigarette butts and ash and shit, fucking gross, and everyone's just like cracking up and going pox, pox, you've got the disease now and so I got up and I was washing my hand and all up my arm and stuff and then this like little water fight starts, I flick some water at someone, you know how it goes, and then Tinny just upends this jug over Easty who just stands there man, it was a full jug, and Easty just stands there with this look, it was classic, and this full on beer fight starts up and everyone's into it and we're just fucking soaked and no one even comes in and there's like an inch of beer all over the floor, there's just liquid everywhere man, the sinks and the toilets overflowing and everyone's slipping over and rolling around in it and kicking beer and water at everyone else and yeah.

Yeah, it was real good. And then we did some more bongs after that and went out to the ballroom all soaking wet, everyone laughing at us and stuff, but no one really cared, it was all just good fun. And then you know things got a bit hazy, can't remember much after that but I was just talking to this chick, this blonde chick, I think she was from Salmond, and she was wearing these like pink satin pajamas, summer ones, like shorty legs and arms and stuff. And she was a real babe. And I must have said something or done something, I don't know, but she freaked out for some reason and I got kicked out. Fucking bitch. No shame though.

Some spinny shit though. And it was just pissing down outside but I was so soaked already it didn't even make any difference so I just went home after that.

"No shame." This is a phrase we have used since around fifth form. We use it in circumstances where shame could really be an option: puking, fucking up a bong, scoring an ugly chick, firetrucking, whatever. Shame, or at least embarrassment. It is a fending action. It says, my actions are typical. It says, any offence you feel at my actions is a function of your own naivety; this is how things are done. It says, this is what is reasonable; this is what is acceptable.

I hope I say it with conviction.

You see, it wasn't really like that. That is how my story will be told, that's how they are always told, and that's how I will tell it. But that story is not real. It does not include my real memories. Memories that are fuzzy and unconnected, just random images that I try and fail to connect, to make a flow, some kind of chronological representation of last night. I am lying here in my bed in my room in Unicol, my hall of residence here in Dunedin, awake and sick. My stereo is faintly playing "Fool's Gold" and must have been on all night. When I turn it off with the remote control the word "goodbye" floats across the LCD screen and disappears, leaving only the time: 6:45 A.M. in tiny glowing green letters that eerily illuminate the mess here in my room. I can see the broken glass lying in the corner and the smear of black-looking blood along the concrete wall. I can see my ripped Speight's "How To Be a Southern Man" poster above it. I can see my books, swept from the shelf and strewn across the floor, some of them swollen into a solid mass of paper pulp from soaking up beer. I can see my copy of *The Queen Is Dead* lying broken in half by the stereo. I can see the jersey I wore last night in a sodden heap near the foot of my bed. I can see my notebook lying beside me on this tiny bed. There is writing visible, writing I must have done last night, but it is an illegible scrawl, like I wrote it with the pen in my fist like a knife.

That is how my story will be told, I'm planning how I'm going to say it here in bed, but it omits certain images, images that I know have profound bearing on what is to come, on the trouble I am in, on what I have become and will become.

Images of my hands, reaching out. Of the bong looming above me. Of the sight of my face reflected in a window, my eyes drooping and bloodshot. Of faces against the black, turning to me, then quickly away. Of blood on my fingertips.

And of the girl, standing, scratching and pulling at her silky pink pajamas and crying, looking directly at me, her wet eyes wide and disbelieving. The black cloud like anesthetic that surrounded her and I, that filled the ballroom, retreating to admit the crowd of strangers whose eyes were full of accusation and anger, who were shouting over the music, which was so, so loud.

I staggered home in the rain, wet as a newborn, my waterlogged jersey slapping against my thighs.

From where I lie I can see a message still blue-tacked to my noticeboard. It reads:

Richard, a girl called Anna rang from Christchurch and needs to get hold of you "urgently"— Have a good night?!! You're a maniac!!

Beside it is an old Sylvia Plath poem that I found and rewrote about me and other boys I know.

> *Into the ash*
> *We fall with our dirty hair*
> *And we eat girls for air.*

I lie here and make plans. I will leave today, this Sunday morning, and take a bus home to my parents in Timaru. If I come back I will leave Unicol and move in with Matt and Nick at Strangeways, their flat on Dundas Street, trapped in the shadow of the old castle. I will get a fifty dollar bag to take home from the gear Nick got from the Caversham drug house before I go.

My name is Richard John Sauer. My nickname here, as it was at school, is Souse. I am eighteen years old. It is April, my first year out of high school.

The things I see coming to pass this year, from what I did to that girl to what I know I will end up doing to other girls—like your daughters, your friends, your sisters, even mothers maybe—have a logic now, that extends directly from my experience, this country, my life. I am going home now to escape the fallout from a drunken rage. I can't stay home forever, and it would make no difference if I did. And when I say "I," it doesn't matter, believe me, because there are many others like me.

So the fall begins.

1

Home
James

There's no one home. My parents' cars are both gone, the street and the garage are empty, and apart from the far-off echoes of church bells ringing Timaru is silent and gray, a smell like watery tinned salmon drifting up from the harbor, 6 P.M. on this Sunday night. I can hear my dog, Snoopy, barking down the bottom of the backyard. I let myself in the back door with the hidden key and enter the house through the laundry. The house smells of dishwashing liquid and new carpet, and standing here on the lino I suddenly realize what's going to go on once Mum and Dad get home. I realize that my clothes are dirty and I reek of cigarettes and alcohol, and that, in spite of my unexplained arrival home just under a month into the university term with plans to leave Unicol and move in to Nick and Matt's flat Strangeways when I return, and in spite of the long thin cuts and the cigarette burns on my left forearm, and in spite of the thing that happened with that girl, I will soon take my familiar place at the kitchen table, silent and sullen—you know, the disappointing son, the under-achiever—and my parents' first reaction to my arrival after one terse phone call at 8 A.M. this morning will probably just be something along the lines of, "Oh Richey, why are you smoking?"

And my reaction will have to be, of course, sullen silence.

It will be bad here, I know, but it's got to be better than walking around varsity tomorrow not knowing who saw what happened, not knowing what people's reactions are going to be, sober, in daylight. It was the same at high school. After bad Saturday nights when I got drunk and either pissed in someone's house or grabbed some ugly chick or whatever I would avoid the boys at the public areas at school during interval and lunchtime, go to the library or Matt's house and basically hide. There were exceptions of course. The First XV aftermatch that Matt and I found out about through Nick who, though you'd never think it to look at his dreads, actually played First XV rugby a few times, this aftermatch that we arrived at so pissed and with drugs and which was actually really quiet and the girls were all bored and the First XV guys were all drinking quiets in the garage, staunch-ly silent, soon became full-on because we put on this old record, "Pretty Flamingo," and Matt and I were so stoned and drunk and we were dancing and doing shotguns in this beige suburban lounge and the girls got into it because of the dancing and so then I vomited on this couch and it all basically turned to shit and noise control came, things got broken and Matt and I left late and all this time Nick had been drinking with Sebastian and the rugbyheads in the garage in staunch silent mode.

And on the Monday morning there were whispers and snide asides through the first couple of periods, but then when I walked out into the quad at interval there was actual applause from almost everyone, apart from Sebastian and Nick who just sort of smirked, and the hostel boys of course, and everyone either thought it was like "classic" or thought I was trying too hard. But I got some respect out of that, and other similar stuff as the year wound down and the drinking got more intense. And when you're someone like me, even though I drink primarily because I like it, and when you're in a school like that and you're no good at rugby or pretty much any sport at all, you take respect where you can get it. But I suppose people have limits to what they are impressed by, and I think I crossed a few limits last night at that "P" party. But if you want extremes, it seems like I'm the guy who'll give you extremes.

And no shame.

So I'm hiding, essentially. I will admit that. But that's not to say that this is easy. From where I'm standing here in the laundry I can see that the hallways have been recarpeted in pale peach, perfect for clumsy dirty shoes like mine. It's all just a lot less stressful to go back outside and down to visit Snoopy.

And as I walk down the path toward the lawn, past the crabapple tree, I remake the vow I made at the end of exams last year. I say it again in my head, testing its power now, after all that has happened since school. And it seems okay, it seems like an achievable goal and it does in fact make me feel kind of cool, walking down toward the dog: a boy with a secret, a hidden power and controlled urges, walking and chanting to himself.

I will not hurt the dog

I will not hurt the dog

But as soon as he starts barking his high-pitched bark along with the coughs and wheezes as he tries to pull against the leash and collar tying him to his kennel I feel a quick sudden wave of anger, sharp and uncontrollable, and I remember the beatings, the rage all comes back so quickly and I remember the drunken weekends when my parents were away, weekends I haven't thought of in months, once my friends all had gone, like 4 A.M., and I would be drunk and angry, or drunk and sad, which sadness can turn to anger at just, say, for a random example, the high-pitched bark of a dog, and I would walk unsteadily down here and

I will not hurt the dog

I will not hurt the dog

Snoopy is a Sydney Silky Terrier cross. He is small and the color of beer. We have had him since my sister basically rescued him from some students she knew in Christchurch who had taught him to chew the taps off wine casks and suck the wine out and to chase his tail. I call his name and he jumps and wrenches at his leash, choking himself, wheezing, his barks turned to coughs, but I don't let him off because he'll instantly leave, gone to find a tennis ball for me to throw and I can't be bothered with that shit right now. So I sit down next to him and he jumps up at me, dirty paws all over my dirty shirt, and breathes foul dog breath up at me as he tries to lick my face and I am gentle with him and I pat him and after a while he relaxes and settles in my lap and just looks up at me as I pat him, and his long pink tongue dangles out the side of his mouth so comically I almost laugh out loud.

—

But there is nothing to do in Timaru.

I am sitting at the dining room table, looking at the pictures of a National Geographic retrospective of Khmer Rouge atrocities in Kampuchea from 1975 to 1979. I've showered, smoked a cigarette (in the shower, exhaling out the steam extractor fan so my parents don't smell the smoke), and reclothed myself in clothes I left behind just a month ago and which are now boxed and bagged with the rest of my stuff in the wardrobe of the room that used to be mine but is now some kind of "guest" room although it's us, me and my sister and occasionally our friends, who are the most likely to come and stay here, but I suppose we don't warrant a *home* anymore since we've moved out into our own *homes*, and but anyway, I have tried to watch TV but on Channel Two there was a Country Calendar rerun with music so familiar it almost gave me a panic attack and on Channel Three there was a current affairs program on liposuction with some really graphic footage of initial incisions that caught my attention but soon turned into an article on superannuation cuts, and on One there was Mobil Showcase, on which was "The Best of a New Generation" and which included a young saxophonist in a button-down shirt playing Mark Knopfler's "Going Home," a dire Maori funk band like Ardijah but called "Concrete Jungle" who also had a saxophonist, a guy in a shirt and string tie playing a lap-steel, and the final straw, at the sight of which I had the TV off within literally seconds, a four-piece called "Sightz and Sounz" with a guitarist, a keyboard player with a strap-on keyboard, and a male and a female singer who were doing synchronized dance steps to a cover of "Funky Town."

And so I rifled through the video cabinet with the TV turned off and after finding nothing but my sister's tapes of "Home and Away" and my father's rally and rugby tapes and my mother's recorded Montana Masterpiece Theatres and because all my music videos are in Dunedin and have been watched so many times I know where to find any video on any tape instinctively anyway, just timing the rewind, I gave up and checked out the bookshelf. There I found mostly *Reader's Digests*, *Wheels* magazines, *Overlander* magazines, *Popular Mechanics* magazines, sewing patterns, my father's old record collection, which I flicked through and saw the name "Herb Alpert and his Tijuana Brass" seven times and "Mantovani" nine times, and a small collection of novels with exactly the same yellowed paper and cheesy covers as the five for 50c stack at secondhand bookstores, and which only had books like Enid Blyton's *Nature Lover's Book*, Jackie Collins' *Hollywood Wives* ("Now a Major Television Miniseries"), Alistair MacLean's *Force Ten from Navarone* ("The Major New Epic from the Author of *The Guns of Navarone*—Now a Major Motion Picture"), Frederick Forsyth's *The Odessa File*, Sven Hassel and *Legion of the Damned*, et cetera, et cetera, until finally I found myself here, looking at pictures of tortures in a *National Geographic*, hunting, and hungry for something.

The magazine is worn; certain pages flop open more easily than others. Looking at the pictures in here calms me. I used to read this article again and again when I was younger, maybe fourteen or fifteen, just after I started high school. I can't remember why I read it then, what feelings it gave me, but now it calms me sitting here, makes me still, quiet and contemplative. Another secret thing for home. Another after what I did to that girl.

There are skulls wrapped with rotting blindfolds, Khmer

Rouge red. Underground chambers filled with skeletons. Torture rooms in a Phnom Penh jail with stains on the concrete. Walls papered in photographs of sad-looking Asian boys subsequently tortured and executed. In the photos the boys' arms seemed missing, like some horrific thing done to their arms, but only now do I realize that they are so tightly tied behind the boys' backs that they can't be seen. There are exhumed mass graves in the flanks of hills. Burned blackened bones sunk in the grass.

The gate clinks and I know one or both of my parents must be finally home and I jerk and I start to blush and I close the magazine and hide it back on the bookshelf like it's pornography and sit quietly, guiltily, at the dining table, waiting for them to come inside.

But they must know I'm home because they use the knocker on the front door rather than unlocking it themselves and so I get up and pad out of the living room into the hallway in socks and unlock the door and swing it wide open.

Mum and Dad both stand there smiling, kind of hovering at the top of the steps that lead up to the front door, behind them a wall of green ivy catching the last of the sun, and their smiles are not completely self-assured, my mother and my father.

"Gidday, mate," Dad says over the top of my mother's head. They are strange to me. They seem both younger and older. Dad's hair is whiter and the flesh on my mother's face seems looser, but their body language seems so casual and relaxed; Dad's got his weight on one foot and his hips cocked casually; his body forms the shape of a parenthesis behind and beyond Mum who stands, shoulders squared to me, her focus completely on me, with that almost smug air of certainty, of someone who knows their back is covered. They look nice though, like that, one in front and one behind, and maybe this is what they were like when they were young and together.

"Hi," I say flatly, with no emotion, and it's what I always say and it's what he always says and how we always say it and I feel the past and all our stale petty domestic traditions wash over us and envelop us again, another kind of certainty, and that brief moment when I saw them together is gone and they are apart again, they feel it too, the division into three, the injection of me, the dead third that sucks their energy, their youth, their money into himself giving nothing back and I turn kind of abruptly back into the living room and then say back over my shoulder, not knowing what to say, not wanting the old times to happen again now but knowing no other way, and cursing myself as I do and trying to remember what I felt like when I was looking at those pictures, that calmness, trying to remember what it felt like to be someone strong, I say, "I um got in about six and got a taxi from the bus station and I had a shower, I hope you don't mind, I didn't let the dog off . . ." and I trail off feeling sick and wasted and my mother is saying "Of course we don't mind, dear, sorry we weren't there to meet you but we decided to go to the late service, the morning one is just too long for us now . . ." as she follows me back into the living room and Dad shuts the front door, sealing us into this house, and a great dread washes over me, all I've learnt and all I've done dribbling down out the leg of my trousers before their implacable familiarity with their life, and I collapse into the leather armchair and know immediately that it's Dad's chair and that I should move but in a monologue that's also horribly familiar I'm thinking or saying to myself in some other's monotone fucking hell it's just a chair and one's as good as another and don't move even as Dad comes into the living room and you can tell he senses an invasion by the tiniest of pauses at the door, his awesomely familiar path stripped of its destination and I say to myself in another voice if I were a good son I would get up courteously and offer him the chair and offer to make tea for them both, take the cups gently from my mother's hands in the kitchen and "usher" her back into the living room and they could cluck away about how lovely it is to have me home and I could "clatter busily" in the kitchen and shout interesting news about how exciting life is at "the varsity" and how many interesting people I've met and how I've "met someone special" and it could be love and studies are going well and money's fine and but instead I wait till Mum walks back into the living room and comes between me and Dad, who is still hovering kind of uncertainly by the door, and I know my collapsed posture in my father's chair, though it feels assumed, appears smug and arrogant, and I choose this, the worst of all moments, to mutter:

"I'm leaving Unicol and I'm going to flat with Matt and Nick in Strangeways."

Silence. They halt, mid-living room. I stare at my stomach. Mum sits down in her armchair, looking at me.

"Oh Richard. Why?"

"Are you sure that's the best decision?" my father says, then, a pause, "Do you think you can sit in that other chair?"

I sigh heavily and get up, my movements exaggerated, and collapse in the "other chair," looking out the window.

"Oh Richey . . . do you think you could lean your head on the doily?" says my mother. "It's just that sometimes greasy marks get left on the furniture from people's hair. Sorry, dear. But we've worked so hard to get things nice, you know. Sorry, dear. Oh—" She gets up, walks into the kitchen. "We've got a letter here for you, from Anna is it? Yes." She comes back in, puts down on the arm of the chair a white envelope with a picture of some lavender in the top left corner. There's a pause. They're watching me. Something's wrong.

"I don't know . . . what a doily is," I mutter.

"Miriam," my father says, and sits in his armchair, extends the footrest with a lever. Then, "Why is it that you want to leave? Are you homesick?"

"I just hate it. I want to live with people I know."

"But those boys are into drugs, Richard," my mother says.

"No they're not."

Dad is staring into the middle distance thinking hard. Mum is leaning toward me. I stare out the window.

"Are you sure that that's what you want to do." It's said like a statement.

"Yup."

"Are you in some kind of trouble?" my father says, turned now, I can tell he's speaking at the back of my head and I feel myself blushing and I look harder out the window at flecks of paint on the glass that are so fucking familiar it makes me want to scream and then down at the letter and then I think in another voice oh how very prescient of you, I'm in trouble, I have done something to a girl and can't remember why or how it happened, I'm drinking larger and larger amounts that amaze even me, I stay in bed until midday almost every day with hang-overs (apart from today though), I sometimes feel like people can't see me or that I might be made of plastic, I cut myself with broken Gillette Sensor razorblades, my friends are strangers to me, I buy pornography from twenty-four-hour service stations when I'm drunk and masturbate until dawn or until my cock hurts too much to touch, and you can't save me or do anything about it and oh it's all trouble and how could I even begin to explain?

"What'd you have in mind?" I say, and laugh.

"You haven't got anyone pregnant have you?"

"No," I sigh. "No, Dad, no one's pregnant."

They're gone, upstairs, in bed. Which is a great relief. It's 11 P.M., and I've shifted Dad's chair into the center of the room, closer to the TV, and I'm splayed out in it, after two beers, with the footrest extended, watching, just barely, *A Nightmare on Elm Street 3*, with pages of Anna's letter lying on my chest. It's dated after our little New Year's fallout.

Hello Richey,

Well it's been nearly two months so I think we can probably talk to each other now?! I've forgiven you. I can't forget it, but I can forgive you. It's just that I think I'm too much of an idealist, and I expect things from life and from people that often just aren't there. Maybe other people are just being realistic and I'm living in this dream world but I don't know, I thought maybe you were a little bit like me. I guess everyone just has to do things their own way ("Your way" just happened to be particularly awful for me, not to mention embarrassing—most of Girls' High knows what happened, you're a tiny bit famous).

Kim and I are kind of still friends, but she's into that whole Girls' High scene—who went to whose party, who scored who, who's wearing what, who got picked up by who and driven where, blah blah blah—and she's leaving school soon to go to England so that's another friendship biting the dust it seems. Did she ever ring or write to you after New Year's? I assume she didn't. We have never spoken about what happened, it's just like one of those things that end up existing between two people, like when you've both read the same book—it's always there but you never talk about it apart from by accident. Then you both know suddenly, and one of you might wink, or laugh, or just sort of smile helplessly, and really it makes me sick. But that's what school's like in general: codes and secrets and manipulation, all these power games and so often it's all about people like you, aren't you flattered? So often it's all about guys, and mostly the only reason is just because of the mere fact that you're guys (I'm just thinking that sounds a bit horrible—you're different of course aren't you?).

I remember third form and how we had this group then; me, Kim, Julia, Mel, Bronny, Celia, that's all but disappeared now. And they always used to say that I was the glue that keeps them all together. So it looks like now I'm not doing my job right? And anyway, although that's kind of flattering, no one ever wonders about the fate of the person who's the glue do they? Everyone's so busy worrying about themselves and their own shit and crying on the glue's shoulder that they never wonder if that person is going to be okay. I mean, what happens if the glue dissolves? Just the usual I guess. People put their failed hopes on to someone who hasn't given up because they haven't got the guts to believe in anything themselves, and then if that person falls apart they just say, oh, I was right all the time, lucky I didn't try, I was right to just cruise. I don't know, this makes me angry I guess, because I do actually believe it's important to believe in something, and sometimes I think that just the appearance of believing in something will get you further. I think that it's very important to <u>feel</u> things.

Okay, enough. Well, I'm not very well again. I'm off to my doctor for an X-ray in a couple of weeks. Did I tell you I'm going to Australia for the summer holidays after sixth form's finished? I'll be staying with my cousins and then traveling around in all the hot, hot weather, doing some wine trails and we're going to some raves in Sydney and I just cannot wait to get out of here. But I've still got this year of goddam internal assessment to go first. Aargh, as they say.

Well, I hope we can be friends again. I mean, honestly, it won't ever be the same again after what happened—she's the third friend of mine you've ended up trying to get with—but I'm sure we can still be some kind of friends.

Please write and tell me some things you believe in, Richey, and what you think happens to people who are glue. Do people just drift away from them when they lose their strength? Do people get disappointed with them, or bored? Are people that lazy?

Please, I'd like to know. Good luck for your first year in the big bad world.

Love, Anna

I lie here, remembering hard, the artificial leather creaking and cracking when I move. The TV murmurs quietly. My parents' room is directly above the living room so the volume has to remain low.

Tonight's argument was bad, even for us. They tried to convince me to abandon university and get a job. They spoke to me of "the inheritance of student loan" I was generating for myself. They sat there in this house and their own personal chairs and told me I was "getting older."

"Employers aren't interested in me now, Richey, because I'm too old. That was why I was made redundant. That's why I'm working in a bloody garage now. You don't think I like it do you? The older you get, the less value you have. You don't want to end up a bloody professional student do you?"

"It's only . . . first year."

"I know that, but it's an important year. It's important that you make the right decisions now, for your future."

"We're not trying to pressure you, Richey. We don't want to pressure you into doing anything you don't want to do. We're just worried about you. We love you, you know that. We just want you to be alright. It's lovely to have you home, but we're worried that you're missing lectures and that sort of thing. Are you missing your lectures?"

". . ."

"Answer your mother."

"Some of them."

"Well can you catch up on the ones you miss? Can you get the notes from your friends?"

"Um, yeah?"

"You don't seem too enthused about any of it. Have you thought that maybe varsity isn't for you? You know your father's got the boy Abernethy working for him now, doing his apprenticeship. He's making eight dollars fifty an hour isn't he, Ian? He's just your age."

"He's the boy whose brother committed suicide last year."

"*Ian.*"

"What, Miriam?"

"You didn't know him did you, Richey? The brother?"

"He was a couple of years ahead of me at school."

"Oh those poor, poor parents. I think that's just about the most selfish thing you can do. They raised him from when he was just a tiny baby and then he goes and does something like that to himself. It's . . . I think it's just . . ."

"It's laziness, and weakness."

"He was smoking drugs they say. You know marijuana lowers the self-esteem chemical in the brain, don't you, Richey?"

"Serotonin it's called."

"Oh come *on.*"

They get angry when I laugh at them. Dad leaning forward. Mum sighing. Dad is the only person I've ever known who actually shakes his fist at things. Dad always gets angry, Mum gets sad and defeated-looking.

"It's true. That's what you don't know. They've researched it."

"She's right, son. You can laugh all you like. We know Nick and Matt smoke weed. Is that what you want? To sit around and smoke pot with your mates till you're just another one of the losers? I can't understand that Nick." Much head-shaking. "He's bright, he's good at sport, and he does his music. But he's into the drugs, and that'll be his downfall."

"Are you still doing something with your music, Richey? There's an Irish band at your father's pub who make some money."

"If you're interested in music why don't you try and make some music that people like? There could be money in that. The thing is that the government aren't going to care if you're making music or not when it comes to handing out money. All they care about is if you're working, if you're paying your taxes."

"What do you care about?"

"What do you mean?"

"Do you *care* if we're 'making music'?"

"Of course we do. All I'm saying is that to have artistic ambitions is all very well, but the fact you've got to face is that if you're not one of the few percent who're either very good, or make something that people are prepared to pay money to see, then it's a dead end."

"It doesn't matter anyway."

"What doesn't?"

"Either way."

"What do you mean? Which way?"

"It just doesn't. Don't worry."

"We're not worried . . . we *are* . . . about *you*, that's not . . ."

". . ."

"How is varsity going then?"

"We . . . haven't done much yet."

"You're getting very thin, Richey."

"That is . . . right."

". . ."

"Are you going to pass this year do you think?"

"How could I possibly know. It's April."

"Well are you going to your lectures?"

"Some of them."

"You having a bloody holiday down there then? If you don't do any bloody schoolwork how are you spending your days?"

"In a . . . daze?"

"Don't get smart with me, boy. I'll bloody thrash you."

"No shame."

"What does that mean?"

"It means there's no shame if you want to thrash me. Go for it. I'll take you to the family court."

"You won't be able to move, son. I'll put you in the bloody hospital."

"Richey."

"While you're under the roof that I paid for you'll obey my rules."

"Richey."

"'Under my roof obey my rules.' Jesus."

"By Christ, you try getting smart to an employer like that and you'll soon find out where it gets you. Smart alec."

"Richey, you're not still hurting yourself are you? You're not still cutting yourself?"

"Oh for *god's* sake, you're *not*."

"Oh *Richey*. Why?"

"Why are you *cutting* yourself? What the hell's wrong with you?"

". . ."

"You'll regret that later in life, you mark my words. What do you think you're going to say when you roll up your sleeves at work and your workmates ask you what that business is all over your arms?"

And then a bad moment when Dad got up and came over to my seat at the window and tried to pull my sleeves up to ascertain what new business I had, and when I hunched in my chair and held my sleeves down and folded my arms and wriggled away like a little kid, hating him, hating him, and whispered *fuck you* he hit me a few times near the temple with a loosely closed fist and Mum said, "Ian, leave him alone," and they began to argue with each other properly, Mum in her chair, her knitting abandoned in her lap, sitting forward and Dad standing in the middle of the living room, angry, animated, turning to her, away from me, and at last I entered blissful third person status.

"He's got some hard bloody lessons to learn. What kind of man's he going to be sitting on his arse smoking dope and drinking beer with those losers and picking holes in his arms?"

"Ian."

"He's turning into a gutless wonder, like all the other useless young buggers in this town. He's got to learn to harden up. He needs a bloody job, he needs . . ."

"*Ian.*"

"What kind of life's he going to have scratching at himself and drinking piss all the time? At his age I'd already been working for three years. My father'd been an orphan since he was *twelve*. He had a job at the freezing works when he was fifteen. I *loved* my father. I re*spect*ed him."

"Thing's are different, Ian. It's not easy to find jobs. It's harder for the young people growing up now."

"I know *exactly* how hard things are. The boy's. . . . If *you're* going to. . . . Alright. I'm going out to the garage. If anything changes, you come and let me know."

He went to the fridge and took out a beer. The fridge door clinked shut then the front door crashed shut, the knocker clattering, and then it was just me and Mum, like so many times before.

"You know he just gets angry when he doesn't understand, Richey."

My adrenaline was high. With him gone it was easier to be angry with him, and I suddenly realized this, and realized that this time I wasn't going to explain and confide in her like those other times; it wasn't going to be my mother—who gardens, who knits, who cooks, the one that always understood—and me, against him anymore; I realized that talking wouldn't change anything even if it made me feel a little better in the short term, and that she's really just as much an enemy as him. She may have understood me, we may have been close in the past, a month ago, but now things are different, now I've done something she cannot forgive, and I remembered this morning and I remembered the girl and I thought of Anna and I felt something that felt like strength and I wouldn't drop my defenses for her. So I got up, said something like "Silence is the New Zealand male's best weapon," or, "Hating him is so predictable it bores me," or, "He is fat but strong and I am neither," but more probably, "I'm going upstairs," and went upstairs.

Families are for the weak.

—

And so here I am, three hours or so later, lying in his chair watching *Elm St.*, only returned to the living room after Mum knocked on my door and told me they were off to bed and actually were leaving in the morning for Christchurch to visit my sister who's doing Profs for Law at Canterbury and to help myself to anything and to look after myself and that they would see me on Friday. And the scene where the mute boy's fantasy about the nurse comes true in his dream and she takes off her uniform and she's blonde and has big porno-type breasts comes on and Anna's letter falls to the floor as I unzip my jeans and take out my dick and I'm hard instantly and I masturbate there watching the scene which soon turns ridiculous, the nurse's tongue shooting out of her mouth and tying the boy's hands and feet to the bed posts and he's spread-eagled, mute, trying to scream, and the bed drops away beneath him and becomes a fiery pit, a portal to hell or whatever, and with my left hand on the remote, still wanking with my right, sinking lower in the chair, I turn the sound off, and gradually turn down the color first, then the contrast, then the brightness until the screen turns from orange to gray to dead black and I wank and think of the girl at the party in the pink silk pajamas who had blonde hair also and I'm fucking her and she's surprised and a little frightened and looking up at me scared but compliant and just before I come I'm reaching down into her face which becomes a black cloud framed by her blonde hair as I claw in the place where her face was, grasping, finding nothing, my hands disappearing in this black oily gas, fucking her roughly, her legs spread so wide it must almost be impossible until I come and come and come and the picture disappears and the white gloop spurts out and floods all over my hand and dribbles down my fist and between my legs and onto the black leather of my father's chair and I lie there sweating, alone, but this time I don't feel guilty or dirty at all.

But four days alone.

The details are sketchy now because I drank and smoked through most of each day. I had the fifty dollar bag that I got on tick from Nick at Strangeways on Sunday morning, on my way to the bus to come home. I had been pale and shaky, he'd been half asleep and pissed off. He hadn't said anything about the party and I hadn't let on that I felt like anything unusual had happened.

Monday started with Mum and Dad leaving, Dad telling me to up and atom, Mum saying let him sleep in. We'll be back on Friday, Mum tells me. Look after yourself and help yourself to the cupboards. And mow the lawns, Dad says.

Bought alcohol from up the road, didn't get asked for ID. Drank during the day, alone, not playing with the dog. Listened to the only tape I brought back with me, a compilation tape of songs I listened to at school. Nirvana, The Smiths, Stone Roses, The Pixies. Bands I had got into through my sister's boyfriends, years after the albums had originally appeared. The Smiths had split up before I'd ever even heard of them. Rolled up the drugs. Smoked lots of cigarettes.

Each day drinking beer and wine then drugs later on at night. I can't drink any more after I've smoked and also if I am drunk and then get stoned I'm more likely to just fall asleep rather than end up eating if the munchies hit. Didn't eat much, mostly just toast and a Lucozade for breakfast each day, which was good.

Tuesday night, I think, I biked to the Maori Hill twenty-four-hour service station and rented three pornos. I got drunk first. I got one that looked high-budget, one for anal stuff, and one for lesbians. Very stressful hiring them out. Ironically, a Maori guy behind the counter. This was about one in the morning, no one around, and I studied him carefully, trying to assess what he thought of me. I dropped off some sly comment like "I drew the short straw," which I thought cleverly implied that (a) I was part of a group that was going to watch these, and (b) the group was a fun-loving drunken group of rugbyhead types that got drunk on Tuesday nights and drew straws to decide who'd have to rent out the porn that we like to sit around and laugh at, innocently, just a good laugh and a few beers, and (c) cleverly implied that I wasn't a solitary fuckup, a lone gunman; not an eighteen-year-old dirty old man wanking frantically into the dawn because the only good feeling he gets these days is the tiny few seconds when he comes, which tiny few seconds gets tinier and tinier and more and more difficult to arrive at after he's come in his hand four or five times over a long night and his cock has little red patches of raw skin on it and nothing even comes out when he orgasms, not a boy who finally looks down at his jerking fist in the flickering light from the TV and sees that the red patches that stung a little have expanded into open wounds that are bleeding freely and sees that he's now wanking his semi-hard dick with lubrication provided by his own blood and yet still doesn't stop, fast-forwarding the cheapest of the videos to the dirtiest and hardest-core scenes just so he can come just once more, so he can disappear just once more; not a boy who finally limps up to bed, his right hand blood-stained, his jeans undone and his raw red and shriveled dick hanging limply out because it hurts too much to put away; not a boy who lies naked on his bed, as the room begins to lighten and the birds begin to chirp, cursing his body and cursing the dawn and praying for sleep.

I hung rather a lot on those words.

And so each day was fairly similar. It was difficult without them here, knowing their rituals but fighting them as if they were still here, as if it meant anything. Getting up at eleven, twelve. Not opening all the living room curtains in the morning. Smoking half a joint and drinking a glass of cask wine for breakfast. Not turning on the National Radio news during breakfast. Avoiding TV altogether. Not putting the milk bottles out at 5:15. Eating toast, staying inside, out of their sun. Not feeding the dog. Listening to the tapes, memories of parties. Not doing the dishes after every "meal." Carrying my carcass from room to poisoned room. Feeling like I knew the girls in the pornos after I'd watched them so many times. Masturbating. Smoking while masturbating. Drinking while masturbating. Finishing masturbating.

Wanting to debase this house, do something real, burn it, destroy it.

I kept the videos hidden under my bed when I wasn't watching them in case they arrived home early, and was able to keep them late without phone calls from the service station because I'd signed the receipt with a name from a rhyme that had been recurring in my head since I'd got home, a rhyme that my mother had sung to me when I was little.

> *James, James*
> *Morrison, Morrison*
> *Weatherby George Dupree*
> *Took great care of his mother*
> *Although he was only three*

So, James Morrison, with a fake phone number and a fake address, which phone number I couldn't be sure belonged to anyone real or not, and if it was real was probably getting some confusing calls re some strangely titled videos, and maybe some suspicious words and veiled accusations were getting bandied about between the elderly residents of some suburban townhouse this week. Timaru has the second most elderly population of any town in the South Island, behind Ashburton, who beat us in suicides too.

The videos I watched each night, every night. I fast-forwarded to the parts when they fucked. I watched hairy guys rubbing their dicks up and down the girls' arses. I looked away and watched the light flickering on the bookshelf. I watched them fuck the girls in their arses. I watched them slap the girls' faces with their cocks. I listened to the moans of yeah, yeah, and scoffed. I watched a girl push a vibrator up her cunt and a vibrator up her arse and when it didn't slide in easily she looked uneasy and said in an unconvincing low and breathy voice, "ooh, it's so tight."

I watched a girl who looked sad and lost when she opened her eyes after she came, as if she'd imagined she was somewhere else.

I watched an intricately staged scene where after mutual oral sex two girls crouched facing each other on a sofa and kissed each other as they were fucked roughly from behind by two guys, one with a moustache and one without, and one of the girls looked up at the other girl about halfway through the fucking and rolled her eyes and obviously the editor of the film—probably out of it or just so bored by this point that he missed it—missed it, and the other girl smiled the same smile that checkout girls smile to each other when they have a difficult customer, and they kissed again like friends until the two guys came onto their backs and the two girls moaned and sighed and looked back at the come on their backs like it was just what they had always wanted, and I would have to look away every time the girl was about to roll her eyes, I would have to not watch, sitting there like their sad and stupid king who didn't know what to feel about any of it.

Each day blended into the next. Going to bed later and later, 6, 7 A.M. Waking up later and later, 11 A.M., 12, 1 P.M., kind of amazed and disgusted at what I'd done all the previous night and vowing not to do it again. But ten beers, some wine, a whole pack of cigarettes and some drugs later and I'd be back in what was literally, during those northwest sultry days, the hot seat: my father's black leather chair, pulled up in front of the TV, surrounded by beer cans, more and more familiar porn going through its motions on the screen, no longer able to shock, barely managing to arouse.

Late at night I would patrol the empty house, an aimless, blank-eyed, silent ghost, drinking white wine and wandering, checking every empty room and watching myself in the full-length mirrors.

On Friday, however, things changed.

Early Friday, two or three in the morning, finds me drunk down the bottom of the garden, sitting with Snoopy. Snoopy is sitting in my lap, leaning against my chest. The drunkest I've been since I got home. I have moved on from beer and now, this latter half of the week, I drink only cask wine and spirits from the liquor cabinet.

Snoopy tries to lick my face and I push the dog's muzzle away.

This is the first time I have sat with Snoopy since I've been home. I've been deliberately avoiding this, in case. But now I'm here I realize how much I've missed these times, just like last year when I would get home from those last increasingly frantic parties over the holidays as people would steadily disappear, into jobs, to Dunedin or Christchurch Teacher's Colleges and university, and those of us who didn't know what to do, or didn't believe that the things we were going to do would get us anywhere, who knew only that we had to get out of Timaru, kept having parties that got smaller but louder and more desperate-seeming, and we would get so drunk, all day, any day we could, and long into the night. Five A.M., 6 A.M., I would come home

and sit down here and talk and cry with Snoopy and he would literally lick tears off my cheeks. But so often I would get angry,
Snoopy would growl at me if I hugged him too hard or if I put
my face too close and it would all end horribly, with beatings and
slaps and kicks and Snoopy growling and yelping and cowering
at my feet until finally I made the vow to leave him alone, not to
hurt him again, and soon after I left for Dunedin and the high
times of Orientation.

Now I'm here again, after this long week, and now here's
Snoopy growling low and softly, deep in his chest as I lean too
hard against him, and as he growls he watches me warily, and his
eyes follow my hands.

   And now here's me standing up quickly, dumping Snoopy off
my lap, and Snoopy scrabbles on the concrete to keep his balance
and backs away from me. And I lean low over Snoopy, swaying a
little, and mutter something like *fuck you*, and Snoopy growls a little louder as I loom over him and I hit him on the back with a
wide stinging slap and everything seems to fall into a predeter-
mined pattern, a very familiar set of behaviors, because the dog
cowers flat to the ground at the first slap and at the second growls
a little and for the third and fourth and fifth slaps is silent but for
tiny whimpers and then as the slaps get harder Snoopy growls
and snaps a little, still cowering, still watching from the corner of
his eye, while I loom above him swaying, slapping, my eyes only
half-open and it takes upward of twenty blows to Snoopy's back
and legs and head before he finally turns on his master and bites
the hand that feeds him only intermittently, and this seems to be

my cue, my final excuse, to stand straight and mutter words and reach into my pocket and pull out the Bik cigarette lighter and lean down near the dog's hindquarters muttering and swaying and it seems, maybe, crying, and I flick the lighter's wheel, holding it by the cowering foamy-mouthed dog's hind leg, and the bright-orange bloom of flame illuminates the little scene briefly and then there is crackling and hissing and fizzing and a screaming yelping noise and finally a splash as I, hunched and looming, up-end the dog's water bowl over the dog and loom and sway and hunch away from the hunched, yelping, cowering dog and stagger back up to the house.

And I am caught and momentarily blinded and when the spots in my vision fade I am staring down at a harsh, lopsided, drooping-shouldered shadow cast by the movement-sensing light attached to the house, which has finally chosen this moment to come on.

And awake, this Friday morning, the morning my parents get home, my sixth day home, I'm lying on the floor in my room half-naked, wearing only a T-shirt.

I roll over and sit up very slowly. My body throbs and my head is full of buzzing. It is early. Everything is slow and gleaming. The curtains are not shut and the sun is streaming in. I close my eyes against the light. I am sweating and dizzy. I lean slowly against the cold metal of the bed and rest my head on the mattress. I squint at the bed and see that it has been stripped completely. I think I sleep again for a while like that: seated, and leaning.

When I am finally well enough to stand it's fairly clear I was so pissed that I firetrucked last night. I find the duvet and under-sheet and underblanket in a wet heap outside the door of my room and my pajama trousers stuffed in the bottom of the toilet. The strange logic to drunken cleanups.

In the razed calm of the hangover I put all the wet things in the washing machine, including the duvet, which may be a bad idea but my options seem fairly limited at this point. I inspect the mattress and there is an ambiguous stain in the middle, the size of a plate. It doesn't seem to smell of anything but wet fabric and so hopefully I had drunk so much by that point that all I pissed was basically water. What if they find out? If *Dad* finds out?

"Dad, I wet the bed."

I don't think so.

Can't do anything but invert the mattress and hope the smell doesn't like, *develop*.

And in the knowledge that my parents are coming home today I extend the cleanup to the rest of the house, collecting beer cans, wine casks, cigarette butts, roaches (which I salvage), and vacuuming and doing the dishes. As I wash the dishes I look out the kitchen window and down the garden. Poor Snoopy is silent today. Normally he can hear when someone is doing the dishes and he barks and watches the windows. He is out of sight, probably in his kennel. I leave the dishes half-finished and realize I haven't yet mown the lawns.

The stock of my father's rifle is dark and slightly oily. The gun is heavy; my left arm shakes a little, supporting it, as I aim it out the window of my parents' bedroom. It is a circa–World War II Lee-Enfield bolt-action rifle that my dead grandfather used in the war. My father keeps it wrapped in oily khaki cloth in his wardrobe with his shotguns and the .22. Ammunition for all the rifles is kept in the cupboard above the wardrobe, supposedly out of reach of children's hands. The rifle takes twenty bullets in its small magazine. Dad has a box of twenty lead-tipped .303 bullets in the top cupboard. The box is full and the gun has never been used in my living memory.

I often played with it when my parents went away for the weekend, always without their knowledge. I did what I'm doing now: load the magazine; insert it in the bottom of the rifle (clapped in hard like an actor); work the bolt up and back; look at the bullet that has risen into the breech, fat, bronze, and oily; push the bolt back in hard and lock it down, all in firm, familiar satisfying movements. Pan the rifle over the valley, taking aim at windows in the houses opposite; aim at people mowing lawns with a live bullet in the breech, safety off, finger sliding up and down on the trigger. Tracing cars coming down the hill; aiming at the front right-hand tire, then the left-hand tire, then the shape of the driver in the windscreen as it appears between flashes of the sun.

Set up the rifle between your legs, stock on the dark brown carpet. The hard steel muzzle clicks against your teeth, oiled coldness rimming the tip of your tongue as you lean uncomfortably down, trying not to turn your head too much, to reach the trigger with your thumb.

Just experimenting.

Then reversing that position, put the barrel of the gun to the floor, wipe the sweat off your fingers—you must be very sure—hold the bolt hard as you can and gently pull the trigger and take the pressure of the bolt—which is always shockingly strong—and gently, very slowly, let it slide inside the gun, where the hammer softly comes to rest against the base of the bullet; the mechanism released, the gun safe again.

Then work the bolt up and back but slow this time because the bolt has a claw that hooks onto the outer edge of the base of the bullet and tries to flick what should be an empty cartridge out of the breech and if you do this too fast and uncontrolled the bullet with its load still heavy and its lead and metal tip still present can flick out and hit and maybe smash the mirror or mark the top of Mum's good dresser and then there's evidence, the whole game is fucked. You remove the bullet by hand, pull the bolt right back until the next bullet ascends from the magazine where the rest of them lie snugly and silently like good little soldiers in a trench and then you send it, too, into the breech.

This is what I do, early Friday afternoon, killing time until they get home. For a buzz, a few tiny adrenaline rushes. And as I'm sitting here, looking out the window over the valley with the gun across my knees like a Mississippi Vietnam vet redneck on his porch, the phone rings deep in the house beneath me, the first rings quiet and muffled, then loud and brash as the phone in this room catches on.

"Hello, you have reached the sour residence."

"Hello, is Richard there please?"

"Yup, speaking."

"Hi . . . Richey. It's Anna here. From Christchurch?"

"Oh. Hi. How's it going."

"I rang you last Saturday in Dunedin. Did you get a message or anything?"

"Um yeah, yeah . . . but I had to come home for something and so . . . and then I forgot about it, you know. I've been drunk for four days."

"Yeah. . . . Oh. I rang Unicol again today but they said you'd gone home. They were kind of. . . . Well the person I spoke to called you a name."

". . ."

"Richey?"

". . ."

"Hello?"

". . ."

". . ."

"They called me a name."

"Um, well yeah. They kind of . . . they sounded kind of mad at you actually."

"What was. . . . What did they call me?"

"I really don't want to say."

"What was it, Anna?"

"Look I didn't ring about that, I wanted to talk to you, to see how you are and that? Richey. You haven't answered any of my letters. And I haven't seen or heard from you since New Year's, remember?"

". . ."

"You know? When you had sex with my best friend on the bed next to me?"

"Oh look, Anna, I never had sex with her. I was too drunk and out of it to do anything anyway."

"Yeah well, not for lack of trying. And I saw and heard you do more than enough anyway. Kim's got enough problems in her life without you adding to it, Richey. She's tried to kill herself four times. And she's on antidepressants now."

". . ."

". . ."

"Did you know I'm leaving Unicol, Anna? I'm moving into a flat."

"Yeah, why."

"Cos it sucked. And I hated it."

"Oh sometimes I think home's just as bad."

"Oh yeah."

"But I'm lucky, I guess, with my parents. You don't really know them but they are good to me. Like they can be really understanding."

"Yeah."

"We've actually gotten really close. Especially now."

". . ."

". . ."

". . ."

"Well. I um . . . rang cos I wanted you to be the first to know. Apart from my parents of course."

". . ."

"Are you still there?"

"Yeah."

". . ."

"Is something wrong, Anna?"

"I . . ."

". . ."

"Well, I've got cancer and they say . . . I'm . . . might die . . . from . . . what I've got. It's a stomach cancer. And they can't really . . . they . . . apparently can't. . . . And, well . . . did you know I was going to go to Australia at the end of the year?"

". . ."

"And now I've got to go and have chemotherapy."

". . ."

"My hair's going to all fall out, Richey, and they know it's not even going to work anyway, they know that."

". . ."

"Are you still there?"

"When . . ."

". . ."

"I . . . I'm . . . I'm sorry? Anna?"

". . ."

". . ."

"Richey . . . I'm going to die before the end of the year . . . and I don't even know what I'm going to be doing till . . . when . . . Richey?"

"Yeah."

"I don't know anymore what to do."

". . ."

". . ."

"Look, Anna, you . . ."

". . ."

". . ."

"What was that?"

"Uuuh . . ."

"What was that *noise,* Richey? Are you alright?"

"Oh. Fuck . . ."

"What's happened? What was that sound? *Richey.*"

"Um, I have to go, Anna. Something's happened, I have to go, I'll call you back."

"Yeah, okay, alright. Bye."

"I *will,* Anna . . . I've fucked something up and I've got to go now."

"Richey, that sounded like a *gun.*"

"Um . . . Bye."

On the bus back to Dunedin I'm thinking about the drunk and stoned night in Christchurch around New Year's, when me, Anna, and two of her friends—one called Kim and someone else I can't remember very well, both who I'd just met that night—had taxied to Kim's parents' expensive Fendalton house around three in the morning and had all four of us collapsed on Kim's bed, which was a white futon but had looked gray lit by the full moon shining through the skylight. And Kim had rolled against me and whispered something in my ear after the four of us had lain there silently for a long time and I had started kissing her; I had undone the buttons of her shirt and she was braless, her skin too appearing gray in the moonlight and her young breasts just gentle swells as she lay there with her eyes closed, and I had undone her belt and the button fly of her jeans, pushed them down to her knees, slid my hand between her legs and inserted one finger in her cunt and had slid it gently in and out, concentrating really hard, trying to do it right, and when I heard her hissing between her teeth it had seemed shockingly loud next to my ear and Anna had woken up, Anna who I'd planned to try and score sometime over this New Year's and finally lose my virginity, and she and the other girl got up as I leaned over Kim and her open shirt, sucking on her nipple, and I heard Anna say guys, guys, don't and then I heard rustling and the door slam, me still sucking on Kim's nipple, Kim who may have been asleep at this point, and but I was too drunk and stoned and couldn't get the condom—this inaugural condom I'd brought with me all the way from Timaru with Anna in mind—to unroll onto my semi-erection once they were gone, me sitting hunched over on the edge of the futon in the strange moonlight playing with my dick, trying and failing to get an erection, and so but I tried to finger her again but she rolled over away from me and pulled her jeans up so I had lain there with wicked head-spins looking at the moon out the skylight before eventually just falling asleep.

And a week later I had got this letter:

Dear Richey,

Well, you're probably wondering why I got so shitty the other night. The thing is that I don't understand how you could do something that should be so personal and special with someone you hardly know.

And for god's sake Richey, couldn't you have moved off the bed? Doing it on the same bed as two other people seems to me to be so fucking cheap. And no, the fact that you'd been smoking up is no excuse, if you ask me you knew exactly what you were doing.

Another thing is that Kim's life is fucked up enough as it is

without you adding to it. I don't know, I probably expect too much
of people, all I know is that I sure expected a hell of a lot more
from you.

Anna

I used to read that letter over and over before university started,
trying to figure out who Anna saw—Anna who remains my
"friend" because she lives in Christchurch and has only just
turned sixteen and is in sixth form this year and hasn't really seen
me enough to find out what I'm really like; Anna who has photographs of me, of us at Tekapo during New Year's in 1991 where
I first met her and thought I might be able to score her, and that
I don't have any control over and feel uneasy about; Anna who
thought that because I liked the Violent Femmes and Lou Reed
and The Smiths I had to be a good person; Anna who cried to
"Asleep" one night as we sat drinking around a dying fire in the
camping ground, quietly singing with her eyes closed—*deep in
the cell of my heart I will feel so . . . glad to go*—Anna who, really,
I've fucked over in thought and word and deed three times that
she knows about and but who still haunts me because I still
sometimes feel kind of guilty; and Anna who's got this disease
and tells me she's going to die—trying to figure out who it was
she saw when she wrote the words "Richey," and "you," and why
I hadn't just kept trying to get her in the sack that night rather
than going for Kim.

Sometimes I listen to my own thoughts and I don't recognize
myself.

It's snowing—can you believe it? The bus is stopped at the
very top of the Kilmog, just a few kilometers from Dunedin and

it is snowing in April, blocking the road, jamming up traffic, which is lined up in front and behind the bus as far as I can see, the snow appearing gray and only white where it is picked out in flurries by cars' headlights. I'm pissing, by the roadside, a little bit drunk. The landscape is a dark gray. The hills are invisible. I feel fantastic actually. I'll be back in Dunedin in time to go out tonight, spend this Friday night with actual people, after such a hell week.

And what a hell day it has been. My parents got home shortly after my little accident and I'd had only enough time to put some Selley's No More Gaps in the holes in the ceiling and the wall and vacuum up all the dust and pieces of Gib board on the carpet. It maybe actually looked kind of funny, me running around the living room (directly beneath my parents' room) trying to vacuum in the plaster dust that clouded the room and was turning the carpet from peach to white, waving the vacuum hose frantically about above my head.

The curtains and the TV were beyond repair however.

And knowing that this time I'd really gone beyond the pale, knowing that at last something concrete had been done, and not, this time, done to someone else like to the blonde girl but just to some of my parents' things, my parents' house, knowing that at last there was a concrete example of my secret life and my secret thoughts was actually really liberating. And so, when I heard the gate clink and I heard their voices and their footsteps coming up the steps I put down the sandpaper, which was clogged and useless anyway because the No More Gaps was still wet, and I adjusted the towel that I'd draped over what was left of the TV and, feeling a just massive adrenaline rush but also feeling strangely calm, I went to the front door, just like the first day, just like five days ago at about this time, and I opened it wide and Mum took one look at my face and just said, "Oh Richey. What have you done."

And thus ensued the argument to end all arguments, a proper argument this time, I assumed full first-person status, and with my blood singing with adrenaline I defended myself, remained defiant, would admit no guilt, blamed the gun, blamed solitude, blamed depression, blamed high school, blamed them, and the argument finally came to a standstill as my parents looked about the ruins of their living room, their spirits broken, my mother crying, my father's shoulders almost sagging, me standing straight and tall but my knees a little weak with all the tension, and finally my father said in a terribly quiet voice, looking away from me, "I think it's time you went back."

And I could only agree and pack my things and think that this was a chance to return the porn to the Mobil, I couldn't leave them here because Mum would clean the "guest room" after I had gone and she would find them underneath the bed. And so I packed my things, pitifully few, the videos stacked in the top of my pack, and I stood at the door to the living room and said look I'm sorry and Dad wouldn't look at me and Mum came out of the kitchen and said leave your phone number at this new flat so we can get in touch with you and I did and she said I hope things get better after this and I nodded or looked away or something and said bye and then just left, just walked out the door and left them there, like that, my mother crying behind her glasses, looking at me, and my father's back to me, silent, standing by the ruined TV with the towel in his hand, looking out the window.

The line of traffic is moving again, along the crest of the Kilmog, just crawling along. It is still snowing. I sit in the very back of the bus, drinking a beer. It's disgusting—Southern Draught—but it was only $9.95 a dozen and it's 4.5 percent and I haven't checked my bank balance but by now it must be running dry. There are like about four other people in the bus and I can see their heads over the seats up near the front in the dim light inside here.

What with the snow falling thickly right outside the window and the darkness and these lights inside I can only see my own reflection in the window, half-darkened, fluttering and flickering, tentative and ghostlike in the flakes of snow closest to the side of the bus.

Returning the videos was far easier than hiring them. They were in generic maroon video cases and plus all I had to do, as James James Morrison Morrison, was saunter casually in and drop them on the counter and leave quickly, before the staff had time to check the videos and discover that: (a) they're two days late, and (b) that they've been ringing a phone number re these videos where some elderly people are getting extremely frantic, having to deny vehemently that they still have "Club Anal," "Gushers II," and "Robyn Hood: Princess of Sluts" out; and before they can run after the fairly rapidly walking boy who's headed into town and who's just dropped the aforesaid videos off, to inquire if indeed he had left the correct phone number and if not, like what's the problem.

No one ran after me. Next stop was the bottle store on the Bay Hill for Southern Draught, and then down the main street to the bus station. The shops were all still open, Friday night, and after I had booked my ticket on the 8:40 P.M. bus to Dunedin, half an hour to waste, I walked back and looked in the shops. On the grass on the Stafford Street–Canon Street corner some high school kids were drinking beer and smoking and talking shit to people that passed and I recognized some of the boys from my Peer Support group at Boys' High. One of them lifted his chin to me, and I did the same, and after I had passed them I heard someone mutter, "Fag," and the girls giggled and I walked on.

In the New Releases section in Whitcoulls and there I saw a red- and black-covered book with raised-print gold letters on the cover saying, *A Book of Murder*, by someone called S. J. Johansson. Packaged in black with embossed gold letters like a Stephen King. On the blurb, standing there as a stranger in my own town I read this:

> Jeffrey Dahmer's butchery . . . David "Son of Sam" Berkowitz's brutal point-blank shootings . . . Edmund Kemper's horrific sexual mutilations and necrophilia . . .
>
> Serial sexual murderers. Lust killers.
>
> Who are they? What do we know about them? What goes on before a sexualized murder?
>
> From leading serial murder researcher and forensic psychologist Dr. S. J. Johansson comes the most comprehensive survey of who serial killers are and why they do what they do. Dr. Johansson has interviewed and delved deep into the lives of over fifty imprisoned killers—rapists,

necrophiles, mutilators, murderers—and has returned with what we need to know about these men.

Who is the serial sexual killer?

A Book of Murder has the answer.

And under this New Release, to somehow coincide with what they're treating as some kind of seminal new book or maybe it's killing season, are more books, three shelves of them with cards underneath that describe the contents, the covers black and dramatic, some of them with portraits of men on the covers, disfigured or blurred or masked or distorted:

> *Bloodlust: Portrait of a Serial Sex Killer*
>
> *American Psycho* (Staff Pick and shrinkwrapped, 18+)
>
> *The Search for the Green River Killer*
>
> *Holes in M'Naghten: Ed Kemper III*
>
> *Fatal Vision*
>
> *Cruel Doubt*
>
> *The Evil That Men Do*
>
> *Jack the Ripper: Revisited*
>
> *Red Dragon* and
>
> *Silence of the Lambs*
>
> *Halloween 4: The Novelization*
>
> *The Ragged Edge of the Nineties*

A Book of Murder cost $21.95 but underneath some of these other books were older and on special so in a kind of like glee I picked up one then another then another, *Bloodlust, American Psycho, The Green River Killer, Cruel Doubt, Holes in M'Naghten, Red Dragon,* and *Silence of the Lambs*, stacking them under my arm, crouching in front of the rack intently, putting the widest book at the bottom and grading them upward by size so I didn't drop any, rocking on my heels with my pack on my back, tucking in one more, almost grinning to myself, why not, one more.

And at the checkout the old woman who scanned them looked from the barcodes to the computer screen and back again and didn't say anything and I didn't say anything and blushed, and widened my eyes and added a Mars bar at the last minute and flexed my jaw again and again and again and as I paid, a fatal total of $74.95, as I pressed the eftpos keys my adrenaline subsided abruptly and I looked up and glanced at her eyes still on the screen and muttered the words, "it's a class project," and then, kind of pathetically when you think about it, "for school."

And Accepted the eftpos miraculously said and into my pack in the big supermarket-size white and red plastic Whitcoulls bag on top of the dozen beers, next to the little clear plastic bag containing all that was left of the fifty dollar bag I got off Nick, just mostly cabbage and stalk but probably some headshake as well, though.

And walking past the high school kids again, back to the bus station, having all this good-seeming heavy stuff in my bag I kept my head high and snorted when the same voice said louder this time, just after I passed, more challenging this time, "Faggot," and as I kept walking he said it again, louder, *"Fag,"* and I looked back once and he was sitting there in the middle of the group of about five boys and three or four girls, all of them only about sixteen, and I didn't recognize him; the two boys from my Peer Support group were watching me to see how I would react; and he stood up and said, "Yeah?" and I snorted again and kept walking and the whole group laughed this time (including my Peer Support boys who I suppose I kind of bullied but I had wanted them to like me and but that was what all the Peer Support leaders did, most of them, anyway) and I was blushing and so angry and weak until I made myself think of the last week, of all the beer and wine and drugs, of the fresh cuts and burns on my left forearm, of the tip of my tongue in the muzzle of a gun, of a shattered television, of stomach cancer, of an almost real-life sexual betrayal, of a blonde-haired girl exploding at the ends of my arms, of almost beating my father just once. I made myself think of all I can do and have done, and of all the stuff in my bag, and all those black books, and *A Book of Murder*.

And it almost worked.

I walk unsteadily down the aisle of the bus, holding onto the heads of the seats for support, as we near where Dundas Street meets the Cumberland Street one-way. The bus driver stops the bus just past the intersection, opposite Rugby Park. The snow has become rain somewhere between the Kilmog and Dunedin and the streets shine blackly. I walk along Dundas Street in the drizzle, listening to parties in houses and passing on the bridge over the Leith River a group of three boys all wearing full-length Drizabones and carrying beers. At the crest of the first Dundas Street hill, opposite Studholme Hall, there are lights in the windows of Strangeways as it looms over the street, the typical dirty cream weatherboard 1940s villa, loomed over in turn by the castle behind it, where Matt says he has sometimes seen lights also. I can hear "Rape Me" playing, muffled, inside.

I climb the wet mossy concrete steps and underneath the wooden hand-lettered STRANGEWAYS sign that hangs by wires from the porch roof I bang on the front door. There is no answer. My slight tipsiness has gone and I actually feel adrenalized and kind of scared by what I'm going to find. Entering a party for the first time is almost always too stressful. And there has been entirely too much adrenaline today.

I knock again, pound the door with my fist. And I hear a female voice and suddenly the door creaks open and the music is really loud, a voice shrieking *am I the only one . . .* and standing there is this short dirty-blonde–haired girl holding a cigarette and a bottle of gin in one hand.

"Yes?" she says. She's drunk, her eyes are kind of unfocused, and she sways a little bit, hanging onto the door, which seems huge next to her. "Can we help you?"

There's light coming from the second door on the left down the dead straight hall, the door that leads to what I thought was my room. The music and voices are coming from this room.

"Are Nick and Matt here?" I ask her, my heart kind of sinking at the thought of a big party in my house without anyone I know.

"I think, they've gone out . . . somewhere," she says, still swaying, looking up at me, her eyes focused somewhere a couple of meters behind me. A boy I don't know comes out of my room with a cigarette in his hand, looking way more sober than this girl.

"Ur-su*la*," he says, kind of camply until he sees me. "Who's this?"

"Wait, wait," says Ursula, swaying. "We're *hav*ing a . . . Kurt

Cobain party. Come on in," and she opens the door, stepping aside to let me in and she loses her balance and falls against the wall and laughs, still clinging to her cigarette and gin bottle, which is Seagar's, I notice, and one-third full.

"No but wait, wait," she says, and stops laughing and looks up at me along the door, her head bobbing. "Did *you* know . . . that Kurt Cobain . . . killed himself today."

It's not a question but I kind of shake my head.

"He blew his head off with a shotgun. We're having a party for him," she says, and now she looks kind of hazily sad. The boy standing there, right in front of me with his feet wide apart, takes a drag of his cigarette, blows it out, and says, "What do you call a man who's shot his own head off with a shotgun?"

I just look at this boy, and then at Ursula, who leans and sways toward me a bit, still holding onto the door for support.

"Curt," she says, and they both crack up, and Ursula collapses back against the wall again and the boy just stands there and I stand there too, looking from one to the other, not getting it at first.

2

Strangeways

"Hey wank, I mean, Nick."

"Welcome to Strangeways, Souse, you bad man. How was lunch?"

"Pretty much hellish. Few beers but I'm still hungover."

"I'm sweet as now. Cricket's on."

"Oh, who?"

"New Zealand Australia, Souse."

"Oh right, yeah."

". . ."

". . ."

"Merv Hughes is just a fat fuck."

"Yeah."

". . ."

"So who's this Ursula chick, Nick?"

"Rang up after she saw the ad. She's sixteen. What do you think?"

"Has she dropped out of school?"

"Yup. She's a transient. Have you got any cigarettes?"

"Yeah, in my room. Oh when I got in last night I was absolutely shitting my pants, well I wasn't shitting my pants but I was kind of weirded out you know? I didn't know where you guys were, and there were all these strangers in my room and stuff."

"Souse. The room is big. It was empty. We didn't know when you'd be back. Just get over it."

"Oh I'm not worried about it, it just, you know it was just weird after like drinking on the bus and stuff I thought I might have like wandered into the wrong house."

"Get. Over. It."

"..."

"..."

"So. Has Ursula got any babe friends?"

"Na. She's from Wellington and all her friends are still there apparently."

"What's she doing here?"

"She's on the dole and apparently going to do a photography course."

"Does she smoke up?"

"Does she what, mate. You interested, Souse?"

"Oh she's a bit young ay."

"Don't worry about that, mate. Old enough to bleed, old enough to butcher."

"What do you mean, 'bad man'?"

—

I was woken this morning at Strangeways by the phone ringing out in the hallway. I had slept in my sleeping bag on the couch in the living room last night, the one Nick and I are here now sitting on, talking shit, watching cricket. My room had been empty apart from some cushions and ashtrays, empty bottles and cans and Matt's stereo. I answered the phone in the hall and it was my mother, ringing from a motel here in Dunedin to say that she and my father had driven down here this morning with a trailer full of a bed and a desk, to help me shift my stuff from Unicol into the flat. I was hungover and feeling vague and hazy. She said nothing about the gun incident or me leaving. I think they may be under the impression that I was trying to kill myself, so this may be an effort to stay close to me. If that is what they think (it's not completely wrong but it's also not . . . *completely* right), and if helping me shift into a new flat is their idea of an "intervention," then they really are a fucking joke.

The flat was silent and smelled of cigarettes and old dead fires. The doors line either side of the hallway like a prison corridor's cells. On one side, Nick's room, my room, the bathroom. On the other, the empty room that must now be Ursula's, Matt's room, then the living room. At the end of the hallway, opposite the front door, the stained glass window in the back door that leads to the cracked concrete of the rear courtyard, dark in the shadow that is cast over Strangeways all day, every day, by the castle that looms behind. You can walk right through this house without entering a room.

I sat and waited in the living room, on the same ragged brown Chesterfield couch we're sitting on now, and watched *Coca Cola Smash Hits*. There were noises from Matt's room and next thing he had clomped ostentatiously down the hall and in here. He was wearing black shell pants and a red Stallones shirt, plus a little red Stallones cap. His eyes were half-shut, hungover like me, and he got a shock when he saw me there on the couch, stopped, shook his head as if to clear something away.

He said "Jesus. Souse. When'd you get in man?" and clomped past me into the kitchen.

"Last night, late."

"Oh man, you should've told us. We went into town ay. Fucking *rude* as Cook." Behind me things clattered in the sink, fridge door opened and shut. "No *fucking* food."

"Didn't know I was coming till last night."

"You clazy kid."

"Yeah man, I live life on the edge. How's Stallones?"

"Absolutely fucking *rude*."

"Bit early for pizza isn't it?"

"I'm on dough."

"Which is . . . ?"

"Dough is . . . standing over a bowl and hocking loogies into future pizza bases." He laughed an evil laugh. The toaster popped and I heard a knife scraping. Then he clomped in with toast and vegemite and collapsed in the armchair beneath the window to the courtyard at the back of the house.

"Using your car?"

"No way, man. Be fucked in a week the way we drive. The dubbie's sacred. Be better money though. I'm on—wait for it—eight dollars fifty be*fore* tax. Je*sus*." He snorted. "Man, you should see the people I have to work with. I've got a fucking high B Bursary. I should be at varsity with you guys."

"I don't know if I'd describe what I've been doing as 'at varsity.'"

"So are you moving in or what, Souse? We need your dosh. Nick's getting money from his olds but we're a couple of weeks behind. Ursula's on the dole. You met her?"

"Kind of."

"She's from Wellington right? And she's down here for like *days* and she's got contacts. We're going out to Caversham this afternoon before my parents get here. Oh Christ what's *this* shit now?"

"Um, this is okay isn't it? I actually think it's quite good."

"Righto, Souse."

"At least they're English."

"It's three chords . . . F sharp, A . . . and B."

"At least they've got guitars."

"That they don't know how to play."

"Better than fucking drum 'n' bass."

"Last night I was getting into some beats, man. We went to the Cook with these guys that came into Ursula's little do, and this guy . . . Brooke . . . something had his girlfriend there right? And we were standing next to each other at the bar . . . she was between us . . . and I had my hand on her arse ay, bit of squeeze and release, you know how it is, she's making out nothing's happening and this guy's on the other side, doesn't even know. Brilliant."

"She probably thought it was him, Easty."

"Na, mate, na, mate. She knew."

"Who'd she leave with?"

"*That*—is not the point."

"What *is* the point?"

"*I* had the moral victory."

"*You*—are so full of shit."

"Oh whatever." He sighed.

". . ."

"I can't stand this anymore. I. Am. *Leaving*."

". . ."

"So what're you up to today, Souse?"

"Moving out of Unicol."

"That should be . . . stressful."

". . ."

". . ."

"What do you mean by that, Matt?"

"Oh. You know, just going back . . . now . . . after everything. Gotta go. Good luck, Souser."

And then he left, leaving me worried. The front door slammed and the sound of his Volkswagen rose briefly then receded. How much did he know? How much did he remember of that night? What had Nick and he said about it? What had they said to other people?

I couldn't tell.

I went and waited outside, and from the porch at Strangeways, sitting underneath the sign on an old armchair, I could see down the length of East Dundas Street, with all its student flats so similar to this one, to the hill with the graveyard. And beyond the hill, the harbor, the Portobello road. It was sunny and quiet. No cars passed on Dundas. Studholme Hall loomed before me, Strangeways and the castle loomed behind me. It must have been ten; no one was up, no students walking the street. Everyone in bed nursing hangovers. To the west, more student flats, the Leith, low and invisible in its concrete trench, two or three construction sites around Castle Street where more student flat complexes are being built.

I was thinking that I don't like it here. I don't like the way people straight out of high schools all over the country come here and in a matter of weeks saunter around as if they've had a long and famous history in this town. I don't like the way people travel always in twos or threes. Apart from freshers, of course (my sister told me this), who travel in packs of ten or more.

I was thinking no, I don't like it. Why was I here then? Because of all my options—joining the *army*, joining the *police force*, becoming a *mechanic*, going to Polytech, or staying at home and going insane on the dole—being a "student" here at Otago University seems to offer me the opportunity to get a lump sum of student loan and drink most nights without being thought a bum and without having to really figure out anything else to do. Students are allowed, expected, even obliged to keep up the image—carry out new feats of bonging, drink the most, the quickest, for the longest duration.

This is a happy coincidence with my current interests and abilities.

Nick's smoking one of my cigarettes and I'm talking again:

"So what's the band doing?"

"Easty's parents are bringing down his brother's amp today. And the drumkit's set up in his room you'll be pleased to know. We've had a few good jams."

"You still want me to drum?"

"Course."

"Where *is* Matt?"

"He's gone out to Caversham with Ursula to get some gear. Apparently she met one of the guys at Gardies."

"..."

"..."

"I think she's quite a babe."

"Do you now, Souse?"

"Well she's alright."

"She's a fucking bush pig, Souse."

"No shame. She's not really. I think she's alright."

"You always go for the blonde chicks don't you?"

"No. Sometimes, maybe. What do you mean, 'go for them'?"

"Planning some late night visits to Ursula's room then, Souse?"

"Good on ya, mate."

"Introduce her to Souse's flesh-pink nightstick."

"Okay, mate."

"You should just go in there one night and put it in her hand. You never know unless you try. If you dream it you can do it. Face your fears and live your dreams."

"..."

"But I suppose there's always the faithful right hand."

"..."

"Done you pretty good service up till now, right, Souse."

"Okay, mate."

After my parents had picked me up we drove straight round to Unicol. My father was mostly silent in the car, as was I, mainly because of my hangover but interpreted by my mother as discomfort, and so she talked and talked, trying to break the tension. We parked in the staff car park and walked in together. Because it was early there were few people about, which was a relief. I saw no one I knew. I suppose I had only really spoken to people I knew from Timaru anyway. There was a piece of paper stuck to the door of my room. I pulled it down and stuck it in my pocket before my parents could see it. I opened up the door and the curtains were still closed and everything was as I left it, beer cans everywhere, brewing sugar all over the floor, blood on the wall all dried and brown, books and papers everywhere, *The Queen Is Dead* still lying broken by my stereo. My room smelled stale and not just musty but actually sour, like rotting carpet. (I had pissed in the corner one big night during Orientation, so wasted that I just got out of bed, flopped it out and pissed on the carpet. I can't remember this, but the damp patch and the smell in the morning were evidence enough. I had nothing to clean it with so I poured washing powder and shaving cream on it and rubbed it in with the heel of my boot. The smell lingers, however.)

Normally my parents would have said something, like "Oh Richey, how can you live like this?"—my mother, or, "What a pit"—my father, but this time they said nothing, my mother just stepped gingerly over the mess and opened up the curtains and the window, and my father started packing up the stereo. I went to the bathrooms to read the note from the door, which read:

Richard Sauer,

Please come and see me in my office immediately upon your return.

Dr. P. Neilsen

—

"Anything happening tonight?"

"Mark's having a keg later on this afternoon for the second innings I think. Interested in that, Souse?"

"Yeah I'll be in."

"How're you feeling now?"

"Bit better."

"You know that most of a hangover is actually withdrawal symptoms from alcohol? Best thing for you. It's like sunburn. The only way to deal with sunburn is to get pissed."

". . ."

". . ."

"Who's going to be there?"

"Probably Mark and the flat and I think Sebastian's coming."

"Probably bring all his new Knox buddies."

"I think he's got a girlfriend now. Have you noticed how he says cat all the time now? He's a cool cat, he's a fucked up cat."

"Yeah, I've met her. He changed as soon as he got here. Like he's all of a sudden the man about town and scoring chicks and getting into fights all the time and stuff. I heard this the other day, Nick, we're at the Cook and he's talking to these Knox cats and they're talking about the gym and he says I'm not going to spend three hundred bucks on a gym membership to get rid of a beer gut that I spent three hundred bucks putting there. And he's like this weedy little guy standing next to these big rugby-head types and they don't know how to take him."

"Bit of repressed anger there, Souse?"

"I don't know, I just remember him at primary school when he was sort of nerdy and now he's like he is."

"Mmm."

"You know he doesn't smoke up but he still like talks like he's all so familiar with it and rolls up joints like he's practiced and stuff but never smokes himself. It's because if he got really stoned he wouldn't be able to keep up the show any longer and everyone'd see through him at last and he'd lose all his credibility."

"Like you, Souse?"

I have never spoken to Doctor Neilsen before this morning. He has been a constant distant silver-haired authority figure, talking only with the King's College or Auckland Grammar boys, strolling through the dining hall during those few meals I ever made it to. A few people, a couple in the office, looked at me as I walked up the stairs in the foyer up to his office. I knocked at his door and inside he said "come" and I walked in and he didn't look up at first, concentrating on writing something on the desk in front of him, and then, still without looking up, said, "sit down." I sat in one of the two chairs, chairs exactly the same as the ones in the dining hall, and waited.

After a couple of minutes he had put down his pen, rocked back in his chair, his fingers laced together in his lap, looking at me over the top of his glasses, and said, "So, Mister Sauer, I hear you've been up to some nasty business."

And I said, "Um . . . yeah, and . . . I'm really sorry about . . . what . . . I was really really drunk, and I've never done anything like that before." Then, brilliantly, "It was completely out of character for me."

He said, "You're not going to weasel out of this, Mister Sauer. We don't accept drunkenness as an excuse for anything here. Otherwise everything would be forgiven. I received a phone call from Mrs. Thompson at Salmond Hall telling me that one of my residents had been up to some nasty stuff at a party they had arranged. This was a week ago. Where have you been? Did you just run off?"

"I went home for a week."

"So you did. Why did you take it upon yourself to go to a party that you weren't even invited to, Mister Sauer? A party organized by and for Salmond Hall residents only? And how do you think this girl feels? She's not very happy. You do know she's just eighteen? Did you ever think about that?"

"I'm sorry, I . . ."

"Don't apologize to *me*. It's most certainly not *me* you should be apologizing to. You're in some trouble. Mrs. Thompson wanted me to get you up in front of the Varsity Disciplinary Committee. She'd like you expelled from the university. How do you feel about that?"

" . . ."

" . . ."

"I could ring her up, and apologize . . ."

"And what makes you think you'll be around here long enough to do that?"

"I'm already in the process of moving out."

"Ah, I see. So you think this is all just going to disappear if you run away for good?"

"No, but I thought that's what I should do."

"Well that's not all you're going to have to do. Where are you going to live?"

"I'm moving into a flat with some friends."

"Lucky friends. I hope they have more success with you. What I'm going to do is this. I'm going to give you Ruth Thompson's number at Salmond Hall and you are going to call and discuss this with her. Then you are going to call the girl concerned and apologize to her. Do you in fact even know her name?"

"No."

"I didn't think so. Her name is Rebecca, Mr. Sauer. Rebecca Gilbert. Given that you're leaving here of your own accord I won't take this any further myself. I will ring Ruth myself and put the ball in her court. If she wants to take disciplinary action against you then that's her prerogative, and you'll just have to take your medicine. As for you, you better make those phone calls and hope that she feels better toward you than I do. When are you leaving?"

"Today."

"Good. I hope not to see you again."

Then I left his office.

"Souse? Hello Souse? Does it speak?"

". . ."

People were up by the time we were loading the last of my stuff into the car, but because I was leaving I didn't seem to get any like dirty looks or comments or anything I could see. People looked through me or past me as I walked through the foyer with my arms full of my stale-smelling stuff. I suppose this was now permanent "that guy" status—not Souse, Richey, even "you" now—just the quiet guy who only talked when he was drunk and stayed in his room lots and did that thing at that Salmond Hall party. Third-person status can be liberating however, I will say again. Free to float, and observe. To watch the same people who won't even look into my eyes anymore.

I don't know if my parents were aware of what was going on as we packed my stuff up. But they were never really aware of any of the stuff that went on at school either.

The silence continued into the car, and to Strangeways. When we pulled up outside, the car full of my stuff, Nick was sitting in the same armchair that I had waited in earlier. Nick helped us unload and shift into my room. I didn't speak much then either; Dad and Nick did plenty of that.

My father says things to Nick that he never says to me. And the things he says to me he says differently to Nick. "Gidday, Nick. How's things." And although I knew Nick would imitate my father's broad New Zealand accent when my parents finally left, my father treated him as an equal. When my father said, "This place could use a clean," Nick said, "Yeah, we're going to get Richey to do it," and my father laughed.

When I think of the two of them together I think of them walking along this street side by side, not looking at each other but one of them quietly laughing at what the other has just said, each knowing when to step aside to let the other up the mossy steps to this new flat of mine, each knowing when the other needs help, knowing when to stand back.

When I think of me and my father, I think of his implacable walk and me capering around him, jesterlike, coming forward to help and then shrinking away when my help was unheeded;

walking behind him resentfully, walking ahead of him faking arrogance; useless, childlike, pathetic. All the things I know Nick is not to my father. When they are like they are together I hate them both with a sick empty intensity that scares me.

So my stuff got shifted in, and the final crowning humiliation for me and assurance of status in my father's eyes for Nick was when Nick's ex-girlfriend came to visit and Nick was nonchalant and dismissive, making her wait in the hallway—where I said hello to her, briefly—as they moved my bed, and then finally retiring into the living room with her after standing talking quietly with my father, surveying their handiwork, a job well done, et cetera, et cetera, leaving me to face lunch at "The Irish Rover" alone with my parents during which I ate only a salad and drank three handles of Speight's before they dropped me back here, the ordeal over, to sit talking with Nick and watching cricket.

"Sounds like Easty's home."

"Sounds like someone's with him."

"You're talking again then, Souse?"

" . . . "

"It'll be his parents with the amp. This is like visiting hours or something. Easty? Are you there, Easter egg?"

" . . . "

"Beasty? Zesty tang? Is that you?"

"Eastern time. Yeasty."

"Last but not east."

"I knew him. A man of infinite yeast."

"His parents *are* here."

"The Easton yeast infection."

". . ."

"Oh alright, Mr. Easton."

"Hello, boys. How's the cricket going?"

"Hundred and twenty-nine for five."

"Right then, the amplifier's here now and I hope you're going to look after it. We'll see you later."

"Bye, Mr. Easton."

"See ya, Mr. Easton."

". . ."

"Whoops. Don't think he was too happy about that."

"Come on. 'Yeast infection'?"

"Matty? Are you there? Come out, Mattias."

"Mateus Rosé?"

"Matty. Hello."

"Aren't you clever and witty, Tinny."

"Come on, Matt, it was Souse too. Have a seat."

". . ."

"How'd the Caversham mission go?"

"Ursula's still there. Little stoner bitch. She's crazy. Could get raped."

"Souse wants to get down her pants."

"Fuck off."

"We got an ounce. Keg still on?"

"Yup."

"I'm getting absolutely out of my box tonight."

". . ."

". . ."

"Shit-faced, mate. Caned. Nailed. Off my fucking nut.

*Mother*fucked. I'm going to induce . . . a . . . a . . . coma. A coma is what I desire."

". . ."

"Do you want to go soon?"

"Souse's had a bad day with the parents."

"Tell me about it. There's only one remedy."

"Are you going to roll up now or later? Let's have a look at it. Mmmm, smell it."

"Lovely brown sticky bud. You can almost squeeze the resin out of it."

"I think I'm having an emotion."

"How much was it?"

"Hundred and twenty."

". . ."

"You getting stoned tonight, Souse? How'd that bag I got you go?"

"Yeah, how was home, Souse? Forgot to ask you this morning. Did you hear about Kurt Cobain?"

"Let's see. Probably; I finished it; it sucked and yes."

". . ."

"On that note."

The three of us sit in silence, waiting for something to happen, waiting for something to change. Me on the Chesterfield sofa facing the TV that's mounted inside the fireplace. Nick to my right, slumps in the armchair beneath the window. Matt to my left, opposite him and facing him, in the other brown armchair, the third of which is sitting out in the porch surveying Dunedin.

There is nothing in here but armchairs and the TV and some rubbish piled in the corner.

And then it's five o'clock and time to drink so we leave together to walk down the hill to Mark's flat on Leith Street; me, Richard "Souse" Sauer, walking in front, and Nick "Tinny" Tin and Matt "Easty" Easton walking together behind me. When Nick and Matt turn down the alley into the back of the section of Mark's flat I sort of panic just a little bit, and have to wait, and tell them I'm just going to go and get some cigarettes from the shop, I'll be back in a minute, and so I leave them going down the alley, the two of them so familiar with each other that when they're not drunk or taking the piss they barely speak. I have known these people since third form, along with Mark; Sebastian I've known since early primary school, but he is a different person every year, especially this one.

So they go in—I already have cigarettes—and I hover around outside for a while, listening to the quiet, watching the trees along the Leith, mustering courage for what will be an ordeal until I have at least a jug, and that's assuming someone's got their act together enough to get a keg. Nick was first XV and first XI cricket, Matt played some soccer, Mark was first XI soccer and cricket. They all of them know arcane and intricate sport in-jokes that I only ever glimpse the actual meaning of. I have only ever played cricket with my father.

I steel myself, take a deep breath, walk down the alley and knock on the back door to Mark's flat, praying for a keg so I can prove myself.

And the door opens and standing there is Sebastian's new girlfriend, Nikki someone, and she is rich, has short dark hair, moleskins, Aertex shirt, brown Last Footwear boots, brown jersey, tan brown skin. I met her at Orientation when he was first scoring her, and but Sebastian was so cool at Orientation he could barely speak anymore so I don't think Nikki thinks we're actually even friends and I realize this even more when her smile disappears and all she says before she turns back into the kitchen is "Oh, it's just you," and I stand there disbelieving and start fucking blushing, wanting to flee, flee, get back to my room, to anywhere, a stack of lagers and my notebook and some music, but I can't because I don't know how my money's holding out and if I play my cards right I could get lots of keg beer—if there's a keg—for nothing, *and I need to drink*, so anyway, standing there like a fucking idiot all I can manage to do is ask her if she wants a fight.

"D'you want a go?" is what I say, is what we always say, and take a step into the kitchen and in the living room is a circle of low armchairs full of boys, surrounding—thank god—a fifty liter keg and silently watching the cricket on a TV in the corner and they all look up at me as Nikki sweeps past them to sit at Sebastian's feet, between his legs, and then Mark laughs and shakes his head as they all look up at me, and says, "First thing he says. D'ya wanna go. Fucking egg, Souse," and they all laugh except Sebastian and Nikki the bitch who's staring at the TV and I try to laugh too and I sit down in a beanbag on the outskirts of the circle as quickly as possible to escape the collective attention.

To my right in the first armchair is Mark's flatmate Dazza who's in the Otago cricket development squad; to his right the TV; opposite me is Sebastian and Nikki; next to them is Reuben, Mark's other flatmate, co-builder with Mark of the MOAB and really good at bonging; next to him is Nick, then Mark, then Easty, then this guy I don't know, a like semi-stoner friend of Sebastian's from Knox who's wearing a beanie, and then me, sitting in this stupid little beanbag with my back to the open space of the kitchen and horribly sober and exposed and alone.

So we watch cricket. Mark leans forward and pours a jug, which gets passed to me. It is mostly quiet apart from the commentary. I take a large mouthful, remembering watching cricket with the boys in Timaru, how nuts we would go, even me, at a wicket or a stumping, and how every player had a nickname and so did we and it felt like being part of something and it was fun. But things are different now, there's a tension in the air and I wonder if it has anything to do with me, or whether it's only me that senses it. Everyone watches the TV. The light flickers on their faces.

Occasionally someone—maybe Easty, Nick, Mark, or Sebastian—mutters something and there is a brief flurry of conversation. It never really matters who; these conversations all follow the same trajectory.

Someone: "Softcocks, I'm drinking even if you're not."

Someone else: "Story. Pour us one while you're there, Mark."

"Oh. Shot."

"He *is* good value."

"Nup. He's a fag."

"I don't rate him ay."

"Na, mate, na, mate. I rate him. See him against South Africa."

"*Brutal* form."

"Nup. Fucking homosexual."

"So he's a homosexual and you *don't* like him."

"Get a great big fat black dog right up your arse."

"No shame in a fat black dog up your arse."

"Shut *up,* cunts."

"Settle down and drink piss."

"Tell him the joke. You might want to leave for this one."

"Nick. Brother told me this. Heard of the bucking bronco? You fuck her doggy style then you lean forward, whisper in her ear, you're the dirtiest ugliest bitch I've ever done this with, then you grab her by the tits and hang on for the ride."

"As if."

"Is that a joke?"

"Na, na. This weekend Mark's gonna get his end away."

"As. Fucking. *If.*"

"*You're* the joke."

"Hey, hey, hear that? Fucking Richey Benaud says 'that's a useful *shout.*' The fuck's that supposed to mean?"

"It's alright, Easty. Don't get too excited."

"Okay, mate."

"Just keep it in your pants, mate."

"D'you wanna go then?"

"Yeah, cunt?"

"Yeah, cunt."

"So you want a smack in the head then."

"Hey, geeks? Suck my cock."

"Geek? Isn't that like a . . . fifth form term?"

"You're . . . a geek, Easty."

"Bimbo, bimbo, bimbo."

"Tin, you . . . are just *rude*."

"Onya, mate. Old lady. Tiny . . . little . . . soft . . . girl's . . . blouse."

"Right, cunt."

"Sit down, sit down."

"Out of the way, out of the way. Trying to watch cricket, girls."

"Whatever, Easty. I'm ready for you."

"We know, Tin. Bums to the wall."

"Ha . . . ha . . . ha."

"Know what happens to people like you in jail, Nicola? Be afraid. Be very afraid."

"You *are* afraid, Easty."

"Okay, softcocks. We'll all just drink as soft as softcocks shall we?"

"You don't always have to be the peacemaker, Mark. Let him look after himself."

"I just want to get *drunk*."

"A machine. You're a machine."

"Few beers, bit a how's your father, that's all we ask."

"Alright. A jug of piss then. Right now. From that keg."

"Why don't you just try fucking up, Easty?"

"Oh Tinny, Tin."

"Geeks suck cocks."

"What a lovely little self-satisfied smile you've got."

". . ."

"You're a winner man. A born leader of men."

"You're a soft on, man. A born soft on. Just shut. The fuck. Up."

"Hey, man. Hey, man. Anyone see that? Man, that guy *is* good ay."

And crashing silence after Sebastian's friend the beanied stoner-type finally speaks up.

There's a moment of quiet in which everyone waits for everyone else.

He's nodding, possibly starting to realize he's made some kind of mistake. "Yup. He's all good. A good cricket player," he repeats.

The silence continues and no one even laughs.

Someone burps.

"A good . . . player . . . of the game . . . of cricket."

More silence.

He's slowly nodding his head in a show of confidence, and there's even more silence before someone—not Sebastian, who's cultivating stoner friends to get in with Nick is my theory—finally says, "Yeah, well, possibly a good player of cricket, but a homosexual all the same."

And everyone cracks up, even the beanie guy who's a bit embarrassed but trying to laugh and whose nickname I find out is "Works" and who doesn't realize that it's *him* that's getting laughed at because, why?—and this sort of shit goes on until the final over when things start gearing up and we're all drunker, New Zealand bowling, Australia 200, trying to make 213 with two wickets in hand, Dean Jones on strike. Easty's now bouncing up and down in his armchair, everyone's leaning forward, hunched, tense, even Nick, who the conflict has elevated,

clapping, shouting on dot balls only half-ironically, and I've finished my jug and halfway through a new one and I'm smoking a
cigarette now, sitting cross-legged in my beanbag and getting
into it, feeling good, and when Dean Jones gets a four I accidentally shout out, excited, "That's a King Kong cut!"—something I
heard my father say once during cricket and everyone laughs and
I laugh too, surprised at them and at myself for speaking up and
then after that the cricket quickly ends, Dean Jones gets a four
and a six in the next two balls and it's over but it doesn't matter
because everyone's getting drunker now and feeling good and
the replays start so people start talking and all kind of pair off;
Easty talking excitedly to Mark who just sits back and drinks his
jug and listens and laughs occasionally; Sebastian's leaning over
Nikki (who just has this constantly pissed off look on her face—
I hate her now) and is telling Nick about joining Law Soc and
how he's also joined some kind of Christian group at Knox and
Nick's just got this look of absolute scorn on his face, leg over
the arm of his chair, and Sebastian's protesting although Nick's
said nothing, telling him no, it's really good, they've in fact got
lots of power around the varsity and they're mostly actually
good cunts and there are some good-looking bitches there too
and always a cask of claret at their meetings and so on and so on
and but Dazza and Reuben and me and Works are pretty much
silently drinking, watching the replays, and I feel a little uncomfortable because Nick and Sebastian and Mark and Easty are supposed to be my friends and I don't want these other boys who're
basically strangers to think that I'm not completely one of them
and cool and calm and stuff and so when they replay Dean Jones'
second last boundary I say again, loudly and fatally, "That *is* a

King Kong cut," and but the talking has gone quiet for a brief second and I haven't spoken for five or ten minutes so my voice sounds strange and out of place and stupendously loud and oh god what a cock I am, the silence goes on and I'm blushing so badly and the silence now is simply crushing and then Sebastian takes the opportunity and says, with just appallingly good timing, "How many times are you going to tell us, Souse," and there are a few sniggers and I think I die there, I freeze-dry onto the bean bag and can't move for the hours it seems to take before Mark finally says, "Alright, girls, how about a drinking game?" and Sebastian says, "Story."

The real drinking begins now. It's 10 P.M. To get started we play Next with bongs. Next is the most straightforward drinking game, the way we play it. No international rules, no beginning your drink before the man on your left finishes—none of this. Each man does a bong of one jug and hands it on to the next. That's it. The skill and the adrenaline are still there though, but in the drinking and not the playing of the game. The middleman has been cut out—the element of chance—and the only variable now is the individual's capacity to get it down and keep it down.

The MOAB is the "Mother of All Bongs"; built by Mark and Reuben and Dazza from materials they bought at Pay Less Plastics. It is made from an arc of a meter of clear industrial plastic tubing two inches in diameter, attached by a proper metal plumbing fastener to a funnel about the size of a large inverted lampshade. Because the plastic tube weighs so much and because the bong gets a lot of use, this fastener has to be repeatedly refastened. The bong can hold over four jugs, about four and a half liters, although this has never been attempted. The standard introductory Next bong is between one and two jugs.

Everyone gets up and stands in a circle around Mark, the keg, and the bong, watching intently while he checks the attachment of the funnel and then carefully, with Reuben holding the end of the tube, pours a jug into the funnel. It gets very quiet. Everyone is quietly doing a personal inventory: how does my stomach feel? am I too bloated already? when was my last bong? how did that one go? am I going to puke it all up straight away after the bong or am I going to lose it mid-bong and end up not only puking but getting the rest of the jug in my face?

No one talks. Reuben holds his palm over the end of the tube while Mark slowly pours the beer in, allowing any air bubbles to gently float up the tube and burst in the funnel. Nikki is the only one not standing. She has taken Sebastian's armchair and sits back looking bored. She pulls at the leg of Sebastian's jeans but he ignores her, staring intently at the bubbles in the inside of the tube. I can feel a loud pulse at the top of the back of my neck. A failed bong can lead to a definite loss of status for the rest of the night, whereas a good, sound one will equal respect, and so, relief.

Silence. No one knows who will go first once the bong is ready. The circle around Reuben and Mark and the equipment is solid, silent, unmoving. No one is any further inside or outside the circle than the boy next to him. No one wants to get picked out, be the first to fuck up, be noticed and remembered for something out of his control. Arms are folded, feet are spread wide apart. The only sound is the fizz and gurgle of beer.

Nick's smoking a cigarette opposite me, but even he's entranced by this scene, staring at the beer in the tube, the cigarette down at his side, smoke clinging to his fingers then drifting in a straight column up the sleeve of his denim jacket until he notices me watching him and takes a drag and says, "You gonna go first, Souse?"

"Na, mate," I say quickly, too quickly, and Sebastian, the fucking predator, looks up quickly and sneers, snorts, says, "Yeah good one, Souse, fucking soft on" and there are a couple of laughs in the form of quick exhalations around me. My adrenaline is still high and I don't want to do it, let alone be first, but I have done it before so I dare to say, "What about you, Sebastian?" and he snorts again, looking at me, still sneering, his head tilted to one side, but he's a little worried too, I can tell, because he shakes his head and looks away from me and then Reuben, still standing there with his hand clamped over the tube opening, breaks out of his tube-staring trance, looks up at no one in particular and says, "I'll do it."

Mark says, "On ya, Rubes," without looking at him, holding the bong up in the dim light, searching for any air bubbles that could disturb the flow of beer, and the spell is broken a little and we all relax, the circle becomes less uniform as we give Rubes room to kneel down, palm on tube. Mark—with one hand supporting the funnel, one hand around the middle of the tube because the bong weighs a bit, the plastic is thick and he's poured about a liter and a half in there—crouches down in front of Rubes who lifts his end, his left hand wrapped around the tube, right palm holding the beer at bay. Mark lowers the bong until the beer recedes a little from the tube end and Reuben removes his palm from the end and grabs the tube with two hands. He waits till the beer is as close to the end as it can be without spilling and then opens his mouth wide and takes the tube inside. Mark, crouched, supporting the weight of the bong, watches his face. Rubes moves his knees a little, breathing fast and heavily through his nose and looks up at Mark and is suddenly still, his eyes wide but calm, his lips white, mouth distended and painfully wide open. He watches Mark, adjusting something invisible inside himself. Mark watches back, waiting patiently for a signal. Rubes exhales one last time through his nose. Looks up at Mark. Blinks once, slowly, then nods.

Who rises, and looks so cool, rises so fluidly, with like ease he ascends from the floor holding the bong before him like an offering, but his eyes are on Rubes as are all our eyes, and Rubes begins to take the beer into himself as the bong reaches the maximum possible position, an elegant elevation in Mark's hands, the tube a gentle arc down into Reuben's upturned face, who might look as if he were praying now if it wasn't for the tube and his distorted mouth, his working throat, the tears coming into his eyes, and the beer level in the bong dropping in sharp one-inch descents before the hydrostatic pressure really kicks in and it just injects itself into him, sinking inside the tube in a continuous rush, and "look at his belly," someone says, and it's true, under his T-shirt his belly is visibly growing, protruding out over his belt, and "go, Rubes, get it down ya" someone shouts, he's over halfway there, and looking at Mark who's now watching the level in the tube, watching him intently from his kneeling position, the beer pumping into him, his mouth grotesquely wide, tears beginning to run down his cheeks.

And the last of the beer dribbles out of sight into his mouth—the end of a bong is always an anticlimax—and he pulls away from the tube gasping, beer running out over his lips and down his chin ("Floorsuck," someone shouts excitedly), and he rocks forward, hands on the carpet, face to the floor, a line of drool hanging from his mouth, Mark standing over him, inspecting what's left in the bong, and we all wait as he moves and gasps and spits, and he rocks back on his heels, his face turned upward, palms on his thighs, eyes closed, beer and tears on his cheeks, and there is a pause, a long pause as he seems to think hard about something and his body goes very still and we wait to see what will happen and his mouth opens and his eyes open to the ceiling and from deep inside him comes a burp, a long liquid gurgling that becomes a roar, an almost spoken word. And he relaxes, and smiles.

"Effort," says Mark. "Jug and a half. No shame in a spit, Rubes. Who's up next."

Stupidly, I wait and let the others go first. Nick's is successful, as is Mark's. Sebastian's gets a bit messy at the end. He gets the dregs down his Sonic Youth T-shirt that he's wearing over an Otago rugby jersey ("Shirtsuck," someone says). I finally step forward, but too late. The boys are starting to lose interest. Half have already bonged and are sitting in armchairs bloated and enjoying headrushes. The other half are gaining in confidence and talking and drinking as no one lets the side down.

Sebastian steps forward to administer mine. But strangely, he pours in less than a jug. I assume the same position as Rubes, copying his techniques: palm over tube, lower the tube, mouth over the end, nod and bring it on. But Sebastian must have been a bit drunk because there's air in the bong about halfway up—surely he didn't do it on purpose?—and the flow is disrupted after I've taken in about half. I take a big mouthful of air and cough and it's all fucked, the pressure is gone and the rest of the beer just splashes down against my teeth and I have to try and gulp it in—which is hard with your mouth this wide open—but there's no point because the whole physics of the thing are compromised.

"Flag it, flag it, bullshit," says Sebastian, slurring, drunk and dismissive. He looks up, around the room, not at me. "Right, who gets the dregs?" No one's taking any notice now.

I take the tube in my mouth—there's some foam and liquid dribbling about inside it—and blow as hard as I can but because the tube and my mouth are so wide it sounds like I'm winded, just a sort of weak, asthmatic wheeze, and a few drips fly out and hit no one in particular.

"Flag it, mate," says Sebastian, not interested, and drops the bong and collapses in the armchair vacated by Nikki. I get up off my knees and wipe my face, strangely somehow shamed, not because I tried and failed or anything as simple as that. Nothing happened, is all that matters. It was boring; no suspense, no effort, not even a failure to laugh at. No story. I pick up my jug and fill it from the keg and sit in the armchair next to Sebastian. I take a long hard drink, somehow isolated by my mediocre bong. No one speaks to me. There is no headrush and hardly any bloated feeling. I feel the same and that, maybe, is what is intolerable. I finish the jug as quick as I can and fill another, which I start into as quickly as possible before the rest of the beer hits my stomach. I turn to Sebastian, who's lying back in the armchair with his arms out and his eyes shut.

"Crook?"

"Na na, mate."

". . ."

". . ."

"Where's Nikki?"

"Picking up friends."

He opens his eyes slowly, looks around, sees Reuben and Dazza and Mark in the kitchen, no Easty, Works and Nick on the opposite side of the living room talking. He sees me sitting next to him, jug in lap, leaning back, trying not to let on that I know or care that he's looking at me.

Sebastian gets up, fills his jug and walks over to sit beside Nick.

I light a cigarette, drink more.

By the time the girls get here I'm getting almost drunk enough to not care that I'm still sitting alone. Easty's still missing. I must be on about my fourth or fifth jug when they arrive in the back door, Nikki first, talking loudly and like flouncing in, her stupid shirt tucked in the front and hanging out at the back, the collar so high and erect she must have impeded peripheral vision. There's music on now, Nirvana again, it's everywhere now he's dead, and I can't hear anything they're saying as they walk kind of uncertainly in, Hannah, another Knox chick I think, Jane who's the sister of a friend of my sister's so we kind of know each other—she looks around the living room, at me slouched in the corner, past me to Nick and Sebastian and Works, and "It's Janus the anus," Sebastian says and she says, "Oh hi, Sebastian," and then looks at me and gives me this uncertain smile, not sure how I'll react, I must look really drunk and brooding or something, and she mouths "hi" and I sort of lift my chin to her but she turns away too quickly to see.

And then comes Sarah, this tall blonde girl, a friend of Jane's from Timaru who I've seen and talked to at parties before and she's wearing blue moleskins and a red checkered Aertex shirt but she does it way better than Nikki, and I think she'd never be interested in Sebastian, she must know how bad he is, and they stand together in the kitchen, she doesn't even look around or into the living room, just starts talking to the other girls. And from where I'm sitting I see Dazza sitting on the kitchen bench, kind of uncomfortable now it's not just the boys, and Reuben leaning on the bench beside him's uncomfortable too and he holds his jug and glass in front of him like a shield. Mark moves easily between the two groups, drinking hard still. He leans back against Jane with this dreamy look on his face and Rubes and Dazza laugh. Then Jane pushes back against him and he turns with this exaggerated surprised look on his face and she puts her hands on her hips and cocks her head—a matronly "oh you boys" look, but still a little uncertain because Mark is only like this when he's drunk—and I laugh to myself over here in the corner because they all look nice and kind of like sweet together.

I don't trust myself to stand up anymore. But I can't stay here, alone, looking foolish, because any chance I'll have of scoring anyone will be gone. So as a first step I lean forward in the

chair and rest my elbows on my knees. I then slowly stand, sucking in my belly in case anyone's looking, trying to make it look
like I'm standing slowly because I'm like stretching or tired or
something. I make it upright. My knees crack. I gather myself
and step confidently forward toward the kitchen but I must be
too drunk or I've been sitting down too long or something
because I misjudge the level of the floor, straighten my leg too
soon like when you think you're at the bottom of some steps but
you're really not, and I lurch forward and stiffly and jarringly
stamp on the floor, and I feel my face wobble, the flesh around
my cheeks jiggles and I cringe inside, wondering if anyone saw,
if the girls think I've got a fat face, if they think I'm fat, and I suck
my cheeks in and walk over to lean beside Reuben and try to be
part of the group.

And out of the blue, from nowhere, Sarah comes over, I
think she must be going to the living room but no, she walks
over, smiling a little shyly and she's just taller than me, she's so,
so beautiful, perfect, beautiful face, beautiful blonde hair, and
she walks up and stands with her weight on one foot in front of
me and she says, "Hi, Richey?"

And I go, "Hey, Sarah," in this interested voice, that pumping banging sound in the back of my neck again, and there's a
second-long pause and then we both say at the same time,
"What have you been up to?" and you know, it's funny and goofy
and we laugh.

"Oh, I'm at Teacher's College. And some arts subjects at varsity. We had to start weeks earlier than you guys," she says.

"Yeah, yeah, it's rude," I say, and there's an uncomfortable
pause. I can feel Reuben and Dazza listening to us, so I say, "Did

you know I've moved in with Nick and Easty?"

"Yeah, I heard that. We're just down the road from you. At the bottom of the hill. But weren't you at Unicol though?"

"Oh yeah, but I . . . you know, it wasn't for me." Did Reuben snort?

"Yeah, Halls aren't for everyone. I like Hayward though, Jane's hall. Ex-maternity hospital, did you know that? Nothing much has changed." I look at her face, wondering if this is a joke or not. I can't tell. She looks around her, then says, "So what's your sister doing?"

"Um, Profs, she's doing Profs at Canterbury."

"Oh. Cool."

There's a pause.

"What are *you* doing, Richey?" she says. She's looking straight at me now and I suddenly realize that she's actually drunk, she's swaying a little, and there's some kind of damp stain I hadn't noticed on her shirt, and her eyes are just a little bit glazed and not focusing on me properly.

"Oh, um, you know, just some first year papers, I don't really know ay, haven't really made my mind up," I say. The truth is I enrolled and put my fees on Student Loan and haven't been to a single lecture.

"But . . . it's . . . *April*, Richey," she says, and laughs again. I blush, and but then Nikki comes over and hands her a glass of beer. Nikki stands there, watching me, waiting for our conversation to continue. I don't know what to say, there's a long pause, they're both looking at me. I can feel Dazza and Reuben listening, so I look at Nikki and raise my jug, and say, "Few beers?" and she looks back at me, her forehead wrinkled, and this kind of amazed look of contempt comes over her face and she says, "Yeah. That's right. *A few beers.*"

"Snakebite actually," Sarah says, and Nikki leads her away

in the bathroom later—with a smashed seven ounce glass—holding the base with my right hand—clawing it up my left forearm—stabbing at my arm—scratching at the skin— blood dribbling and dripping into the sink—staring into the mirror, still drinking—lighting a cigarette—holding the lit end hard against my arm while the hairs sizzle and smoke till it almost goes out, watching my eyes—the blood dribbles down to mix with the ash—taking a few drags to bring the cigarette back to life—burning my arm again and again until I calm down and can see my reflection more clearly

and back out to the party I can go straight up to Nikki who's standing alone in the kitchen now pouring snakebites because everyone's gone outside where there's a bonfire being lit and I'm a different person now I stand tall and my body is strong and I'm neither smoking nor drinking and the blood is congealing and drying on my forearm and the hairs tickle but I feel nothing absolutely nothing I am clean and cool and empty and I can go right up to her in her fucking moleskins and fucking awful stinking homespun jersey knotted around her neck and her fucking pathetic attempt to hide her fat arse with that clichéd stupid checkered shirt and her tiny mind and her clichéd Last Footwear boots and I can calmly say,

"I like your chukkas. I've got some ordered with Foster heels and pads."

She concentrates on pouring the beer and the cider but I can tell she's listening.

"They're going to be about two hundred and ninety bucks."

"They last forever though," she says.

"Yeah, my sister's had hers for a couple of years. How old are yours?"

"Oh, I got them for my seventeenth birthday which must have been, oh, couple of years?"

"Yeah well, they're cool," I say and move toward the back door and she says to my back, "Um, Souse, do you think you could give me a hand carrying these out?" and she's holding a couple of stubbies filled with snakebite, still not looking at me, but there's beer stains on her moleskins and she was pouring the drinks unsteadily and her voice has changed and I know that I've beaten her, I've won.

The bonfire is just getting started. It's built in a hole dug in the lawn of the flat, and the party is bigger now, about twenty or twenty-five people, and they stand in groups of three and four and five, dimly lit by the struggling fire, and in most cases watching. Sitting around the fire on the edge of the pit are most of the girls, and Nick and Works. Easty has materialized and is throwing bits of tree branch and planks and rubbish into the hole, all businesslike, talking to Jane, or some of the girls any-way. Nikki jogs lightly past me toward them holding two of the snakebite stubbies. I am holding two more. It is raining very lightly.

"Souser, how's the keg going?" shouts Nick over to me. He

and Works are looking at me from where they sit. He sounds in a good mood.

"A good third I'd say," I say confidently, although I haven't checked it, don't care now. Then they watch as Nikki kind of skips and jogs back round to me to get these two stubbies I'm holding. She takes them carefully, says "Thanks, Souse," and goes back to the girls. Nick and Works are still watching, Nick with this exaggerated look of surprise on his face.

"You made friends pretty fast, Souser," he says before they turn back to the fire. Before I say anything I squeeze my left forearm hard.

"Hmmm," is all I say, and sit down next to Works. Nick gets up straight away on the opposite side of Works, and says, "Piss?" and I say "yup" and Works says "Yeah man," and then Nick leans in close behind me and says very quietly into my left ear, *"Guess who's here? Henry and the Salmond boys. Over behind you."* I shrug, and he strolls inside.

That night was one week ago almost to the hour. I turn to Works to start a conversation, in case they're looking.

"You're Works ay."

"Yeah man. How's it going. You are . . . Souse." He is wearing a Wu-Tang Clan beanie pulled low down his forehead almost to his eyes and he has a wispy ginger goatee and moustache. He's also wearing a gray Nike sweatshirt and brown cargo pants. He sits with his knees together, leaning on them with his forearms smoking a little rollie like a joint; he leans his head back, holds it between his thumb and first finger like a roach and concentrates hard on it when he inhales. His voice is low and strained, his eyes half-closed like he's always stoned.

"Yup," I say.

"So Nick tells me you smoke a bit of ganja, man?" he says, leaning back, looking down his goatee at me with this small smile.

"Been known to, been known to," I say. "You at Knox with Sebastian?"

"Yeah, yeah. Good cunt."

"Yup, good cunt," I say, not knowing if he really means this or if he thinks me and Sebastian are friends and is being tactful. There is a small silence. There is no music now, but the fire is getting bigger and louder. People stare at it, as do I. I can't tell if Henry and those Salmond guys are still behind me or not. I say half-sarcastically, "Uh, so what's your real name then, Works?"

He turns to me quite abruptly and snorts. He smiles this little boy smile. "Um, Hamish," he says, and the stoner drawl disappears for once.

"I'm Richard. Or Richey."

"Okay. Yeah, it's funny, ay, how the nicknames just take over."

"Yeah, yeah. How'd you get Works?"

"Oh shit, it was just like . . . you know . . . school."

"What year did it happen?"

"Oh, was about fifth form I think ay." He's rolling a cigarette, talking past the filter in his lips now as he rummages in the plastic envelope of Drum in his lap. "Yeah, yeah, fifth form. About . . ." He looks up. "Two and a half years ago." Concentrates on rolling again.

"Tailor?" I offer him my B&H's. He holds his hand up.

"No man, no man, it's cool. This is how I got the name ay.

Cos in lunchtimes me and a couple of friends would like disappear down this alley that used to run down beside our school? And we'd roll up these little racehorse joints and get stoned before the afternoon periods."

I laugh.

"Yeah, and I was the one who always had the gear and the papers, man, from my older brother, in a little thirty gram Drum bag like this ay. And we had these fucking wanker seniors ay, they'd come and steal our shit, and we couldn't do anything about it cos they were seniors ay, and they'd just dob us in if we didn't hand it over. Or just smack the shit out of us. And cos I always had the gear they started calling me Works."

"So you got stoned every day at school."

"Yeah, yeah, mostly ay. Apart from when the shit got nicked though ay, which was more than what I would've liked." He turns and laughs to the fire at this, and then lights his tatty-looking rollie, exhaling with a thoughtful expression on his face.

"I used to play badminton once. In fourth form. I just remembered that." He turns to me, smiling. "Yeah man, badminton. Used to be called fag tennis."

"That's cos it fucking is, mate," I can say, and the smile disappears.

In third form there was a Maori boy in our class in home period, which was science, who walked down each aisle in the class and punched every one of us apart from the last two rows, who were the tougher boys. I was sitting in the third last row, on the very end, always on the edge of the select, and Nick was sitting beside me. I was the last one he could possibly punch safely. He was the only Maori in our class, maybe in our form. I had been given advice by my dentist before I started third form. He was an old boy from TBHS and he'd told me as I lay there in the dentist chair, with my mother waiting for me in the waiting room, "Just keep quiet. It's part of high school. You won't get picked on so much if you keep your mouth shut. Try not to be noticed and you'll be alright."

I followed that advice and never questioned it, and so by the time this boy got to me he didn't know how I'd react. He put his left hand on my shoulder, adjusting me so he could give me the deadest dead arm, and then smiled, a little unsure, and punched me lightly. I had gotten off easily. In third form we were mostly hit by senior guys: dumped off chairs, slammed into walls as we queued outside classrooms, given dead arms and dead legs. They would tell us wait till you're a senior, then you can do it to the third formers. To assuage their guilt, maybe. We would talk, and plan what we would do to the turds next year. But in fourth form the hierarchies were all in place and everyone knew who could get picked on, who wouldn't fight back, so as a form we turned on ourselves. There was no unity; there was only getting hit, then hitting the next you could be sure wouldn't hit you back. I would come home and cry, in those early days, and my father would tell me that when he was in high school he had one fight—that he won, of course—and then no one touched him again. He told me that's what I should do. Beat up one person properly and I'd be alright from then on.

I would have dreams where I sat in the back of Accounting with a huge revolver—so big that I could barely get my hand around the handle—and carefully and deliberately shot certain boys in the back of the head. Their heads would explode and blood and brain would splatter onto the boy at the desk in front of them, who would never notice, and quietly keep writing with his head bowed as the dead headless boy behind him lolled and swayed and thick blood ran down his gray shirt and onto his pencil case and folder.

Other dreams were mostly about running away from faceless boys with no hair, trying to hide in corrugated iron alleyways with no exits, losing fights against boys I hardly knew, that got arranged by older boys I hardly knew, and waking up sweating every morning then going to school where things like that happened every day.

Nick returns with three full jugs, gives us one each and leans down beside me and whispers dramatically, *"They're still there, Souser."* I shrug, take the beer, drink a big swig and light a cigarette, watch Works take a big drink too. Nick walks past behind us around the bonfire that's giving off no heat at all to where the girls are sitting. I can see Easty on the other side of the fire. He has a long stick in one hand that he's poking the smoldering planks with. He's looking directly at me, and nods his head up, looking at me, then past me over my head. I nod and mouth, "I know, I know." He shrugs his shoulders, turns away. It's funny how in times of crisis we— me, Nick, Easty—actually seem like real friends. They seem like they're trying to help me. But I know something. The Salmond boys haven't done anything or said anything to me, and Nick at least just wants to get something going on.

Works isn't talking, just staring into the sparks and the ash. I feel very alone, as you always do before a fight.

I finish off my jug and decide to go inside and get more, defuse anything that might be going to happen. I stand, I turn and it is Henry, and three other boys, standing over by the fence, but I turn away quickly before any kind of eye contact is made. Easty shouts over the fire, "Piss, Souse?" and I say, "Yup," in a voice loud enough for them to hear and understand that I'm confident here, with my friends who are also confident, and I'm not ashamed of anything that might have happened, not ashamed because it's cool you know, I do what I want, and Easty throws his stick into the fire and jogs round to join me by the back door and whispers, "Niggle, Souse?" and I reply, "Looks like it, maybe," and we go inside.

And once inside we decide to get the fuck out, things are winding down anyway, Dazza's disappeared, probably gone to bed, Reuben's asleep in one of the armchairs with a bucket in his lap, so we fill four milk bottles from the keg, which is on its last legs, hide them in our jackets, one under each arm, and we go back out the back door. Works has disappeared. We walk past the fire together, arms clamped to our sides. On the other side, beyond where Nikki and Hannah and Jane are still sitting watching the fire I can see in the dim flickery orange light Nick is scoring Sarah, they're back underneath the trees rolling around together, his dark dreads hanging down over her blonde hair spread over the black and orange grass, and we keep walking, Easty striding ahead of me, and I shoot a glance back the other way and Sebastian is standing with the Salmond boys by the fence now, they're all of them, Henry, Sebastian, the three boys I don't recognize, standing and staring after us as we march away with arms stiffly held to our sides, beer splashing onto my shirt and down my jeans from the open milk bottles, and one of them, one of the boys I don't know, sees me look and takes a step forward, drops his half-full jug on the grass and shouts out, "Yeah, cunt?" leaning toward us, rolling up his sleeves as we leave, and as I'm turning away from Sebastian's smiling and his leaning and his sideways whispering to this boy I hear him shout, "Good on ya, cunt," and we just keep walking, down the lawn and away.

And at the end of the lawn we turn hard right onto Leith Street and the throb is back in my neck and Easty whispers back to me as he walks briskly ahead of me along the footpath, "Are they coming?" and I whisper, "Na, na, don't think so," and he slows and walks next to me, extracts one of the milk bottles, turning to me, milk bottle in mouth, says, "Do you even remember what you actually did, Souse?" before taking a swig and I'm shaking my head as I'm thinking of something to say, and all it is is, "There's . . . no shame . . ." and when he won't stop looking at me I mutter, "I won't . . . just . . . don't give me any of your shit, Matt."

We are sitting, me and Matt, at the foot of the mossy concrete wall that encloses the Leith River. The river is just a trickle at this time of year. We're drinking the milk bottle beer and watching the river glittering blackly in the light from the streetlights on Dundas. Matt has puked already, felt sick and stuck his fingers down his throat, and he's telling me this thing bitterly, thinking for some reason that I'm angry at Nick.

"It was when Nick first started getting into rugby instead of soccer. And they made some kind of agreement, Tinny, Dan and Cameron, Mark, Sebastian, fucking *Will Parker*," he counts them off on his fingers, "and I just came to school one day and they stopped talking to me. You know, I just walked into class and went up the back and said hi and that, and they didn't say anything back. They like . . . just talked amongst themselves. The whole class was watching. Man, it was . . . horrible."

"Will was really into that I remember."

"Fucking little greasy cunt. I *know*, I know. You know, we've been friends since we started playing soccer in, like, standard one? And then it was this silence, because *Nich*olas decides I'm not cool enough to hang around with them anymore."

I'm wishing he wouldn't talk about this, and I'm remembering another boy in our class, Antony Brown, and the time in third form when Matt—just Matt then, not "Easty" or any of the other nicknames—when Matt came running into first period before school all excited, telling us *Brown's a fag, Brown's a fag*. Matt had gone to his house on the weekend or something, to watch a video or play soccer, maybe, and after they had played for a while Mrs. Brown had made them some popcorn, and Antony had offered to put a bit of the popcorn in Matt's mouth, and then, sealing his fate for the rest of high school, had told Matt to close his eyes.

"Close your eyes and I'll put it in," Matt, center of attention, quoted for the class, everyone laughing, shocked. There was skepticism and then fear on Antony's face, and he'd totally denied it then and there but it was too late because all the boys got into it, anyone who needed the attention of the cool boys paid to someone else, and the chant started in the class, *fag*, *fag*,

fag, fag, and got louder and louder and went on until Mr. Bennett arrived, shut everyone up and told silent, crying Antony to pull himself together.

But it was like a new toy for the boys, and for the rest of that period at odd times someone would call out quietly, *fag,* and out in the quad at interval the chant was huge, the hostel boys getting into it up by the caf, even.

And Antony, who had up till then been just quiet, ignored mostly, was Fag Brown all day every day until the end of seventh form, until his real name became strange to us—*Antony*—and maybe to himself as well, and he maybe is still Fag Brown now, wherever he is, even though Matt had formed some kind of strange kinship with him in sixth form after he was cut off from Nick and the group, after he was rejected too. Matt, the actual instigator of the whole thing, maybe thinking he was paying some kind of penance with Fag Brown after getting a taste of the same sort of thing from Nick. But sometime in seventh form Matt was slyly allowed back into the group, eased slowly back in but reduced, humiliated publicly, taught a lesson as to his own personal status in relation to Nick, Will, Sebastian, all of them. Nothing as good as that happened to Fag.

A memory. Antony Brown showing anger, finally, in fifth form. Guys standing around him in the quad shouting *fag, fag, fag, fag* at him; him standing, chin to his chest, caught coming back from the caf by this spontaneous attack that for whatever reason finally drove him over the edge, and him grabbing at the closest person to him, Willy Parker, not prepared for that kind of outburst and getting hit by Fag Brown's frantic little fifteen-year-old roundhouses as the crowd goes quiet, waiting to see who gets the upper hand, waiting to see whose side to take, waiting to see who was to be laughed at; and Will failing, recoiling from Antony's tiny breakout, ducking, hands over his face, and shrieking, *what a psycho, what a psycho*, looking around himself just as frantically as Fag, looking for support, his eyes just as wide, his composure just as completely lost.

And everyone had laughed, a gorgeous community laugh from the quad up to the hostels by the caf, everyone grabbed hold of it: *psycho, psycho, psycho*, and Antony panted and stood in an empty circle of concrete as we, as *I*, laughed, and chose him, chose him over Will, to meet this random contempt, our glad betrayal.

I never just watched. I was part of it all too. In those early years I got hit too, but I still punched the arms of those I could be sure wouldn't punch me back, and called Brown fag, knowing by then it was too late for him to raise his eyes to me. I remember amazement he didn't just kill himself, almost wishing he would. But later I grew more and more silent, hovering on the fringes, pulling in my average marks—my low A bursary that disappointed my parents: I just scraped in with a 323—and gaining a strange collective acceptance for my attitude to drinking, which translated into a kind of marginal status in this group. From chess club I went to the prefects' room, and all it really took was my attitude to drinking. I tend to drink as much as I can, as long as I can. It may not be as much as you or someone you know can drink, but all that mattered was my attitude. I showed no fear. I could be drunk and they liked that. And it could be something for someone who has nothing to talk about.

—

"I'd say I've had about . . . six jugs tonight," Matt says. "Man, I feel so much better now after that spit."

Another memory. Matt in third form being held by one of the prefects over the banister of the balcony outside one of the prefabs, his art folder ripped and his pictures blowing away over the concrete. He was reaching back, trying to grab the railing when the senior boy dropped him, but he had reached back too far, his hands groping past the banister, and when he fell the banister caught him up in the armpits and wrenched both his arms up behind him and he fell forward onto the concrete, his gray shirt actually torn under the arms. I remember the white threads, Matt crying, amazed.

Today, including the beers at lunch with my parents, I would say I've had five jugs from the keg, plus the three handles, which equals one and a half jugs, plus the two milk bottles, which are empty now. So, allowing for spillage, about seven jugs. But this is over a long period.

We stare at the river, smoking my B&H's, ashing into the water, and I try, haltingly, self-consciously, to quote this *Paradise Lost* quote I suddenly half-remember from when we did it at school, which I thought was drinking, was wise.

"The slow and silent stream . . . Leith, the river of oblivion . . . rolls. Her water, whereof who drinks forgets. . . . Both joy and grief, and pleasure and pain . . . and his former being. . . . Beyond this . . . Beyond this . . . um . . ."

" . . ."

"That's . . . I think that's mostly wrong. But it's something like that."

"Jesus, Souse. Shut *up*."

—

Matt gets hungry after his puke and suggests that we walk to the twenty-four-hour dairy on George Street to get some food and cigarettes. I tell him I'm sober enough to drive his car and probably because it's raining again he believes me. We walk up the hill to Strangeways and Matt goes inside to get his keys. He owns the Draize Train, a light blue Volkswagen. We get in and Matt starts singing sarcastically the school rugby song, "Ee Ah La Spatio," which is this faux-Maori chant we were taught to sing during rugby games that actually has a lyric, "moo-ree-oo." But he stops singing when I pull this hard U-turn on top of Dundas hill without looking, and says, "Jesus, Souse . . ." but doesn't say anything more as I crunch through the gears, riding the clutch trying to find third, veering all over the road, until when just before Cumberland Street I'm peering down in the half-dark looking for fourth, can't find it, can't get in gear, and he shouts, "Souse, *stop!*" and we're almost onto the one-way but the soles of my boots are too thick and I can't feel where my feet are so I press the accelerator and the clutch instead of the brake and the clutch and the car slows and the engine screams and whines and we drift slowly onto the intersection and Easty's shouting "*Oh fuck fuck fuck* . . ." and but there's no one coming, we're in luck, I find third and release the clutch and we shoot through the intersection, Easty's panting, holding the dashboard and the door handle going, "Oh my fucking god, that was so lucky, that was so lucky . . ." and I say, "Don't worry man."

And at the two-four there's a security guard on the door and a gay porno mag open on the magazine rack to a centerfold of a close-up of a huge flaccid cock, and Easty whispers loudly, "*Soft-cock,*" and the guard turns to see and Easty waves a hand at the magazine and says, "I was just ob*serv*ing . . . a soft cock," and the guard turns away again and I'm good, I've only had a salad and beer today so when Easty gets fish and chips I just get a Lucozade hoping I can minimize the hangover from all this and some cigarettes, which comes to $8.95 and the guy behind the counter taps the keys on the eftpos as four boys with no hair come in the door wearing trousers and chambray shirts and rugby club ties and Easty standing behind me goes, "Je-*sus*," and whispers in my ear, "I *have* to get stoned when we get home," and but when I turn back to the guy behind the counter he's holding up the screen of the eftpos to me, wagging a finger, his face unreadable.

On the little L.C.D. screen the word materializes out of the gray.

It says Declined.

3
A
Frozen
Continent

On this Monday morning I have a really bad dream.

In my dream my dick has grown into a massive tube that arcs out from my pubic hair. My dick grows and I can feel the erection, I can feel this new weight and density and it's not an unpleasant feeling, just like a normal erection, and some part of my dreaming brain tells me I should be enjoying this since my dick's so big, that this must and should be a good thing.

But as it grows and grows up toward and before my face I feel something else in the head, and the slit on the end that is now right before my eyes, bobbing and weaving lightly with my heartbeat, is reddened and swollen and sore-looking, and as I stare at it I feel something inside, something trying to get out. And the tiny reddened slit is forced open just a little and there protrudes a little black pin, coming out of the end. The pin waves a little, gestures left, then right, and is then joined by a second black pin alongside it, and I can see now that something is writhing and alive, moving inside my body, and I realize the pins must be the antennae of some evil black centipede, struggling to be born, and dreaming I mutely scream as I throttle my dick with two hands, trying to hold the creature inside, but which throttling just seems to squeeze the creature's glossy black head out, which pops from the stretched slit at the tip, two shiny blind eyes and then two claw-like legs gesturing vaguely before I wake up with an aching erection.

And so I lie here, in my strange new room in Strangeways, in dusky red light from the sun outside on the tattered red velvet curtains. The clock on my stereo at the base of the wall opposite reads 10:03 A.M. The room is vast compared to Unicol, and is only the third bedroom I have known. I have an open fire, my father's large desk, my sister's old double bed with the head in the bay window. Above my stereo is a poster of Matt's, Lou Reed, from the cover of *Coney Island Baby*, in a T-shirt with a tuxedo print. The carpet was white and shag pile but is now gray and flattened. The ceiling is extremely high. The room is bad, but sixty dollars a week.

I lie here naked beneath my stained duvet, needing to piss, put off the thought of masturbating like I do most mornings. These are the kinds of dreams I suppose you have when you're a man. I listen hard. There are no sounds in the house. Matt's room is opposite mine, on the other side of the hall. Nick's is next door. At least this morning I won't have to worry about either of them hearing me do it.

Occasionally I hear voices passing by outside on the street.

And it's when I roll over onto my left side that I see the bag with the remains of the dope from home, my notebook, the stack of new books, *Bloodlust: Portrait of a Serial Sex Killer*, *American Psycho*, *Holes in M'Naghten*, *Red Dragon*, *The Ragged Edge of the Nineties*, *A Book of Murder*, sitting in a pile on the upturned cardboard box I use for a bedside table. I stare at it, the top book, for a while. It's a paperback, mostly black on the cover, gold raised lettering just like a Stephen King. On the spine I read the author's name: S. J. Johansson; then beside it, in bigger lettering, the title. I reach for the book and draw it beneath the duvet and toward me until it appears next to the pillow I'm lying on.

On the cover is the image of a clown collapsed against a wall. His big feet are splayed before him, his hands limp by his sides, his head lolls. From his sleeves blood is running, which forms a pool around his feet. All in black and red, it looks like the cover of a bad eighties metal album. I turn the book over with my one available hand and read the back.

> Jeffrey Dahmer's butchery . . . David "Son of Sam" Berkowitz's brutal point-blank shootings . . . Edmund Kemper's horrific sexual mutilations and necrophilia . . .

Drama, I'm thinking. I flick through the pages, find the contents page. I flick to:

> Commonalities are the things that these murderers have in common. They are basic statistical and qualitative attributes that these men (for in 99 percent of cases the perpetrators are men—the first commonality) share. These attributes include the most obvious measurements of human beings—sex, race, age, socioeconomic status—

but also extend to the murderers' own histories; their lives, their families, their beliefs and attitudes, their behaviors from early adolescence until they commit their first serious sexual murder.

Our first discovery is that these murdering men were at one point boys that were, in many fundamental ways, very much alike.

I remember third formers would get this terrible shocked look on their face when you hit them as you walked past, by the bike stands or just in the hallways, you could just shove them out of your way, onto the ground even. It was so random, so unjustified it was exciting. They'd look up, shocked, and angry if they were unaccustomed to it; but then they'd see your uniform, see your blazer, and the angry look would modify rapidly when you leaned over them and said all you needed to say.

—In all cases studied the perpetrators (hereafter referred to as "the subject" or "the subjects") were male, Caucasian, and came from two-parent families.

—The subjects all possessed average or above average intelligence. Most finished high school. Some attended universities. Most did not achieve their academic potential.

—The subjects' families were often economically advantaged, lower-middle or middle class with a stable income. Subjects' mothers were often homemakers, their fathers working at either skilled or unskilled jobs, mostly blue-collar, but a significant percentage were lower-echelon professionals.

—At the time of his first serious offence—a rape, or rape-murder, with or without evidence of mutilation or sadism pre- or postmortem—the subject will most often be in his early twenties, unemployed, or doing substandard work in a job that does not reflect his abilities. Many of the subjects we interviewed had escaped capture and conviction for this offence; those who had escaped had consistently escalated their behaviors. Those who had been caught proceeded to escalate after their release from either prison or psychiatric care.

—At the time of this first serious offence there was (in 83 percent of subjects) an example in the subjects' recent history—their mid- to late-teens, usually—of some form of assault, breaking and entering, sexual harassment, and/or rape or attempted rape.

—Most subjects reported difficulties with and anger at male authority figures, ranging from fathers and guardians to teachers and police.

—89 percent of subjects reported histories of drug and/or alcohol abuse.

These boys had virtually all the benefits society has to offer. Blessed sons of modern Western culture: socioeconomically privileged, white, male, intelligent.

There's more, but I'm closing the book, putting it back on the box and checking the clock. It's 10:35. If I flag a shower and hurry I can make my eleven o'clock Marketing lecture in Castle 3. It will be my first lecture of the year but maybe I can catch up on what I've missed.

So I'm getting up, dressing with the curtains closed, clothes that are carefully casual: jeans, brown boots, blue knit Speight's shirt with the collar in an ambiguous position—not fully up but not completely folded back flat; just kind of . . . *crumpled*—and my denim jacket.

Into the living room and Nick is up, sitting calmly in front of the TV eating toast.

"Oh, shit, you gave me a fright." Fright. Jesus. I was caught off guard. He just grunts.

"You got a lecture?"

He grunts again, watching the TV.

"Got an eleven o'clock if you want to go now."

"Turning over a new leaf, Souse? When did this happen?"

"Oh, this morning. Decided not to rest on the laurels of my class privilege."

"That's ridiculous. Just because we've got what many haven't got, it doesn't follow that we should give it up."

"Okay, mate."

"It's not cool to be stupid either, Souse. And at least the poor don't hate themselves like the middle class do. They have something to hate. That's a privilege."

"Fuck's sake. Coming or not."

"Yeah well I might actually."

"And anyway, Nick, you're middle class and you don't hate yourself."

"That's because I've got punk rock."

We walk to university in silence.

At the Registry he's turning into the old varsity lecture theaters for his Philosophy lecture and I'm walking fast over the bridge, past Hocken toward the castle lecture theaters. An advantage of being late is that there's hardly anyone around, less chance of any Salmond or Unicol resident encounters.

I'm climbing the outside stairs and I enter the lecture theater at the back. It is vast and packed out. People fill every seat, all up the aisles and are two-deep sitting cross-legged right in front of the lecturer, who's already begun talking. I stay at the very back, leaning against the back wall. More people arrive after me and sit on the floor as well.

The lecturer is writing something on the board. I'm noticing an incredible amount of caps in the theater. There are caps on almost half the heads I can see from where I'm standing. There are Starter caps, Nike caps, Speight's caps, leather caps, blue, red, black, and brown caps. And the eerie thing is that most of them are pointed this way.

At least a third of the people in this room are wearing reversed caps.

The lecturer is writing still:

Wednesday 7 P.M.

A–D C3

E–I C1

J–N C2

O–R COMM 225 (2nd floor Commerce)

S–Z COMM 226 (2nd Commerce)

1 hour

40%

There are groans and sighs from the audience, which is now studiously copying down this stuff, which is slowly dawning on me as applying to a fucking test, a test on Wednesday, for a subject that I'm as of now in my first lecture for, *a 40 percent test*.

I'm writing on my hand because I've forgotten to bring any paper, COMM 226 1hr 40%. The lecturer, this Nordic-looking tanned blonde young guy with a ponytail and a green linen suit turns to the audience and gestures with his hands in a calming motion and then he says, "Ya, ya, I know, I know. Forty percent iz fery hard, but remember, test is only for syllabus up to unt including Fviday's lecture . . ." and I'm halfway out the door and onto the landing before he can say, "so if you vont to leaf now I vill unterstand, yes?"

In Student Loans in the Registry building, talking to this older woman behind the counter.

"Well, I'm a first year student, and I paid for my fees on loan, and then I got out some more to pay for some time I . . . spent at . . . um . . . Unicol, but I can't remember exactly how much, and now I've just ran out of money, um, on Saturday night, and, I was wondering if I . . . well how much more I can get, and if maybe I could get an allowance. I got an A Bursary."

"Okay. Well, an A Bursary is only going to get you two hundred dollars in one lump sum, and you will already have received that. If you could give me your name and student number?"

"Um, Richard Sauer. Hold on . . . 940584."

" . . . okay . . . Well, Richard. You have two thousand seven hundred and fifty dollars drawn down for your compulsory fees. Plus you've drawn down the thousand dollars for course-related costs . . . and you've drawn down . . . fourteen hundred dollars of your living costs component . . ."

". . ."

"You *have* been busy."

". . ."

"Leaving you four hundred and fifty dollars available to draw upon until the next trimester begins."

"And when's that?"

"The . . . twenty-eighth of May."

". . ."

"..."

"But I've got to pay . . . four hundred and eighty bucks in rent before then."

"Oh. Well, perhaps I can give you this pamphlet on budgeting advice."

"Yeah, but, like, I have to budget four hundred and eighty bucks into four hundred and fifty?"

"Okay, perhaps you should have budgeted more carefully earlier in the year."

"Well, then . . . I just didn't know . . . you know . . . I just like ticked the little box and signed my name and it just, you know . . . it all gets done for you."

"So you haven't really looked into your obligations under the student loan scheme?"

"No, no I haven't."

"Well, look, I'll give you this booklet. There are no limitations because of parental income, creditworthiness, absence of security, age, sex, or race of course . . ."

"Can I get a student allowance?"

"Okay. Let's see now. Have you had an allowance before?"

"No. I haven't done any of this before."

"Alright, okay. Well you'll have to take this booklet and fill it out. There's a list on the back of documents you and your parents will have to provide. We'll need an original birth certificate, some second form of identification like a driver's license or passport, confirmation of your IRD number, a bank-generated deposit slip, confirmation of your own previous income and assets, confirmation of your parents' incomes and assets—are your parents married or separated?"

"They're married."

"Confirmation of both their incomes if they both work—are both of your parents working?"

"No, no, my mother's a . . . a . . . homemaker . . ."

". . ."

"I think . . . I think I might be too privileged to get one of these."

". . ."

". . ."

"Well, okay, but if you do get into trouble, remember to call us on our toll-free number—here's my card—and, also, I have heard some rumors that the Students' Association are attempting to set up a food bank."

I have to walk back over the bridge and along beside the Leith to get in the back way to the Commerce Building and avoid passing Unicol. The Building looms above me, gray and pink, a monstrosity I think. Nick says it's a monstrosity.

Inside there are walls made of glass bricks and an atrium, a vast emptiness stretching up to gray Dunedin sky. There are food machines here, tables and chairs, some stunted, gnarled trees in pots filled with cigarette butts. There are people in suits and ties walking around inside it, young guys, like they've already got marketing jobs, but they stop and talk to guys in rugby jerseys and shorts and boat shoes.

The lift doors are shiny aluminum—four lifts—and by the time I find the Marketing floor on the aluminum contents page for the building riveted to the aluminum lift wall by the floor buttons the lift's passed it and I'm on the tenth floor. A guy in a suit gets out and I press the sixth floor button.

The doors open onto gray industrial carpet, and the smell of paint. It is silent. The carpet is springy beneath my feet, and leads down one corridor to my left, lined with identical pink doors, little metal plaques with three-digit numbers riveted to them; and an identical corridor to my right, same doors, plaques, rivets, but, I assume, different numbers. Before me is a massive window and a widening of the corridor out to the edge of the atrium. The wall of glass must be for those who are waiting to pass the time by looking down into the atrium, up at the leaden sky, or just at the inside of the Commerce Building opposite. There are two low chairs and nothing—literally nothing—else. No coffee table, no magazines. On the wall is riveted a map of the Marketing floor. I locate Dr. Martin, Convener MART 101, Rm. 6.14.

Where I'm standing, the map tells me, is the "Waiting Area." Beyond that, where the atrium begins, it reads, "Void."

I knock three times at his door, the sound flat and dead in this pink and gray and paint-smelling hall. A voice calls something out. I hesitate, not sure what the voice said. I knock again, just once. *"Come,"* I hear the voice say irritably.

I open the door just enough to let me in and sidle through. Dr. Martin sits at a desk facing a computer, his left side to me, his right to a large window that looks out over the Leith, student flats, and town. His office is just as sparse as the corridor. The gray carpet. Bookshelves line the wall behind him. The other walls are pink. A suit jacket hangs on a hook on the pink door behind me. He is slightly balding and has splotched, mottled skin. He is wearing black suit pants, a blue shirt with a white collar, and a yellow and green tie.

"If you'll just excuse me for one second . . ." he says slowly, staring at the screen and typing. I don't say anything. As he stops typing and moves the mouse, he speaks slowly, his eyes still moving rapidly over the screen, punctuating his words with clicks on the mouse.

"You know that . . . in certain penitentiaries in Ameri . . . ca . . . the administrators of the facilities were so advised . . . that certain shades of . . . pink . . . had a . . . calming effect on inmates. . . . And they thus . . . proceeded to . . . paint . . . certain key rooms with this particular shade of pink . . . of course, rooms like isolation cells, I imagine . . . before particularly dangerous or disturbed inmates . . . were admitted into them . . ."

I watch him. He leans toward the screen and gives the mouse one malicious final click, before swinging around in his chair to face me, smiling broadly.

"And do you know what they did? The inmates, I mean?"

I shake my head and try to snort, to indicate that I'm amused. He smiles even more broadly.

"They ate the paint. They chewed the paint off the walls with their teeth and ate it. Now what can I do for you, young man?"

"Well. Um." I try and laugh for him. He looks at me, smiling, waiting. "Well, I'm enrolled in . . . um, Mart 101 . . ."

"Ah, excellent course, *ex*cellent course. Yes?"

"Yeah, and I found out to*day*—"

"*That* you've got a 40 percent quiz on Wednesday night and you're utterly unprepared for it."

"Well, yeah, but it's like, I missed some lectures and stuff . . ."

"Okay. And . . . ?"

" . . ."

"You would *like* . . . ?" He's cocking his head at me, leaning forward in his chair, and I'm blushing, sweating, he's making me feel fucking stupid.

"I was wondering if I could get . . . some copies . . . of like the handouts and overheads that I've missed."

"Well. Of course." He swivels around in his chair to some stacks of paper underneath the window. "Can you tell me the dates of the missed lectures?"

And with him facing away from me I find it much easier to say in a deep voice, "All of them up until last Friday."

"And that's what I had guessed, judging from your pale complexion and harried demeanor," he says, taking one piece of paper from each pile and stacking them on his desk.

"I wouldn't worry terribly much, though. You're one of many that are using this valuable service we provide." He looks back at me from his bent-over position, then turns back to the stacks. "You may take solace in the fact that the rugby-jerseyed hordes will be lined up at my door in their hundreds in half an hour or so."

I stare at his back, picturing myself holding a cigarette lighter to his shirt, flames running up his back and over his scalp and catching in his thin gray hair. He spins around and hands me a sheaf of papers. "There you are, my denim friend. More product, price, place, and promotion than you can shake a beer jug at."

I suddenly feel a solidarity with all those reversed caps. I don't return his smile. I growl, "Cheers, mate," and turn and leave.

And I whisper, "You fucking gay faggot," as I walk back down the empty gray corridor.

And outside the wind is blowing harder now and the sky's gray is darker and more leaden, a gray darker even than the concrete of Unicol's two massive towers that loom over me from the top of their little hill. I stand there, on the footpath, as some fat raindrops start to splash about me, the sheaf of papers in my hand flapping and pulling in the wind.

Something enters me at my feet and makes its way up through the veins in my legs. It tingles in my groin briefly, sucks my stomach in, and then grabs hold and freezes my heart like a cold bone lump. Inside my head there is roaring. I cannot feel the rain that is staining my denim clothes black and blurring the ink on the papers I carry. It feels like everything in my body contracting, clenching, then disintegrating, and tiny pieces fluttering down, falling like ash inside me. I feel empty now, freezing, a void, and it feels so good, it feels real, it feels like something I need.

I walk away, toward Strangeways. The papers congeal to the footpath, spitting and stained with the raindrops that become hail by the time I reach the top of Clyde Road and see home.

—

A single candle burns on top of Matt's wardrobe. From where I sit behind the drum kit waiting for Matt and Nick to tune their guitars to each other I can see in the dim flickering light the pictures that line the walls of Matt's room, paintings he has painted but never talks about, all self-portraits, all different sizes, from the size of the cover of a book to one painted on the back of a U2 tour poster, every wall, from floor to ceiling. The paintings surround us, staring in at Matt's little single bed that he has placed in the very center of the room like an altar. Each portrait's face is half-shadowed, backgrounded in black. There is a record here of all Matt's different haircuts if anyone chose to look. From total woolly mammoth with sideburns at school through a number four to what he's got now, a mohawk, which we all find kind of ridiculous but which suits him in a strange way.

So now we're waiting, me and Nick, for Matt to get his guitar tuned properly. He's crouched in front of his brother's amp, picking harmonics through the feedback. I'm sipping beer that Matt bought, hunched in my seat, looking through the drum kit at them. Nick's on the other side of the bed, getting irritated now at having to wait. Matt's faces stare down at us in this thin tall room; sad, half-shadowed, hollow-cheeked and haunted-looking; peering out ghostlike and uncertain.

Nick throws an empty beer can at Matt. It bounces off his back, spraying drips of beer onto his white scalp and his mohawk. He doesn't move, picks another harmonic, tunes it up a little. I can see Nick leaning over the bed, his mouth moving, shouting, but I can't hear his voice over the feedback. He shouts into the microphone but it's not turned on. He turns to me and

I shrug and he throws his hands up in the air, stalks over to the beers stacked on the little Casio keyboard in the corner and opens one, one hand on his hip, shaking his head, dreads flying, his Gibson acoustic that he fitted a pickup to dangling from its strap and bumping against his flat, hard stomach.

Some boys seem born to wear guitars.

Hours later. We are all in Ursula's room, me, Nick, Matt, and her. She sits on her bed—a bare waterbed, a cheap one—drinking red wine from the bottle. She wears black jeans, a long brown jersey, a skirt over her jeans. Smokes a cigarette. We sit in various positions around the base of the wall. In this room there is nothing but the waterbed base and bladder, a pile of clothes, a box of paper and books.

"Fuck man, starting to get cold," Matt says. There's a silence. "How'd you feel about that jam?"

"I think we should stop doing covers," Nick mutters.

"I quite like them though," I say.

"Souse, you only like them because you know exactly how to drum to them," he says, without looking at me.

"No shame in them. They're good songs," I say.

"They're *covers*, Souse. Forget it. It's just wasting—fucking—time," Nick growls. Ursula laughs.

"He's right, Souse," Matt says.

"Covers warm you up. That's all they're good for."

"And for money."

"Exactly. You're never going to be anyone if you do covers."

"Kurt Cobain cared more about the covers they did than his own songs."

"But they still *had songs*, Matt."

"Their drummer's great though," I say and Nick sighs loudly.

"Souse, drums are a tool. They're not an instrument. You can't speak with drums. They're for angry mutes." He looks at me and I look away. "And you only like what? English stuff? American stuff? You can't even decide."

"Yeah well, he's got a point, Tin. We mostly listen to . . . like . . . English stuff . . ." Matt trails off.

"One day. . . . Oh for fuck's. . . . Who've we got? Split Enz. The Enemy. The Clean. The Verlaines. The Chills. They're all dead or middle-aged. They still *play* when they're middle-aged. They're depressing to watch. Like Martin Phillips at Orientation wearing this pink fluffy angora jersey with these little nipples on it. It's just embarrassing. Crowded House, my mother has a Crowded House CD. And the only people that like The Dead C are The Dead C. And their girlfriends."

"Sonic Youth like them."

"Sonic Youth like them because they think that not being able to afford proper instruments is a political statement. Sonic Youth are like fifty."

"Let's face it then, the only way to make money is to be crap."

"I remember when I was about twelve and my sister was having a party down in our garage, and she invited me down to have a beer with her friends. So I went down and they had a table set up and all Karen's friends were sitting around drinking crate beer and they were all muso types and it was summer and it was warm and they were listening to this INXS song. It goes . . . falling down the mountain. End up kissing dirt. And all her friends were giving me beers and talking music and it was all just so cool. And that song's always been . . . I don't know, it's always been what I thought parties should be like. It was that song that made me want to be in a band. Yeah . . . *Falling down the mountain . . . end up kissing dirt.*"

Ursula looks up when he sings.

"One day New Zealand music's gonna be . . . something . . . like . . ." He trails off.

A long silence.

"Let's go for a walk up to the graveyard. Smoke up."

"Man, it's getting so cold." Matt shivers, hugs himself.

Ursula is silent as they leave. I take a long drink of the beer, give up. My Monday is over.

In my room, rummaging around in one of my still packed boxes of shit from Unicol I find an old letter from Anna that I received last year, before the New Year's incident and Kim, after a late night drunken phone call from me. I must have been in a pretty bad way, but I honestly don't remember much of anything we said.

Dear Richey,

Well, it's first thing Sunday morning and I'm writing—talk about your instant reaction. I'm really worried about you and feel pretty helpless. I want you to know that I'm always here for you, if you ever need to talk. Thank you for trusting me enough to ring last night, it means a lot. Please write to me and tell me what's going on—it's hard to know what to say when I don't know where you're at. You sounded pretty bad on the phone but I want you to know that there are a lot of people out there that are built on hurt—but there are also a hell of a lot who really care and love.

Whatever's going on it can't be all that bad—yeah, I know, that's just me being the eternal optimist but you're never alone okay? (I know, I know, sorry about the goddam clichés but sometimes they seem like the only way to express this kind of thing.) I feel really bad for you and want to give you a big hug—as that's kind of impossible I'm sending you mental ones constantly so I hope you get some of them.

So anyway, time for lucky you to hear some of my problems.

I'm having a really bad time at Girls' High lately. Fifth form sucks. And the people are driving me slowly insane. Everyone is so wrapped up in their images and shit and I just can't pretend to be a part of it anymore. I've really cut a lot of my connections here now and it gets pretty lonely but I hang out with a lot of older people from varsity—you'd probably call them hippy types!—but yeah, we go to gigs and they can be really supportive and cool—and plus they can buy drinks for little me.

Anyway, on Friday night there was a record release party for this new music label and there were all these amazing bands and people and not a Merivale or a rugbyhead in sight. I was truly happy. The bands were great—I don't know how many of them

you know cos of that thing you have about New Zealand music—
you blasphemer! (only joking) so I won't bother listing them all
but it was a great night and it was a really high stage so short
people like me could see it all—yipee!

I don't know if I've told you about Andrew—the "love of my
life" who I started going out with about two months ago—but
anyway he is a yucky person who put me through heaps of shit
which I'm sure you would love to not hear about, but anyway, to
put it briefly, he gets pretty psychotic when drunk and is not a
very pleasant person to be around. To cut a long dreary story
short—on different occasions he got stuck into two of my friends
and surprise surprise we broke up. For a while after it I was pretty cut up about it all but now I can see him for what he is: on Friday night he was there with his new girlfriend who was
hysterical the whole night because good old honey Andy had
made the moves on her best friend. What a man I do say—I sure
pick them!

I'm thinking of you pretty much constantly at the moment
and am very worried.

Write soon and let me know how you are.

Lots of love, Anna

I can't help but think that she knew nothing about me then. Not
what I'm really like or what I really do. And I remember thinking that she had a fat arse.

Sometimes I don't recognize my thoughts as I think them,
other than knowing they are mine.

—

Back in Ursula's room, three or later in the morning. Nick and Matt still out on their "walk."

This room parallels Nick's on the other side of the front door and the hallway, overlooking our steep tiny little lawn that plunges down onto Dundas. Ursula is sitting cross-legged in the middle of her waterbed, which is stripped of blankets and sheets. She is slumped over, her hair hanging over her face, a mostly empty red wine bottle nestled between her thighs. A cigarette between her fingertips dangles dangerously close to the plastic waterbed bladder.

"Ursula," I say, taking off my jacket, sitting down on the floor opposite her, leaning back against the wall. "Ursula."

"Mmm?" she murmurs, and laughs to herself.

"You awake?" I say, knowing I sound like an actor playing a horny man trying to wake up his wife but not caring.

"Yeah man," she says, with this slow stoner drawl.

"I was just thinking we've never really talked," I say to the crown of her head, to the tiny round bald spot pointing directly at me. She convulses a little, laughing I think.

"No, no man," she says.

"So. You like the flat?"

"Oh yeah, it's alright." Just a low drawling murmur.

"So . . . and you're from Wellington?"

"Yep, yep. The old windy shithole. Mount Vic, actually." She either shudders or laughs, it's hard to tell. I'm restless, pissed off, might be horny I suppose.

"Have you got a . . . boyfriend there?"

"Aaah . . . *had* one." She takes a drag with an unsteady hand, a column of ash teetering over the waterbed's plastic before she flicks it off out onto the carpet.

"What? You break it up or him?"

"Well. Something . . . I can't tell you, man." Her head lifts just barely and she peers through her hair at me with glazed eyes. "Man, I barely know you." I wait, wanting to know, but not to let on that I even care.

"Oh, well, we're going to be flatmates so we'll find out all each other's sordid little details, all each other's little routines, and habits . . ." I'm listening to myself, cringing.

"You're funny."

"Why?"

"You just are, man."

"Why?"

"Well first you hardly say anything when Matt and Nick're around and now you're all, like, talkative." I start fumbling in my denim jacket beside me for cigarettes. She's still watching me. I snort as I fumble, trying to show that I'm laughing. "And now you're all shy."

"Oh okay, okay. I just wanted to talk, get to know you since we're going to be living together and everything." I light my cigarette, puff out some smoke, try to look irritated.

"No, oh sorry, man. Oh fuck . . . I was only joking, man," she's saying, nodding her head, still slumped over. She drinks from her wine bottle, shakes her head, mumbling to herself. "I'm so fucking rude ay . . . I always just push people away . . . and I'm in a new flat and I don't even know you or anything . . . I'm sorry, man, Richey, ay . . ." She's looking up now and I look away, embarrassed. She's almost got tears in her eyes, really drunk.

"Oh don't worry about it, it's . . . nothing . . ." I say in a rush. She looks down in her lap.

"It's just I've been fucked over by so many guys ay, like this last guy in Wellington, we'd been going out for two months, and he's just started this course at the Wellington Polytech, and like we had sex just the day before I left and then he just fucks off? Didn't come to the airport. Didn't even want my address down here or anything. . . . Not that I had one then . . ." The little laughter convulsions are starting again.

A pause. "I just thought you wanted to jump my bones."

I snort, glad she's not looking at my face anymore. There's another pause. I'm looking hard at the carpet when she says, "What happened to your arm, man?" She's staring at my forearm wrapped around my knees.

"Oh . . . I caught it . . . in the window . . . at the party."

She's looking at me through her hair. She smiles, sneers.

"Yeah. Right."

There's a long, long silence and I jump when the front door crashes open and Nick and Matt fill the hallway with clumping boots, Easty chirruping happily now, Nick shouting something about a "Tin Pan Man." "The Tin Pan Man's gonna get you." Easty knocks and puts his head in the door, sees us alone in here together and there's a second's pause as he looks at me, then her, then me again before he speaks.

"Drugs in Tinny's room, Souse, and it's green and brown and dripping with lovely THC."

"Yep, okay," I say, jumping up. Ursula's head turns, wobbling, toward the door. "Any for little ole me?" she says, her accent changed and almost normal now.

"There's plenty for *every*body," comes Easty's voice from the hallway.

Oh horrible. That's all I can manage. That's all I can tell. It was too awful.

Once I had put my jacket back on and we sat in a circle on Nick's double bed and did a few cones—I wasn't drunk enough, dammit—and Nick and Matt started showing off and juving out, this just freezing, aching paranoia came over me and it was all I could do to just try and smile and I was so aware of how we worked together that it hurt and I could see the voids between us, how Nick and Matt jousted with each other, how I took sides, but constantly swapped, how Ursula was outside of us and how they laughed at her and how I wanted to laugh at her to get in with them but knew—*knew*—that I was still prepared to fuck her if I got the chance.

Ursula smoked her cone in a way they found funny. She said, "This cone's for Kurt Cobain." Nick smirked, Matt snickered. I saw them and giggled, which is pretty much all I can do when I'm stoned but not drunk and which is just impossible to stop when I see anyone else laughing. Ursula passed the pipe to me and saw us laughing, not knowing what we are like she didn't realize it was her we were laughing at and so started laughing too, hunching over with the little convulsions, smoke puffing out her nostrils and mouth, hair dangling and the smoke rising through it and it was then after two cones that I could feel my eyes widening, the eyelids peeling back and my eyeballs bulging and straining out so far they hung over my cheeks and not only could I see round a full 180 degrees but I felt that each person I turned to could see my bulging, hideously huge eyeballs, wobbling like water balloons, red-veined and naked, and but what was worst of all was that a little straight and sober part of me, deep inside, looking desperately through those bulbous distorted bags of eye fluid, knew exactly how I looked, how I was turning to each one and staring with banal, blank and bloodshot eyes and a sick and helpless smile.

And because I couldn't speak they started to speak to me and I couldn't bear it, trying frantically to act just like a stoned fun-loving kind of guy but ending up just sitting there, smiling, my eyelids peeled back, the three of them getting up and literally capering and dancing around the bed, chanting, "Speak Souse speak Souse speak sow speak sow speak sow speak sow speak sow speak sow speak sow . . ."

So I got up and just left, staggered a little, my knees cracking and sore from sitting, and Matt said, "Oh Souse don't *go* . . ." but I did, I left, out the door and into my room to lie on my bed.

I didn't want to tell that. I don't want to know that I have no friends. I know how important friends are supposed to be. It's been said it's your mates, then the piss, then the chicks. The boys, the beer, and only then the bitches. I know all that. But there you are. Here I am. I've somehow managed to cling to my friends, like props, for my life to be acted out amongst. But the props are warm and they're not interested in my sordid little play. Neither is the audience. The stage disintegrates; the people disappear; I only have the nerve to do my little song and dance alone in the dark.

—

Later.

I must have fallen asleep because I am woken early in the morning, still in my jeans and Speight's shirt, by the phone in the hallway ringing. I lie here, hoping someone else gets it. I am yet to be rung by anyone other than my parents in my new flat. The phone rings on and on. Just hang up. Anyone that knows us will know we won't be up until at least eleven. The phone has rung upward of eight times before I hear Easty's door open on the other side of the hallway and the meaty thuds of his stomping—the way he walks in boots or bare feet—then a plastic crash as the phone gets dropped, then some scrabbling sounds, clicks and clacks, and finally, a strained, forced voice saying, "Hell . . . o?"

There's a tiny pause.

"No, no, hold on." A plastic clunk on the hallway floor and three stomps to my door. Three quick knocks. "Souse. For you." Four stomps and his door rattles shut. His bedsprings squeak once, then silence. I swing my legs over the side of the bed and rise. Open my door, and it's bright, the doors all shut, the hallway filled with mottled sunlight that glints in the marbled semicircle of glass above the front door. Squinting, I pick up the phone handset that's resting on the floor by the phone table, the only decoration in this hallway.

"Hello?"

"Hello, am I speaking with Richard Sauer?" A professional voice, not friendly, not impolite, a voice used to being up and about at, what? eight o'clock?

"Yeah." Sounding tired.

"Hello, Mr. Sauer. My name is Paul Morris. I'm the Sexual Harassment Prevention Officer on the Varsity Disciplinary

Committee for Otago University. I'm afraid you've had a complaint laid against you, Mr. Sauer, concerning an incident . . . nine days ago at a function organized by the Salmond Hall of Residence. I'm sure you recall the incident I'm referring to?"

"Umm . . . well, kind of—"

Stupid.

"Well, whether or not—it seems as if you do—a complaint has been laid by Mrs. Thompson, the head of Salmond Hall, on behalf of one of her residents. I was contacted by her after . . . you were previously a resident of University College?"

"Yeah."

"Doctor Neilsen has informed us that you were spoken to, given strict, clear instructions regarding your obligations in this matter, and Mrs. Thompson has confirmed that you have failed to meet these obligations. The matter has now been referred to me. Mr. Sauer, you are required to attend a University Disciplinary Committee hearing in the North Committee Room, which is room 105 on the first floor of the University Registry building."

". . ."

"Do you know where that is?"

"Yip."

"This hearing is scheduled for 4 P.M. on Wednesday the twenty-seventh of July. You have plenty of time to ensure that you are free then. If you should fail to attend, other actions will commence. I urge you to be there, for your own sake."

"Yeah."

"Good-bye, Mr. Sauer."

"Okay."

And that's it.

—

How much could Easty have heard? Just a few "yeahs" from me. But maybe—what did this guy say to him? What are my "obligations"? I shut my door on the glare of the hallway, climb back onto my bed in the red dim of my room. Neilsen said ring them up. But maybe I was going to. I spoke to him three days ago. This is utter bullshit. Christ if only my parents knew. At the moment it might not surprise them too much.

All this seems so ridiculous, so unreal, like someone's got hold of my name and made it the center of all this attention. Richard Sauer. A character, borrowing my name, and things attributed to him belong to me. Live his life.

Seems like it's got actually nothing to do with *me*. I've just been trying to get by, and now they want to put me in a hearing for Christ's sake, they're probably thinking of fucking *prosecuting* me. What? A fine? *Jail?*

I'll not be able to get back to sleep. I write the date and time of the hearing on my lecture timetable, which is taped to the wall above my desk. I lie back on my bed. Why do people read? Times like this. Pick up *A Book of Murder*, flip to the first page, start reading.

> Introduction
>> Statistically,

"Statistically." A great word to start a book about murder.

> of all homicides reported in the last twenty years, the F.B.I.'s research has indicated that the major growth category has been in homicides without a clear motive. The "unknown motive" category of homicide as reported in the F.B.I.'s Uniform Crime Reports publication has consistently grown throughout the 1980s and 1990s.

Within the broad penumbra of "unknown motive" we find what is commonly known as the serial killer, or serial sexual killer, meaning a certain type of murderer whose violent antisocial behavior has escalated from early juvenile delinquence[1] to assault and/or sexual assault through to sexualized murder.

The escalation is characteristic.

I turn to the end of the chapter to look up the endnote.

1 q.v. the F.B.I.'s "homicidal triad," p. 11. supra.

Bored bored bored

For our purposes, we define a serial sexual killer as (almost invariably) a man who commits murder that evidence suggests contains a sexual component. Evidence that suggests the sexual nature of a homicide includes: removal of the victim's clothing; reclothing of the victim's body in symbolic apparel; exposure of the victim's genitalia; sexualized posing of the victim's body; sexually specific mutilation or sadism; evidence of sexual intercourse— oral, anal, or vaginal—pre- or postmortem. Sometimes evidence that, to the layman, may not point specifically toward a sexual connotation to the murder may in fact be the result of the murderer's activities that have a sexual symbolism only for him. This evidence may include obliteration of the victim's facial features, amputation of limbs (especially legs or feet), removal of hair, certain kinds of stabbing. The murderer's specific needs are served by these activities, whether or not they include the actual murder of the victim.

After a murder, the subject goes through a cooling-off period that may or may not be characterized by extreme remorse, guilt, feelings of hopelessness or worthlessness (an emotional state very close to clinical depression). However, we have found that with most of the subjects we interviewed, whether or not these feelings of regret were present (in many cases, the "cooling-off" period was characterized mainly only by fear of capture), the subjects went on to murder again, often improving their technique, learning from their first mistakes. Much like learning a sport.

Much like learning a sport. I find my hand creeping beneath the duvet at oral, anal, or vaginal. Sometimes all it takes are the words. And then *obliteration of the victim's facial features*.

Repeated brutal, sexually symbolic torture and murder of women by white middle-class men, although perhaps not wholly a twentieth-century phenomenon, is on the increase this decade, all over the world. Serial murder is now of course the province of pop culture. We find serial killers' faces on T-shirts, their murders in made-for-TV movies. They are figures of intrigue and humor. Do they remain compelling only, however, at a distance, until they touch our lives personally? These are men who will attack and murder our loved ones from a compulsion so strong that to deny it is, for them, a kind of death in life. More than ever now, we need to know why.

Oral anal or vaginal oral anal or vaginal oral anal or vaginal.

I masturbate, finally, and I think of Sarah, then remembering Nick and her, and so Ursula, lying back naked on her waterbed bladder with her legs spread open and her eyes shut, comatose and silent. When I come I don't see anything at all and I think of *obliteration of the victim's facial features*. I think of *obliteration*.

That's the end of the introduction.

The clock says 9:03 A.M. I find myself picking up the book again almost immediately. Past Commonalities I find a new section entitled

Experiences and Behaviors
in Adolescence and Early Adulthood

We believed that the experiences and behaviors of these murderers during adolescence (age thirteen to nineteen years) and early adulthood (age nineteen to twenty-five years) could provide important information to help us attempt to generalize about the kind of young male who grows up to murder. A questionnaire was given to the men that covered a wide range of topics. Embedded in this questionnaire were several key experience- and behavior-oriented questions. These questions were designed to find, in the context of a general personal life history, the presence and frequency of several key behaviors and experiences we had come to believe were held in common by these murderers. The results are listed below.

Experience and Behaviors Checklist

(expressed as percentages of the 57 murderers inter-viewed)

A quick summary of the table shows

I'm copying it into my notebook

that many of the behaviors we theorized were held in common were in fact extreme-ly prevalent. Over three-quarters of the men reported binging behavior using alcohol during adolescence, including the use of other drugs such as marijuana, hash, L.S.D., ecstasy, and, much more rarely, cocaine. This fig-ure climbs to 90 percent in early adulthood.

Three-quarters is also the figure we encounter for ado-lescent anxieties over body shape. This figure relates to both ends of the spectrum, from anxieties over weight gain to anxieties over perceived thinness. Many of the men linked any troubles with relating to females directly to what they saw as their own inadequate body shape.

This is reflected in the reporting of eating-disordered behavior, most commonly regarded as a problem affecting females. Forty percent of the men reported disordered eating during adolescence, ranging from solitary binging to fasting to induced vomiting or bulimia. This figure climbs to 45 percent in the adult male. We theorize that at a time when many men are in relationships and are thus to a certain extent relieved of the pressure to compete for female attention, the murderer, isolated as he is, feels the pressure to be physically beautiful more keenly.

The "Psychiatric care or intervention" statistic was intended to discover how many of these men had come into contact with the psychiatric profession before and/or during periods where violent behavior occurred. The figures are low, but we must bear in mind that these men were not identified as a risk to society at the time they were seen by professionals, and that they went on to be responsible for a great deal of suffering. (See Appendix III for DSM-IV diagnoses and misdiagnoses. Also, Chap. 5, Serial Killer Worlds: Case Studies)

Other figures powerfully reinforce the F.B.I.'s "homicidal triad" (three key adolescent behaviors shared by men who went on to become sexual murderers): cruelty to animals—56 percent; bedwetting beyond the normally appropriate age—38 percent; firesetting or arson—53 percent.

A knock at my door.

"Come in?"

"Souse. Letter for you."

"Can you bring it in? I'm in bed."

"I'm not going to be disturbed by what I see in here am I," Nick's saying as he opens my door. The curtains are still shut so the hallway is a bright glare. Nick is waving a letter.

"I can't see anything, Souse."

"Just put it on the bed."

"I'm not going anywhere near your bed. Who was that on the phone?" He throws the letter toward the bed and it lands near my feet.

"Oh, just . . . student allowances."

"Good, because the landlord's coming later this week for you and Ursula to sign the lease, and he's going to want money. You do know he shot his wife with a shotgun don't you?"

"Yeah right."

"It's true. He's a crazy man. What . . . are you writing?"

"Oh, I was just like . . . taking some notes from this book."

"So no literature then."

"No, mate."

"I only ask because we thought we might have heard some beat poetry being composed in here about half an hour ago."

" . . ."

The door shuts.

Oh god. Damn, damn, damn. There's no way I'm going out there now. Take my cigarettes and light one. It's okay, it's okay. Murder, murder, murder.

The category of "Violence experienced" is necessarily broad, taking in any violence occurring in the home or outside the home, inflicted by or upon the subject. This is reflected by the large statistics—75 percent for the adolescent, 84 percent for the young adult. Crucial to our understanding of the murderer is the fact that physical violence has become for him a part of the texture of his life, whether that violence be domestic, such as the beating of the subject's mother, siblings or the subject himself by his father or guardian; or whether that violence occurred outside the domestic sphere, such as school bullying in adolescence, or violence in bars, public houses, etc. For the purposes of this checklist physical violence only was investigated. Other, more subtle forms of violence such as sexual harassment or emotional violence may have had just as much an impression, providing a similar context for later violent behavior.

The key point to note here is that for these young men violence is a socially acceptable means of expression. In terms of the subject's own personal feelings—rage, jealousy, resentment, depression, loneliness, guilt, self-hatred, and, crucially, sexual desire—a connection is made whereby these feelings that may confuse and alienate the young man find their only expression in violent behaviors learned socially. To put it more precisely: confusing feelings that exist in an environment where they cannot be talked about or expressed openly generate a feeling of paralysis, unbearable tension, and guilt. This unbearable tension is ultimately alleviable by the only tool the boy has been provided with: violence. During this period the boy's cognitive distortions with regard to violence were often supported and reinforced by nonintervening and nonprotective attitudes on the part of adults. The boy often reaches ambiguous conclusions regarding accountability for acts of violence.

The letter is addressed to Richey Sauer, readdressed from my parents' house. On the back it says simply Anna.

Dear Richey,

How is home? I'm spending pretty much all of my time alternating between my parents' and the hospital now so I can sympathize. Hope everything's okay, you sounded a bit weird on the phone. I wonder if I'll ever find out what it was you "fucked up"?

I've had to leave sixth form after only a month and I have a lot of time to myself right now as you can probably imagine, so I'm writing to a lot of the people in my life that I haven't seen or talked to in a while, which includes you, you lucky boy. I have been thinking a lot about my life and the past and about you and me and our friendship. I think friendships are very important, and it makes me sad to think that ours had to turn so bad just over sex. Kim has all but disappeared from my life. She has gone to England. I've had a couple of letters from her but it seems she is no longer interested in anything that's going on over here in old New Zealand. Which is understandable I suppose, what with all the exciting things there must be to do in London. She is working in a bar and has seen lots of bands already, plus she got lots of candy and cool food duty-free.

Lately I've been too sick to eat much, which really sucks because my parents have been taking extra care of me, making pancakes with real maple syrup and really good Stewart's coffee (though I like the smell far better than the taste of coffee, which I suppose is actually lucky given everything) and Bronny and Celia brought me round flowers and chocolate (I was glad about the chocolate, otherwise it might have seemed like a funeral! Ha bloody ha).

Sometimes it seems like the only way I can think about things is as if it's just that I can't go to Australia anymore. No Brisbane for me. I love the names of some of those Australian cities. I love Perth, and Brisbane (but not in an Aussie accent mind you), and Canberra, and Adelaide sounds like a beautiful old grandma wearing a lacey nightie don't you think? It should have a sister city—Adelaide and Marmalade, two old ladies in rocking chairs on a porch.

You'd hardly recognize me now I don't think. I've lost a lot of weight. I've got a lot of teacosy hats that I wear now, white ones, purple ones, my friend Adam bought me a Rasta one but I don't think that's really me do you? Besides, good little Girls' High girls never smoke up. No of course they don't.

My doctor's really nice. He seems really absent-minded like all brilliant people probably do, but he is really nice, sort of sweet and bumbly. He calls me Princess Anne, but I don't like her, she's so severe and has horrific hair, but I let him. Better than Anne of Green Gables I suppose.

But anyway, what I really wanted to say was that I forgive you and would love to see you next time you are up in Christchurch or whatever, but if you're uncomfortable with that then I'll understand.

Remember there are lots of awful things out there but you have to concentrate on the good things in life or it can all just overwhelm you. That's my philosophy at the moment anyway.

Please write back soon,

Love, Anna

I put the letter down on the bed next to me and turn back to the book, flick to another random page.

Angry Memories

In our interviews with the murderers we discovered what we refer to as a "cognitive filter" that we believe began to form in response to early troubling experiences in the murderers' lives. When we say cognitive filter

Get on with it

we mean a process of mental screening whereby experiences and social interactions and in particular memories become severely limited in interpretation by the murderer or murderer-to-be. This process seemed to begin during mid- to late-adolescence, a period of extreme intensity in terms of relating to the social world. The murderers we interviewed tended to obscure or pass over early childhood memories, some that we later found to be crucial to the formation of their interpretative mechanisms. They did, however, relate in detail certain other experiences from their teenage years that they had come to view as central, pivotal or at the very least highly influential in their lives. What we found interesting was the way particular teenage experiences— which the bare facts of might suggest as being fairly pleasant or at least harmless—were interpreted in terms of horror, fear, isolation, and later, anger. One murderer told us:

"We had a school camp when I was thirteen, and we had to sit in these groups for dinner. And there was this one guy that was constantly picking at me, you know? And he swore a lot, and I was never allowed to swear at home so I started to use some of his swear-words back on him. He used to say, 'Good shit [murderer's name]' in this [expletive deleted] sarcastic voice whenever I said anything, so I started to say that back to him, just because I didn't know what else to do. And then he started using that back at me. And all the time I was just so . . . like there was something filling me up on the inside, and I couldn't ever even breathe properly. And the end of the camp there was a game we had to play down in the swamp, and we were supposed to take off our shirts, but I didn't want to, you know, I was embarrassed about my body because I was chubby then. . . . And he had a very muscled body, and I was jealous and didn't want to do the game so I ended up faking a sicky and working in the kitchens, and then you know I got [expletive deleted] picked on for *that*. And I just used to imagine [expletive deleted] blowing him away across the table with one of the teacher's rifles . . ."

Teachers from the man's secondary school told us that they remembered the boy as quiet and helpful. The murderer's school exercise books from the period were found at his family's home and included remarkably advanced sketches of the area where the school camp was held. The sketches were rendered in black pen and depicted storms and smoke above the camp cabins, a sole figure standing on the roof of a cabin, surrounded by black birds. Also in the exercise books was a diary that the boys were asked to keep during the camp. One excerpt:

"Camp is good. Today we walked up the track to do some archery, and we saw a deer. Weather sunny today."

We noted that during the relating of his memories of camp the man's mood shifted. He became angry and tense. Both in what he specifically remembered of the camp and chose to relate to us, and in the effect those memories had on his mood as he related them, we see the formation and implementation of

I find myself skipping to testimony, looking for speech marks. At our camp in third form I remember Will Parker falling off the flying fox into the river, everyone laughing at him as he crawled crying up the bank, soaked in mud, draped in green weed. Everyone accusing everyone else of wanking in the dorm at night. Why shouldn't he have bad memories? Why shouldn't a cognitive filter just be your own truth? I flick back a few pages to find out what chapter I'm reading. It's

4. Feeling

When we talk about "feeling" we are referring to a kind of emotional landscape in the serial killer. Within a normal emotionally mature adult we might find a thorough emotional range that includes anything from utter depression through sadness through indifference to compassion, fondness, and ultimately, ecstatic love. To these men, these are words without denotation. They are marks on the page but also more: a connoted accusation, or an indictment. Vocabulary assessments conducted on the interview transcripts of our fifty-seven murderers found zero to statistically insignificant numbers of occurrences of the following words: loving, sad, hope, proud, dignity, joy, honor, noble, soul.

The key term to keep in mind in the understanding of the emotional state of the serial sexual killer, we came to see, would be paralysis. Murders were a way of breaking this paralysis, easing tension, and/or inducing heightened states of emotional arousal.

One murderer, a thirty-four-year-old man convicted of the rape, mutilation, and murders of fourteen female backpackers and the murders of six male backpackers in a National Park adjoining his property in Alberta, Canada, told us:

"For a long time it was like I was on hold. That was what it was like. At school no one seemed to see me, apart from when they picked on me. And I used to be in plays, but then because I couldn't sing I didn't get any parts, any big parts, you know what I mean? I was always in the chorus, mouthing along. Just mouthing along. The first one [murder] was just . . . I just wanted to talk. . . . This was before it turned really bad."

The "first one" was a female English tourist, aged nineteen, and her male companion, aged twenty-one. The man kidnapped and held the two for four days chained to a beam in his basement while he went on a drinking binge in nearby Slave Lake. Upon his return he shot the man and buried the body in a forest nearby. The woman he held for a further eight days, intermittently raping and torturing her with hunting equipment before dismembering her body and burying it also.

What we may observe from his words is the sense of stultified expression that finds its way to the surface eventually as murderous, sexualized rage. We asked him how he felt about the woman during those latter eight days when it was just him and the woman alone in the house:

"I felt . . . most of the time, well some of the time I felt . . . excited that there was someone here with me, that I had my own secret in the house, something for me. It felt . . . I could go out into Slave [Lake] and to work and walk around feeling good, you know? But then I'd get the feeling like she was laughing at me, at how I was pathetic, and I'd get mad and come home and do some of the stuff, you know? And I'd feel bad about that too, after. . . . It was a really stressful period for me. But it was . . . I don't know, it was . . . I mean, next to town, and work, it was . . . it's hard to find a word for it. Not possible to be denied. Irrefutable?"

Thus, we see the feelings aroused by the rape and murder are seen as more real than other aspects of the man's life. Another murderer told us:

"I felt [after the first murders] as if I had been skinned alive, and I was standing there, over the bits of the bodies, naked and skinless and more as if I was really there than I'd ever been before."

We noted the Canadian murderer's sincerity as he related his feelings during this period. He was lucid, unaffected, and in no way hostile as he had been previous to this confession. We observed from his body language and what he revealed a relaxation and loosening of the inhibition he had shown during earlier interviews.

This and other interviews conducted supported our thesis of murder as expression.

Flicking pages past the memories bit to the end of the chapter

An adolescence spent in an environment saturated in violence and sexism leads to a mindset where ordinary sexual fantasizing is helplessly associated with physical harm. This same environment hinders the development of emotion at the level of verbal expression. If a word is not said for long enough the word and what it signifies may cease to exist for the speaker. Thus, to break out of the straitjacket of silence that leads the wearer to doubt his own reality, the ultimate expression is required. It is no accident that societies with high rape–murder statistics also have high suicide rates.

Richard Sauer Richard Sauer Richard Sauer. Helplessly associated with physical harm. Lying in bed all morning. Say my name. Someone come and find me. Someone say my name.

The phone is ringing again. I glance at the clock past the book that seems to have been half-read because I've been skipping pages trying to find the good parts. It is 10:44. There is stomping in the hall, clattering, a voice, Matt's.

"Hello? Oh hi. Yeah good thanks, good thanks. No, no, I'm working. It's a pizza delivery place. For Stallones. Oh it's alright. Do you want to speak to . . . Richard? Yup . . . yeah. Okay, I'll just get him."

Knocks.

"Souse? If you haven't got your hands full in there the phone's for you."

Stomping, a door, the living room's, shuts. Laughing, I can hear laughing. I climb dully from the bed, still in jeans and shirt, open the door and bring the phone back into my room.

"Yeah."

"Hello, Richard. It's Mum here."

"Hi."

"Are you alright, dear?"

"Uh-huh."

"Are you sure you're alright? You sound a little off-color."

"I've just been reading some . . . strange stuff."

"Is it for school?"

"Not really. But . . . it could apply."

"Well you should probably concentrate on your schoolwork, Richey."

"Would you say we were middle class?"

"Well, I don't really know if we have . . . classes as such in New Zealand, Richey."

"But we'd probably be middle class or . . . lower-middle class if we did?"

"Well, I suppose."

"And you're a homemaker aren't you?"

"I suppose . . . that's probably a nice word for it. I'm a mother."

"And Dad's . . . he does skilled work, doesn't he?"

"Yes, yes. He . . . probably does . . . less skilled work now than what he did before he was made redundant. He was more of a . . ."

"A professional?"

"Yes, I suppose. But that's all different now, and your father is happy. But look, Richard. We've just rung to see how you're getting on, that sort of thing, and . . . oh, by the way, you didn't notice Snoopy getting into any fights with any other bigger dogs or anything like that while you were home did you?"

"No."

"Oh, it's . . . well he's got this mark on his little back leg we just can't figure out. . . . Are you sure you didn't notice any-thing?"

"No."

"No you're not sure or no you didn't notice anything?"

"What did you want, Mum?"

"Oh. Well. . . . In light of your . . . the . . . accident, you know, that happened . . . well your father and I have been more than a little worried about you and where you're going in your life . . . and that sort of thing, Richey, we do worry about you, you know that. . . . Well, we've talked and talked and I don't want to rush you into anything or anything like that . . . but we just want you to consider . . . well, what we've done is we've booked you in for an appointment with a student counselor at the university."

". . ."

"Richey?"

"Why?"

"Well. . . . It was just . . . what we thought would be good for you. We spoke to a man named Todd Johnson who's a . . . he's a registered psychiatrist, and he was very nice on the phone, and we thought . . . he told us that mental . . . that more young people are having . . . difficulties now than ever before . . . and that it can be very good for you to talk about these things, and talk them over with someone who perhaps . . . understands . . . things a bit more . . . than what your parents might. . . . Hold on, your father wants to have a word."

". . ."

"Gidday, mate."

"Yeah, hi."

"Well, mate, we spoke to this Mr. Johnson, and he seems like a nice enough bloke to me, and your mother and I talked this out and we've decided that the best thing for you would be to talk to someone . . . about your wee problems you're having, mate."

". . ."

"Are you going to answer me?"

"Yes."

"Good. Well what do you think of that?"

"Whatever."

"You're going to have to give me better than whatever, son. I want a firm commitment to this."

". . ."

"Son?"

"Well when is it?"

"A . . . couple of weeks, around the fourteenth of June. Shortest day I think that is, Miriam."

". . ."

"How's that fit your schedule?"

"I don't have a schedule."

"Don't get smart with me. We're trying to help you here. We're trying to help you get your life on track. If you've got something someone can help with then you're bloody well going to get it sorted out. Break you out of whatever's. . . . What have you been doing? Is your flat sorted out?"

"It's fine."

"Right then, your mother wants another word so all I'll say is that this could be just the thing you need if you give it your all, mate. You've just got to try a little bit harder."

". . ."

"Hello?"

"Yes."

"Well the doctor said if you just turn up to Student Health on the fourteenth at . . . 11 A.M. and it will all be arranged for you. So just turn up then, Richard, please, for us?"

"Okey dokey."

"Well. Apart from . . . how are you?"

"Fine."

"Richard, you didn't have the dog inside when you were at home, did you?"

"No. Why."

"Well we can smell this funny smell in your room that smells a bit like . . . well it's like *urine*, Richey, and we thought the dog might have peed in your room."

"I wouldn't know."

"Okay, well, never mind about that. Please, you will just turn up for that appointment won't you, dear?"

"Mmm."

"Alright. Well good luck for it. Bye?"

"Bye."

"And Richey?"

"Mmm?"

"You will grow out of all this you know. I'm sure lots of young men are having troubles too. Just remember that you will grow out of this."

"Okay, Mum."

"Bye."

I go back to bed and sleep for four hours, probably because of the drugs and my hangover.

—

When you try to piece together your life, the things that come to you somehow seem important but they never seem to be relevant, never seem to apply.

I remember one night in summer when I was sixteen and in fifth form, in the summer just weeks before I met Anna at Alexandrina, I went on my first road trip with Matt and his little brother and a guy from school who was older and knew Matt's older brother. This guy literally had a Holden and he invited us to come with him to take a girl out to the reservoir past the scenic reserve. He picked us up from school although it was the holidays—maybe school was all we had in common—in the Holden that was huge and old and dirty. It smelled like an old shed, metallic and earthy at the same time, and there was hay on the floor and the rearview mirrors were filled with dusty limp spider webs. We were drinking beer and hipflasks of Johnnie Walker and we were excited and trying not to show it because, as Nick told Ursula right in front of me and the TV a few nights ago, "Souse is a late bloomer." Because their parents are or at least were religious, Matt's brother's name is Pieta.

I remember that out at the reservoir it was warm and still and incredibly dark, and I could see stars reflected in the water because it was so still, there were no ripples at all.

I remember this all with an incredible terrible kind of nostalgia, as if it was really better than it was, as if it was carefree or a last blowout or I learned something, or as if it was a rite of passage. But the way I remember it now is really because I was so nervous it is branded in my brain, and this is the only reason it has stayed, and why it seems so much like two memories: the one where I find it hard to breathe and feel tiny on the huge vinyl seats, where I wish I was at home and then wish I wasn't some-one who wished that, the one where there is no romance, just paranoia, estrangement, fear, the desire not to be asked to scull Johnnie Walker straight. The other memory is just the facts, a string of words and read facial expressions, a story to be told on Monday morning supercool, to elicit the silence in boys with no cars and no hipflasks that means they're impressed and bewil-dered and you've won.

At the time we went out to the reservoir Matt's brother was only fourteen. He was too shy to talk to us but he would whis-per things kind of loudly to Matt in the back of the car as if he thought it didn't matter that we could hear. Matt would lean toward him and nod, or whisper things back, and then smile and roll his eyes to me in the rearview mirror, and it made me feel kind of older and experienced and empty at the same time. I remember I sat in the car differently with that weirdly unself-conscious boy than I do with Matt or Nick on our own. I had different posture. I had an urge to put my arm on the win-dowsill, but we've taken the piss out of guys that do that so much it would have made Matt tell Nick later, and make a fool of me. I felt kind of giggly and stupid and excited and deter-mined—it was vital—not to show this in front of Matt, the older boy, or Pieta.

The boy played a Creedence Clearwater Revival tape that was jammed in the stereo. When he spoke he always called us "boy," because this was a new thing at Boys' High, then.

"Give us a beer, boy."

He never said much to the girl, and he was younger than I am now.

We left the reservoir in like ten minutes because there isn't anything there but water and barbed wire and we drove fast out to Hanging Rock on winding empty country roads. He knew them, and country people die on country roads is a drunk driving ad on television right now but wasn't then. The headlights were full beam and lit up the trees and macrocarpa from beneath and the car rattled and rolled and seemed indestructible and the trees shifted shape as we neared them, moving eerily in the still night, Creedence, beer and cigarettes, grit under my feet on the vibrating metal tray of the floor, my silence misinterpreted for a little while as confidence, as personality.

And I remember thinking that the words are romantic, the story is romantic, but that I expected—based on those stories—things like this to feel different to how they really do. I suppose I was realizing that it is really better to tell the story, more fun to tell the story, and because of this, later, you can forget who you really were then and *be* the story.

The girl's name was Skye. When we got to Hanging Rock we were on dirt roads in a big bad car, and with all the windows down it smelled of cowshit and smoke from the barbecues of old people at picnic tables who stared at us as we drove slowly past. We found a place where the river seemed deep and slow and the car was parked so the headlights shone out over where we chilled the dozen cans of Southern Draught in the shallows. We sat by the river listening to the Creedence repeating, repeating, drinking—me silently—until Matt was sick in the trees.

This older guy was a farmer's son, and he told us a story kind of trying to impress the girl and probably us about how he and his older brother had to muster sheep on a paddock on their father's farm that ended in a cliff. They were just young, but they separated one sheep from the rest and threw stones at it (he told us) until it had to fall off the cliff.

"It was awesome, man," he said, kind of laughing, to show that it was alright, because he wasn't quite sure. No one had really anything to say to this, because we weren't sure if it was alright or not. "It was sweet as. It was old."

And the river was so slow and deep and black it didn't even look like it was moving at all, and we could hear one of the older guys back at the picnic tables was drunk and shouting, and later that night or it could have been a different night or even with my parents when we were younger, but I have connected these memories, and anyway, it doesn't really matter, later we found the body of a sheep in the river. It was caught underwater and floating there and it was the only thing that made ripples. I would have thought Matt would have got excited but I don't remember that; what I do remember is the sheep itself. It was floating on its side with its head leaned way back. The reason it was the only thing that made ripples (for a weird, electrifying moment we, together, thought it was alive) was because it was being eaten by an eel. The eel had eaten into the sheep's chest between its front legs and up inside its neck. It was making the sheep's neck straighten like it was stretching, and the eel was kind of thrashing and causing the sheep to move, to nod and lean further back, to jiggle in the water like it was still just alive, to make the slow black river water ripple.

The sheep's eyes were open and expressionless and sleepy-looking, and it nodded with its mouth open and it seemed to have too many stained teeth.

And I guess if you're a farmer or you live in the country you get used to seeing things like that, but I am a city kid from half a city, and I remember the memory of a feeling that it was the same sheep the boy had killed with his brother, even though the boy's farm was, I think, near Mount Horrible, and he had definitely told us that they killed it way back when they and we were young.

3. Relationships
Father, Mother, Sibling, Authority figure, Peer

Father

The murderers' relationships with their fathers or father substitutes generally involved the absence of a father figure, a lack of identification with their father, and/or a sense of their failure to live up to the real or imagined expectations of that father figure. Many of the men expressed their sense of weakness or frailty in comparison to their fathers' examples of masculinity and the expectations of that masculinity. One man said:

"Right from when I was a young age my dad used to say that boys should be strong and take care of themselves. And when I started getting into fights in high school he laughed it off and said it was good for me and it would help me grow up. And I'd be lying in bed at night, worried about school the next day and imagining going in to his room in the middle of the night and shooting his fat guts with his own rifle, or somehow just trying to damage him."

Because of a sense of themselves as being "unmanly," "feminine," or "weak," imprinted by their relationship with the archetype of masculinity in their lives, the men develop a sense of their own worthlessness and inadequacy that is transferred to many other areas of their lives, including social interaction with peers, academic performance, and employment. One man, speaking of his father, said:

"I never felt like I could ever, ever be good enough, but that's, you know, how it was

I skip pages

Most of the murderers stated that they felt closest to their mothers as adolescents, although in many cases the murderer perceived the mother as weak in comparison to the father.

relationship to their own underachievement was complex: a failure to achieve in a system (be that system school, the workplace, or social interaction, especially with females) is attributed to the nature of the system in itself, which prevents any significant achievement. Thus, the young man sees no point in pursuing unattainable goals and develops a deep resentment toward the system that sets up these unattainable goals as measures of personal worth:

"When I was still at school my father would say, I still remember it, 'There's no prizes for second place, son' or 'If you're not top of the pile you're slipping off it,' all that sort of shit."

develop a preference for isolation, where the man can manifest some control in his life
many of the men were very well-read, especially

"I came to believe that I wasn't as real, I couldn't seem to feel the way I thought other people did. But that was at school, and then later it kind of reversed, the way I looked at it. I couldn't see how they could be

skipping

triad: cruelty to animals, enuresis (bedwetting), firesetting.

strong narcissistic traits, including grandiosity in private fantasies, where the man is stronger, more powerful, more handsome. The men fantasized about being headmasters of schools, police officers, famous artists, famous sportsmen, high-powered corporate executives, gods, angels, witches, demons, and, finally, murderers. Rape fantasies often begin out of the adolescent linkage of sex and violence and develop as a means of having power and control, having *affect*

contradictory conclusions as to what constitutes *strength*

conundrum for one of these men receiving psychi-atric counseling. He asked, "But what if a dream you really want to fulfill is just a narcissistic fantasy?"

and DSM-IV diagnoses   unipolar, bipolar, self-mutilation, anorexia, bulimia, depression, manic depressive illness, schizophrenia, atten-tion deficit disorder, passive-aggressive personality disor-der, paranoid personality disorder, histrionic personality disorder, panic attacks, anxiety attacks,   attacks

hypersensitivity to the evaluation of others, especially in environments

fantasies of revenge for real and supposed wrongs against the man are not acted upon and remain unrealized,   tension grows
resentment coupled with a sense of isolation   dangerous sense that the man is entitled to satisfy   valueless,   in a culture of ruthless individualism a moral imperative is

generated that states that the individual's responsibility
is especially and even only to himself, which is particularly dangerous when that individual resents

    because the world has, in a sense, failed him

and Prozac, Zoloft, tricyclics, lithium, ECT, lobotomy,
    serotonin

       and fear

      a sense of ultimate absence of feeling;
paralysis, numbness, petrifaction, without even the
words to express

   Financial troubles, conflict with males, conflict with
females,
      alcohol and/or drug binges, employment
problems, academic problems,   heightened
paranoia relating to early offences, a growing sense of
isolation and even persecution

    once I was inside her I'd make her still, make her
quiet, make her notice me for once, see what I had
inside me, and I knew that she never would in a normal
situation, and that it'd take way more than sex

      I felt guilty about the things I wanted, about
the way I felt and the things I fantasized about. I couldn't
tell anyone, I had to hide it even from my friends."

     never been so unhappy

      panting, straining

   just so I could breathe, and not be so tense all

      she was an accident, but when she was
there I wanted her gone, I wanted to take her out of
existence and destroy her, make her into dust and ash

a sharpened broomstick that I made

looking for something in her body, I was hunting in
there for something more real, rummaging among her
intestines, real grisly like but real you know looking for
something to happen in me

while I wore a mask I cut her and carved some
messages in her back while

rigged up all the chains and pulleys in
my basement, and the gutters which were quite hard to
do. I'd never done   felt

for three days, trying to hold it in, drinking till I couldn't move

couldn't get it up because I was so
drunk and then I wake up and she's all dead and cut on
the bed next to me, and I'd slept in blood and it was
tacky like the skin on cooked milk

time changed while I had them. I seemed to have
more opportunities

anything. Haven't you ever wondered what it would be
like to be able to do anything you've ever wanted to a
girl

trapped in it, tied down
and numb
but before the times were bad, and after
they were a different kind of bad

time running out and I had never even been

and wanting more
a hunger

escape, escape properly, to find something for myself

no longer . . . no longer frozen

Winter.

Time passes. That's all that can be said of it. Days loom, pause, chuckle, and wait to loom some more. Or flee into tiny drunken flashes. The weeks grow ever smaller, the weekends expand. The distinctions between the two are challenged. Sleep lasts two hours or twelve. I walk around like a baffled person, averting my eyes from other people's eyes, clenching my fists. Ursula spends her benefit money on fifty-dollar bags and bourbon each week and gets behind in the rent. In her more lucid moments she tells us about her family and her little sisters and her abortion and Oriental Parade and her plans for T.Col, but we get very used to seeing her drunk and asleep on the couch. In late May she starts talking about prostitution to pay the beer-stained bills that litter the hallway around the phone table and I try to make a joke about getting cold in fishnet stockings. Matt cuts shifts at Stallones and spends increasing amounts of time alone in his room, listening to music, The Smiths mostly, painting pictures that get more and more abstract. Nick is hardly ever home. He has three short relationships with girls he meets at the Bowler and never brings back to our flat. We get stoned—first me, Matt and Ursula, then just me and Ursula—in Nick's almost empty room and play firing squad with cushions at four in the morning, trying to laugh sincerely. Which soon loses its fun and we stop.

Things shut down. We go out less, drink and smoke more. We struggle with our power bills and our landlord. My checks start bouncing. Knocks at the door drop stomachs. When the phone rings, hearts sink.

(I hang up the phone in the middle of a heated conversation with my sister, drunk, lifting and dropping the handset as it rings two, three more times.)

Traffic thins as our side of Dundas Street is lethally frozen for weeks. Fogs roll in over the hills and down the North East Valley, fogs that smell carcinogenic and make my skin greasy. The castle behind Strangeways is always damp, and green mossy growths climb the walls. At some point two cars and an ambulance arrive and park at the back of the castle. The ambulance leaves without a siren or lights, slowly maneuvering across the overgrown lawn. People from the two cars are seen walking around the castle in the fog, pointing at collapsed spouting, wiping windows and peering inside, touching lightly the mossy growths and wiping their hands on their jeans. After they leave there are no more lights in the windows.

In my longer sleeps I dream of events where I find myself misunderstood, "accidental" rapes, in my room on the bed, with my hand over a girl's mouth I listen for sounds outside my window, turning back to her once I'm satisfied there is nothing out there and finding the girl is made of fabric, like a cushion, with buttons for eyes.

A girl's body—maybe Ursula, maybe not—turns into a substance like overcooked fish, white and soft, that flakes and squashes under my hands.

Rooms in a vast building, spiders covering the walls and floors, shifting like static.

And I dream that I have a son, a boy of ten or eleven, and I'm holding him between my legs and kneeling over him and I punch him with a closed fist as if I have to, but it feels as if I am punching in water, I can't hit with any force so I grind my fist into his face, all my weight over him and his small body is bleeding and motionless underneath me while with my other arm I hold a red-scaled demon by the neck, a demon who screams stuff at me and rips at my wrist with claws, shrieking and giggling *give him to me, give him to me*, trying to climb down over my man's body to get to this boy, this son of mine, and I know he will eat his heart if I let him.

And then, always abruptly, the demon is gone and the room filled with people, my parents and my sister, cousins, uncles, aunts, Anna, the rector of my school, a priest, and I'm simply kneeling over the broken body of a little boy, my arms covered in his and my blood, and I can't explain as they stand over me in mute accusation, I can't explain what happened here, I try to, I want to, but I can't explain that I was trying to do a noble thing, that my guilt is not simple, that this is something you grow into, not out of, that there is no way out for me, that anyway it maybe is for the best, and that to fall, to fall is what?

To fall is better than to stand still.

There was a summer when I was twelve years old that my mother and father took me and my sister to Lake Alexandrina for a week's holiday. We stayed at a bach owned by the Angler's Club. It had only two rooms and my sister and I slept on a foldout couch in the living room, which was also the kitchen. It was late in the summer, the only time my father could get the bach, and there were only two or three other families in the area. The caravans in the camping ground were all shut up. All the curtains in the windows were closed. There were piles of beer cans and egg cartons and bread bags and other rubbish around the camp-ground toilets.

My sister was seventeen and she complained about having to sleep next to me.

"We can't make him sleep on the floor, dear," my mother said, and smiled at me.

At night the northwest wind would blow for hours, shaking the hut, roaring in the pines. My father would snore and I would be sunburned and awake long into the night, listening to the trees creaking and the waves breaking down by the outlet.

During the days my mother and sister would sit on the verandah in the sun, my mother to knit, or read, my sister sunbathing, looking at magazines. My father got up at dawn every day and went out to fish in the Angler's Club boat. I would pretend to be asleep while he shuffled around the end of the couch to get to the kitchen for the packed lunch my mother prepared for him at night. He always ate the first sandwich standing at the wide glass sliding doors, looking out at the hills.

I would watch his back as he ate. As he opened and closed the sliding door as gently as he could.

During the days while my father fished and my mother and sister sat on the verandah I would go for walks along the path beside the lake and up the hill. There were willows at the lake's edge that hung down into the water. Paint was peeling off the boatsheds and the miles and miles of hills looked faded yellow because of the tussock and matagouri. The hills shimmered in the heat and at the top I could see the end of the lake and the sky was empty and so blue it seemed white. The sky went on and on until the mountains, which looked purple and gray.

At the top of the hill there were no sounds once the wind

stopped. It became so quiet that I sometimes thought my ears needed to pop. I would hold my nose and close my mouth and blow until my head throbbed as I stood there at the top of the hill in the sun under an empty sky.

But it never worked. Once the throbbing went away the quiet flowed back like the water and I could not tell if I was awake or dreaming.

My two earliest memories are of the first time we ever went to Lake Alexandrina. I was maybe five years old and we drove up and back in one day. It was summer and it had been too hot in the car; dust had come in the window and my sister had complained about my father smoking.

At the outlet my sister paddled and tried to catch cockabullies in her hands. My mother sat on the bridge and watched her. My mother's skirt was rolled up above her knees and she was touching the soles of her feet on the water. My father took a long time to put on waders and then he went and fished away on his own.

I climbed up a tree by the lake, and on the insides of the branches of the tree I found thousands of husks of cicadas that had shed their skins, clinging to the bark. They were perfect copies of the insects, with eyes and wings and legs, but they were empty and translucent.

I pulled off as many as I could and the ones that didn't crumble in my fingers I put in my pockets so that I could take them home.

The other memory I have is of when we got home from the lake. I looked in my pockets for the insects I had tried to bring home and all I found was dust.

—

Sometime in June I leave Strangeways in a morning of snow and sleet and ice for my appointment with Dr. Todd Johnson the psychiatrist and it's like this:

"Richard Sauer?"

"Yes."

"Hi. I'm Todd Johnson. Come on through."

". . ."

"Take a seat, there."

". . ."

"Terrible weather isn't it?"

"Mmm."

"Okay, well Richard. Your mother made this appointment as you know, but we're more interested here in you, in how you're feeling, how things are going for you. First of all I'll just get down some details . . ."

". . ."

"It's Sauer, S–A–U–E–R?"

"Yup."

"Richard John. Eighteen years old."

"Yes."

"And you're at . . . 126 Dundas Street?"

"Yeah."

"Heart of studentsville. Isn't that right by the old castle up there?"

"Mm hmm."

"Is there anyone living there do you know? It seems very run down."

"I . . . don't think so. Not anymore."

"I always thought it would make a great bar. Okay, anyway. That should be all we need for now in the way of details,

Richard. So. How have you been feeling lately? It's been quite a while since the appointment was actually made, which I'm sorry about, we've got a lot on around here at the moment. How have you been feeling?"

"What do you mean, feeling?"

"Just generally, how do you feel about your life, your studies, that sort of thing."

"I'm not 'studying' if that's what they want to know."

"We're here for you, Richard, not your parents. You're not attending lectures then?"

"Sometimes when I'm bored."

"So university isn't really important to you right now."

"Did you really use to work in jails? I read that on your card."

"Yes. For three years."

"Well what am I to you then?"

"What do you mean?"

"I'm nothing. I've done nothing."

"Are you sure?"

". . ."

"You wouldn't have agreed to come, I'm guessing, if you didn't feel there was something to talk about."

"What do you mean, 'are you sure'?"

"How have you been sleeping lately?"

"I've spent the last month in bed."

". . ."

"That's important then, if you have to write it down."

"How's the drinking?"

"Frequent. Vigorous. Unrepentant."

"How frequent?"

"Until my bank returned my checks to the liquor delivery place, pretty much . . . often."

"Any drugs?"

"I was thinking that would be sorted out by the end of this fifty minutes."

"We don't dispense drugs without serious consideration of their possible benefit to the patient."

"Oh. Patient."

"You seem . . . angry at something, Richard."

"One of the things is you calling me Richard."

"What would you like to be called?"

"Forget it."

"What else is there?"

"What do my parents want fixed?"

"It's you we're interested in here, Richard. Let's just take a moment here."

". . ."

"Have you ever felt like your thoughts were moving too fast for you to keep track of them?"

"Maybe."

"Have you felt more agitated, irritable, or restless lately?"

"I know what you're trying to find out. Mind if I stand up for a bit?"

"No, of course. What am I trying to find out?"

"Bipolar, unipolar."

"Well, you know a little about psychiatry? Is that what you're studying?"

"Why do you think I'm pacing? And what I'm *not* studying is marketing. Oh forget it. Give me pills."

"What would I give you pills for?"

"Manic depression. Look how agitated I am. Give me lithium. You know I had a gun in my mouth days after he did?"

"Who . . . Richard?"

"Kurt, *Todd*."

"Cobain?"

"Yup."

"So what happened at your house was a kind of suicide attempt?"

"Not really."

"What was it?"

" . . . "

"Do you feel you know?"

"It . . . was a game."

"Did you want to kill yourself?"

"I want to every day. Everyone does."

" . . . "

"Oh I see, another important thing to note down."

"Why do you feel like you want to kill yourself?"

"Why does anyone?"

"Why do *you?*"

" . . . "

" . . . "

"So I can stop this feeling like I'm falling and falling and there won't be anything for me to hit, ever, just the falling, forever."

" . . . "

" . . . "

"You find that funny, Richard?"

" . . . "

"Where is it that you feel you're falling from?"

"From . . . from somewhere that was . . . like in a dream. Somewhere . . . unreal, a place where there could be . . ."

". . ."

". . ."

"I didn't hear that?"

"Just where things could be different. It doesn't even exist."

"Okay. And what does the falling feel like to you?"

"Like . . . being paralyzed. Or plastic. Jail, or . . . sort of . . . suffocation. Being invisible, or engineered. Losing something. I don't know. I haven't got the words."

"Is there anything else you want to tell me about that feeling?"

"It's not even like a feeling. It's more like being held away from a proper feeling. Like being so cold that you can't think about anything but the cold. You know how they say that once you're in a certain stage of hypothermia when you're going to die soon, and the feeling of coldness drifts away and you feel good? You feel warm and certain, and like everything's going to be fine? And you die happy?"

"Yes, I've heard that. What I think we should do at this juncture, what we normally suggest, is that we organize a kind of journal for you to keep, Richard, like a diary, to record your feelings day to day, through your days until our next appointment."

"Don't you want to talk about my family?"

"Do you want to talk about them? We're here for *you*."

"They are . . . textbook. Married. Steady income. Two kids, middle class, white."

". . ."

"See what that's like? You can't blame them for anything.

There's nothing . . . there's nothing you can identify that's wrong with them. What can you say about them? They stand for nothing. They watch channel one. Dad likes rugby and Mum likes knitting. They like kiwiburger ads. Dad says things like 'bloody wailing maoris.' They . . . make me angry."

"..."

"Sometimes I wish they'd split up, or Dad had molested me or . . . just something concrete, you know? Something real to hate them for. Something to define myself against. Some reason for why I'm . . . why I . . ."

"..."

"It's like being a test tube baby, being their son. What can you blame glass for? Being transparent?"

"..."

"Lately I feel like there's more bad things coming and there's nothing you can do about it or I can do about it, no one's responsible, there are no causes, only effects, people get used to things, there's nothing anyone can say is to blame. Things are vast and they move. And you fall through it all. This is all there is to it."

"..."

"Can you even call that a feeling?"

"..."

"*Todd?*"

"..."

"And you want to read a journal that says that day after day after day?"

"..."

"Okay, I've talked too much."

"Richard, I think you've only just begun."

The psychiatrist draws a plan with columns for days and rows for hours, staring intently at the whiteboard. I stand up, sit down, look out his window. Outside the sky is still dark and sleeting and the grass is yellow and dead in big patches. Coke bottles and beer cans and litter float in the flooded Leith, trapped in the backwash of a weir. *Sauer. Richard John.*

The back of his suit jacket is creased and his pen squeaks on the whiteboard.

His computer hums.

Otago are to play South Africa at Carisbrook Stadium, "The House of Pain," on Wednesday the twenty-seventh of July.

I have a ticket.

Nick said, "You in, Souse?" and I sipped my beer and made my choice, thinking about a man's businesslike voice, a voice happy to be up and around at 8 A.M., telling me your "hearing" is scheduled for 4 P.M. on Wednesday the twenty-seventh of July and I urge you to be there, for your own sake.

I said, "Yeah, I'll be in."

I said it with barely a pause, and the only reasoning I can offer is that to fall is better than to stand still, and the dreams are bad but they are at least my own, but mostly that saying yes is easier than saying no, because in this world when you say yes no one ever asks you your reasons.

4

Boys Light Up

Waiting on the porch for the maxitaxi to arrive and for Callum and the boys from down the hill to put out the bonfire they've made from the boards of the fence in front of their flat and come up the hill to join Matt, Nick, and I, I watch the mailman—who is actually a woman and is having to walk her mountainbike because the north side of Dundas Street is frozen and lethal— push an envelope into our frozen-circular-filled mailbox, which I can see from where we silently stand in the porch, smoking ciga- rettes, wrapped in duffel coats, scarves, and beanies, and waiting.

Smoke from the fire rises in great clouds up the hill to where we are standing, stamping our feet in the cold. Occasionally through the smoke one of the boys is visible running around excitedly, or heaving a bucket of water over the smoldering pile of boards. Callum's flat is on the eastern, level section of Dundas, opposite where Sarah lives.

The clouds over Dunedin are low, darkened, indistinct. It is bitterly cold; frost encrusts the grass alongside Strangeways and the steps are icy as I gingerly pick my way down them, clinging with a gloved hand to the wrought-iron fencing. The letter stuffed in the box is another from Anna. It is approximately 2 P.M. and the streets of Dunedin are icy and empty. The only activity visible from the Strangeways porch is the mailwoman negotiating the footpath outside Sarah's flat; the occasional taxi; the tiny blue and yellow forms of the boys down the hill who are now congregating out on the street with jugs in their hands and whistling at the mailwoman; and the smoke, which drifts over the Forth Street rooftops and lazily rises to merge invisibly with the deep dark grayness that spans the city.

Today is Wednesday the twenty-seventh of July. We are waiting for a maxitaxi that we are going to share with Callum and the boys from down the road who Matt met last night at Gardies. The taxi is to take us to the embankment at Carisbrook to see Otago play South Africa at 4 P.M. In the same pocket where I put the new letter is my ticket.

"And just who the fuck are these guys, Matt?" says Nick, who is hunch-shouldered, rocking on his heels, exhaling steam and cigarette smoke from his position in the doorway. He, like all of us, is wearing a long dark-gray duffelcoat with a hood and wooden toggles. Nick and Matt have decided to wear our blue and white TBHS scarves despite the fact that they could be interpreted as signs of Auckland support. My scarf is tartan, six dollars from Farmers.

Matt watches them as they begin to climb the hill, as they stagger out onto the street and smoke their cigarettes, carrying jugs of beer at hip-height, as they start to turn their attention toward us high on the hill above them where Matt leans against the left pillar of the porch, and me against the right.

"They're harmless. I got talking to them in the upstairs bar. They're here from Southland Boys'."

My stomach is rolling and acidic. I haven't eaten today and I feel vaguely high and nervous. In the last month I have lost six k.g., which is good.

"Jesus H. *Christ,* mate," says Nick, turning to us, incredulous, starting to laugh as it becomes clear that not only are all ten or so of them wearing Otago rugby jerseys, light blue jeans, brown leather belts and boots, but they all of them have also painted their faces in blue and yellow zinc. There is some variety here: blue and yellow diagonal, horizontal and vertical stripes; half the face blue, the other yellow; spots, circles, lines, and words on foreheads: Otago, Daz, Wank, Strop, Thrust, Macca. They reach the top of the hill, beneath Studholme, and cross toward us, a disturbing sight, a squad of blue and yellow masked boys who all look almost exactly the same. And it's then, as Nick's still laughing and turning into the hallway while they cross the road toward us, as they hear him laughing and their postures firm, as their smiles disappear, as their voices quiet or deepen, it's then I realize that, to them, the three of us standing above them on this porch beneath this sign that reads STRANGEWAYS must also look almost exactly the same as each other.

—

The taxi arrives as we wait on the porch and they mutter to each other, unsmiling, and finish cigarettes and their jugs, which hang from string looped around their necks. Matt and Callum have greeted each other but little else has been said.

Nick takes the front seat alongside the driver who refuses to make any kind of eye contact with any of us, but when it becomes apparent that the taxi is going to be too full, Nick gets out and lets one of the zinc-masked boys get in the middle before climbing back in again. The boy looks kind of nervous next to Nick, who is silent and menacing. I am seated in the second to last row, against the left side window. Matt is a row ahead of me on the other side. We are isolated pockets of gray in a mass of blue, yellow, and dirty-looking hair, and these guys see us as a group I can tell, but it would be difficult to explain that it is only our difference from them that makes us so.

The sliding door rolls shut, the engine is started, and with the noise and the breaking up of the three of us the boys start talking again, and it's like this, one at a time, then all at once.

"Where are you from, you giant arse."

"I need a fucking piss already."

"You need a strop, mate, that's what you're trying to tell us."

"Oh, didn't catch the name, girl's blouse was it?"

"Cunts, we are on our way."

"We're losing crucial drinking time."

"Macca, you look crook."

"Na, mate, sweet as."

"Puke and you're out."

"Up ya, mate. A big black dog."

". . . stop the bus I've got a hard on . . ."

"Gonna watch footy, drink piss, score me a bitch."

"No bitch is gonna touch you, man. Look at you."

"Hey? Wank? Just stop talking."

"I'm totally cruising for a bit of Janelle tonight."

"She's the fucktarget, man."

"Wouldn't kick her out of bed for farting, mate."

"I'd pay her to, mate."

"Piss on my fish and chips any day, mate."

"You'd let anyone piss on your fish and chips because you're a fat ugly wanker."

"I'm a fat ugly wanker who's gonna smack your fucking head in once this bus stops."

"You're a total fucking winner, mate. You're born to lead."

". . . girls, girls, girls . . ."

". . . geeks suck cocks . . ."

"*Where* . . . are . . . you . . . *from* . . ."

Down Cumberland Street the university buildings loom over us and the clouds are so dark and thick it's almost like twilight already and heading south I can see massive smokestacks in the distance pouring smoke out over the city and I take off my beanie and press my forehead to the freezing glass of the taxi's window and watch the empty streets closely.

Beneath the laughing in here I can hear the hissing of the tires on the road. Reflected on the insides of the taxi's windows against the gathering darkness blue and yellow forms bob and jerk and twist behind the unmoving grayness that is me. My right hand is in my pocket, bending and crumpling the letter from Anna. The taxi wheels around Gowland Street and on to Castle Street and the one-way stretches far ahead of us as commercial buildings begin to hurtle past, first a bank, then Hayward Hall and the hospital, Liquor King, a mall, a carpet cleaner's, the fire station, Cadbury's, factories jumping into view from the fog, and I pull the envelope from my pocket and screw it up to break the seal because I don't want to take my gloves off. I unfold the letter and smooth it on my knee face down, away from the boy who is sitting next to me with his legs splayed apart, jogging his jug up and down between his knees and obviously uncomfortable at having to sit next to me, thinking I'm just another alternative loser, just another resentful fag. I'm hoping this situation doesn't end up in a fight. The longer we aren't speaking, the greater their confidence seems to be growing.

I turn the letter over.

Dear Richey,

Well I've been waiting for a letter to arrive but it hasn't come so I guess you must be superbusy or something so I decided I would write first and . . . break the ice? Ho ho ho oh no. God I hate winter. I am home again now, I can't remember what I told you in my last letter but now I am officially in remission! Yay! (That's not a town in Texas or anything by the way . . .) No more chemo for a while at least, so maybe I can start eating again and not feel so weak all the time.

It is so freezing in here and although I'm sitting up in bed with a hottie and the heater on full blast my fingers are still white which I'm sure you can sympathize with being down there in chilly old Dunedin. My hair is starting to grow back now but it is still very short and stubbly but at least still red, or maybe auburn if you're from Merivale. I thought it might grow back in blonde ringlets or something horrible like that so thank god.

Musically I haven't been up to much apart from a rave we went to at The Ministry last week. It was so cool, such a different attitude to most gigs. People were all so loving and supportive and there were even little kids wandering around, raving away. I get tired very quickly so I didn't dance much but it was cool just to be there with my friends.

Aren't people in relationships sometimes so sickening? You may remember Bronny . . . you know, one of the three of my friends you've got your hooks into (just a wee dig there man), well, she's going out with this sort of friend of ours now and they are just so all over each other, I mean it's . . . lovely and everything, but like twenty-four hours a day? It gets so surreal seeing them together all the time, one in the other's lap like she's given birth to him and he's just grown out and up over her like a vine . . . . And it's not that I'm jealous cos I'm not. It just seems that people cling so very hard to all the wrong things.

Well, I could have been in Australia right now, in a pool in twenty-five-degree heat. It's almost impossible to imagine how a person could walk around outside in only a T-shirt here.

Here's a winter Pooh poem for you. Please drop me a line. I'm not going to disappear just yet.

> The more it
> Snows—tiddeley pom
> The more it
> Goes—tiddeley pom
> On

Snowing
And nobody
Knows—tiddeley pom
How cold my
Toes—tiddeley pom
How cold my
Toes—tiddeley pom
Are
Growing.

Lots of warm love,

Anna

I sense something and look up from the letter. Some of the boys are singing and turned to look at me sitting here reading this letter and it takes me a moment to realize what it is they are singing.

"Dear John . . . how I hate to write . . ."

They see me notice them and when I look away out the window, embarrassed, the singing gets louder and rougher. Nick and Matt stare straight ahead and the taxi hisses down lower Cumberland Street beneath the jetty overpass and the sky is growing darker and small groups of people can be seen now, scattered along the footpaths in clumps, all heading in the same direction as us.

They finish the song and ignore me again, continuing conversations, shouting commands to the driver and again I sense something behind me so I turn slightly to face forward and can see that the boy next to me, the left side of his face blue and the right yellow, is watching me.

I can tell he knows I've noticed him watching but he doesn't move. Adrenaline begins to wash through me. I stare at the gloved fingers in my lap. Then I turn slightly, and say, "Have you got . . . a problem?"

His eyes are red and tiny beads of sweat have squeezed out through the zinc and rest there on his painted face, inches from me. And he smiles brightly and says, "Yeah it's you, you snobby cunt."

And I don't know what to do here, what, how to reply, because he's called me a cunt but he's also called me snobby, and he's said it in such an unassuming, almost pleasant way that I don't know how to react, don't know what this is, whether this might be a fight or what and we're nearing the end of Cumberland Street and Anderson's Bay Road is ahead and so we're not far from where we'll be getting out so I have to play for time and the pavements are thick with people now and blue and yellow are the colors that dominate.

"Why . . . am I your problem," I say.

"Because you're a snobby cunt," he says, and the taxi's getting quiet, the others in here starting to take notice, to look our way.

"I'm just being . . . quiet," I say.

"No. No. You're just *being* . . . a snobby cunt," he says, nodding sincerely, and we are being closely watched by the whole back of the taxi now and someone behind me says, "He's a faggot."

We shoot beneath the railway overbridge and slow as halted traffic appears banked up ahead of us. Someone leans heavily on the back of my seat and I hear spit being hocked in a throat behind me. I shake my head slightly, exhale, face forward. The boy leans around next to me and imitates this, shaking his head with his eyes wide and his mouth hanging open, exhaling two or three times, the smell of beer, adrenaline, silence.

"That all you've got to say?" he says. "Faggot?"

Behind me the hocking noise again.

"Faggot?"

I can't stare ahead, three boys in the seat in front of me are turned, leaning over, staring back at me. I look down at the letter in my lap and I fold it in half and then in half again.

"Faggot? I'm talking to you." The hocking noise again then the seat moves and there's the noise of someone spitting directly behind me and I feel it hit the back of my head and I lean forward quickly but too late, turning, my hand to the back of my head then back before me but there's nothing on the black woollen glove and they're laughing, all around me and the boy next to me's shaking his head, leaning back, intoning *"dork"* in this American accent and the taxi turns into Hillside Road but can get no farther because there are cars and buses and taxis and maxitaxis and hundreds and hundreds of people spilling out over the footpaths and onto the street and hotdog stands and police and Salvation Army ambulances and the taxi comes to a halt at the edge of all this, money is passed forward to the driver, I put a two dollar coin in a hand in front of me, and the sliding door rolls back and as I climb out with my knees shaking with adrenaline I am shoved a few times before I can walk off into the crowd and away from the taxi to somewhere to wait for Matt and Nick who have said nothing all this time.

—

"Is there something in your face that attracts this kind of shit, Souse?" is the first thing Nick says to me when they find me smoking hard by a hotdog caravan and I try to laugh, and say, "I don't know, do I look like someone or something," and Nick loses interest and turns away scanning the crowd and says, "You're just you, Souse. You don't look like anyone."

A group of blue and yellow boys carrying an old pink Para couch with two more boys lolling about on it run through the crowd shouting, ordering people out of their way. The crowd parts indulgently to let them through. There are thousands of people here, they mill about amongst the caravans and the taxis, slowly moving toward the stadium gates. A fire smolders and smokes on the front lawn of a dilapidated house on the corner and people are ducking and covering their mouths to run through the smoke that floats up and drifts over Carisbrook. Police stand in groups of two and three, wearing deep blue overcoats. There is one mounted policeman in a wide circle of space on the road. People eye the horse warily; the horse ignores it all.

"You should've smacked the cunt," Nick says, up on tiptoes looking toward the gates.

Matt, who is slouching next to me, smoking also, says, "Good one, Tin, in a taxi with ten of his mates."

Nick turns to him and sneers and says, "They're your mates too, *Matty,* and don't forget that," and Matt shakes his head, looks away.

I say, "We need some piss," and Matt says, "No shit," so we join the slow movement toward the gates and the crowd gets denser and the numbers of boys our age and older wearing

Otago jerseys and carrying beers grows, and the older men in the crowd pull their children a little closer and smile and shake their heads and join in occasionally when two or three or more of the boys shout out, *"Ta . . . go. . . . Woh ta . . . go . . ."*

The corrugated iron gates to Carisbrook are in the northeast corner and are open and people are tightly queued in what appear to be tollbooths. Beyond and over the heads of the crowd I can make out the tops of more food stands and a blue Speight's tent inside the grounds where people are milling about, less densely packed than out here.

I spot Callum and the boy from the maxitaxi and others nearing the tollbooths. They are practicing lineout lifts on each other; every few minutes a blue-yellow body rises above and falls back into the crowd. As they enter the gates and the tollbooths I hear them shouting over the general noise around us and standing on tiptoes I can see one of the boys pressing his face against the bars of the booth, leaning over this middle-aged woman taking tickets and he's shouting down at her, face mashed against the bars, eyes closed, *"Taaa . . . go. . . . Taaa . . . go. . . ."* She's ignoring him, taking tickets from either side of his hips. He grabs the bars and tries to climb the side of the tollbooth but loses interest once he sees that Callum and the others have left and gone inside, drops down and bows, saunters off.

We are silent, the three of us, although Nick is getting visibly excited. He's standing very erect, eyes above the crowd and focused middle-distance, trying to maintain dignity while surrounded by all these people.

There are hats. Mostly worn by men. Speight's beanies.

Speight's caps. Speight's twenty-four-pack cartons with head-holes cut in the bottom. Conical blue dunce's hats with peeling Speight's labels stuck on them. A sombrero with empty Speight's cans hanging from the strings around the brim instead of corks.

"Sports day in hell," I hear Matt say next to me, and I turn sharply to him, then to the ground before him that he's studying intently, shuffling his feet.

"What did you say?" I say after a moment.

"Short stay in hell," I think I hear him mutter, still studying his feet. I wait another moment.

"What . . . was that?"

He sighs heavily, turns to me and says, "Jesus, Souse. Can . . . you . . . *smell* . . . that . . . *smell*."

"Oh." And I can smell something, something acrid and tangy.

"I think someone's burning plastic," I say, looking around over the crowd. It's the smoke from the fire on the corner waft-ing over us and on over the gates and into Carisbrook. A couple of people are smoking cigarettes in the queue and because it's so cold our breath is steaming; a mist is rising the length of the queue and floating up to meld with the black smoke boiling above us.

"That's what I imagine anesthetic to look like," I say to Matt, watching the clouds.

"Piss. Piss," he mutters.

"I'm . . . scared, I think," I say.

"Are you?" He turns to me, looking concerned for the first time, or maybe just interested.

"Why are we even here?" I ask him, leaning forward so no one can hear.

"To watch the bloody footy, mate," he says, sneering. The queue shuffles forward.

"I think I'm—"

"What?"

"What's the time?" I say.

He moves his glove, looks at his watch. "It's about three o'clock."

"Do you . . . I . . . do you know where I'm supposed to be?" I ask, staring at the heels of the person in front of me.

"Where?" He says. "Where else could you possibly *want* to be?" He waves a hand.

"I'm . . ."

"*What*, Souse?"

"I'm supposed to be . . . I should've . . ."

"For Christ's sake, *what*?"

"I should've probably . . . smacked that guy, shouldn't I? That's like . . . a . . . an unrealized revenge fantasy . . . that . . . creates . . . tension . . . alleviable only by . . ."

"The fuck are you talking about, Souse?" His forehead's all crinkled, staring at me incredulously.

"I think . . ." I lean in closer to him, adrenaline pounding. "I think . . . something's started . . . that . . . Matt . . . I don't know, I . . . I'm supposed to be at . . ."

Nick suddenly turns, leans over to us, grinning. "Guys. Guess what. A little surprise." From his coat pockets he reveals one, then two, then three cans of Speight's.

"Tinny," Matt says. "You are just too tinny." He takes two and hands me one. "Just relax, Souse. There'll be plenty of opportunities to get beaten up today. Don't rush it."

We open the beers and I light a cigarette and I may be wrong but when we do this I get a definite sense that the people around us give us a little more room to move.

And then we're in, just like that, the queue surges forward and we produce our tickets with our beers up our sleeves and we're in. The embankment stretches away to the right, an open blasted wasteland all along the north side of the field. Stands to our left and along the south side. Down the other end beneath the motorway a massive scoreboard faces us, flashing OTAGO V STH AFRICA on and off. People mill about here; long, long queues to the Speight's tent; a sign that reads TWO CANS—$5; the field sur-really empty next to the crowds and the embankment, which is steadily filling up. I see the boys with the Para couch halfway down, six of them squashed into it with beers in their laps.

I take out my beer again, drink half of it quickly, light a cig-arette, burp out smoke, shiver once, feel a little better.

"Story, mate," says Nick, still grinning, eyes roving over everything.

"You're loving this aren't you?" says Matt, sneering. "It's your element, you fucking *kiwi*."

Nick deepens his voice, unruffled. "Too bloody right, mate, game a footy, few beers, bit a how's your father, bit a niggle, mate, few more beers down the pub, cruise the chicks, mate, balls, boys, beers, bitches . . ."

"No, you really *are*," says Matt. "*We* hate this, Nick. This is all that's shit about New Zealand, right here, one big perfor-mance of hate and force and violence. Big men with nothing in their heads hitting other big men. Big men watching it. I've got less"—he's leaning forward, muttering, really angry—"against the guys that play it than the guys that buy into all the bullshit around it. So they're hard. You're not hard. Half of these guys"—he points toward the Para couch boys—"just do this kind of shit because there's nothing else for them. There's not enough people in this fucking country to even refer to to find out anything else to even do. No one's got the imagination to *think* of anything else to do anymore. No one even realizes how fucking *warped* this all is. *You* do, but you don't care. You just buy into it because you can get along, because you know it's easier than doing anything real. You're a lazy cunt, really. And Souse just goes along with the whole thing cos he hasn't got a clue who the fuck he is."

There's a silence after this. A long pause while Nick looks at him. And then Nick slowly smiles, and finally says, "Well if you don't like it why don't you just fuck off and paint some pictures. *Matty*."

And Matt shakes his head at him, looks away over the field and says, unconvincingly, "Good on ya . . . mate . . ." but nothing more, his little outburst over, and then there's nothing to do but end up queuing for ten more minutes to spend fifteen dollars each for six cans of beer.

And past the few girls who are dressed the same as the guys, and past the young boys running along the edge of the field beyond the advertising hoardings, and past the older men who look over and past us as if we're not there, and past the younger men our age who do one of three things when they meet our eyes:

A tiny, reluctant raise of the chin.

A squinting of eyes, widening of stance, deeper mutters, louder laughs.

A straightforward staredown.

Past all this we walk, between the hoardings and the embankment, before all these eyes that look away or sneer.

At the halfway mark Nick stops and turns up some steps and into the crowd. Matt and I follow closely, eyes to the concrete. The familiarity of the men around us with all that's going on is as palpable as our lack of familiarity. I avoid eye contact with anyone, keep my beer in front of me, and keep drinking as I walk. None of us speak during this whole journey. We just silently follow Nick, off the steps toward the scoreboard, deeper into the crowd, toward a gap only he can see.

We find a small stretch of gravel terrace on which to stand. We're boxed in by people: older men, men my father's age in woollen jerseys and jeans and Reeboks, boys our age with shaven heads and faces painted in zinc, one or two women.

Along from us I can see the Para couch boys and they're standing on it now, bouncing up and down, dropping beers, falling off into people. Some of the men around us watch the crowd and point out fights to their friends.

Nick stands to my right, feet spread and arms folded, a beer and a cigarette in his right hand. He moves little, focuses his eyes middle-distance, looking more for who may be looking at him, who may be a problem in the immediate vicinity, than what is before him. Matt's to my left, mostly staring at the gravel. I stay hunched and inconspicuous.

A voice over the loudspeaker announces the name of the winner of the Speight's Kick for Goal Competition, for which the prize is a pallet of Speight's cans. A boy in an Otago shirt, shorts, and socks jogs out with a referee and a guy in a Speight's tracksuit carrying a bucket and a ball. The tracksuit guy pours some sand out at the center of the centerline and passes the ball to the boy. Their mouths move to each other and they seem very far away. The boy places the ball with exaggerated care and steps back away from it, exaggeratedly looking from the ball to the posts at the scoreboard end then back again. The referee blows his whistle and he runs and kicks. The ball bounces along the ground and rolls to a halt before the twenty-two and the crowd is booing and laughing in a huge combined roar. The boy turns his back to the crowd and bends over and pulls his shorts down and moons the embankment and the roar shifts note to one of approval and peters out into laughter.

The three of them jog off and the loudspeaker announces the Speight's Otago Cheerleading Squad to a noise that is unspeakable.

Teams jogging out side by side from a tunnel in the stands opposite the embankment. We are jostled and there is roaring, a wash of sound, cans flying into the air, drops of beer raining down onto us. Nick's jumping up and down to see, Matt's lost his beanie and holding on to someone's jersey to stay upright, I stare up at the black boiling sky above me, the clouds rolling and shifting shape, growing, rising.

The game has begun, I know, because some of the crowd in front of us can see properly and are shouting together in pulses when something happens. The scoreboard down at the end of the field changes and displays statistics for a game that has only just begun:

OTAGO	0
STH AFRICA	0

TERRITORY

OTAGO	0%
STH AFRICA	0%

POSSESSION

OTAGO	0%
STH AFRICA	0%

SCRUMS

COLLAPSED	0
TWISTED	0

Now the crowd surges to the right in front of us and we get a view of the whole field for brief seconds. Far away there is a scrum, down beneath the stands at the west end. The empty expanse of grass between us and the players is vast, and steam is rising from the scrum as it jerkily scuttles forward and backward, and I'm thinking of a crab, or a spider, in an oven or roasting on a hotplate. Then the crowd rolls back and our brief view is gone.

The air is freezing and bitter caustic smoke is drifting above us.

The men are so huge. Jeff Wilson is placing the ball for a penalty and behind him they stand breathing steam, hands on their knees, and though they are mostly bent double I can still see the size of their legs, the divisions in the musculature of their thighs, the width of their calves, the simple bulk of their chests and shoulders. Heads are mostly shaven. Insulation tape and bandages wrapped around. Jaws are broad, dirty. They squint their eyes a lot. Some of the men are very low. Jeff Wilson kicks, and the muttering and booing and grunts of *fag, fag, fag,* reluctantly shift into applause and I suppose it's because he has blonde hair or maybe it's just something indefinable in his face they don't like.

It's so cold now that I can't feel my toes and when I see a scrum all I see is a stirring in a fog.

"Niggle! Niggle, Easty. Souse, look . . ."

"Fuck man, listen to them . . ."

"They never show this shit on TV."

"Should never have long hair when you play rugby. Always looks worse when you get hit."

"Oooh, oooh, oh . . ."

"Oh . . ."

"Bullshit, man."

"*Pienaar!*"

"Get him, get . . ."

"Fuck *off,* ref."

"I don't think they can even feel it. He's smiling. They're enjoying it."

"Adrenaline's too high, man. You're probably right."

"That's a fucking eye gouge."

"Blood bin, blood bin."

"Rough justice's what it's called, mate."

"Christ, look at him . . ."

"I can't see . . ."

"Here . . ."

". . ."

"They're . . . do you see how . . . big they are, Nick?"

"Yeah man."

"This is . . . fuck . . . terrible . . ."

And now you'll find me staring at the scoreboard, maybe half a smile on my face.

COLLAPSED	1
TWISTED	1

Urine, I suppose, and beer, is running through the gravel we're standing on, leaching up to darken our shoes.

A boy in front of us with long dirty-blonde hair, wearing tan moleskins and an Arana Hall rugby jersey is fiddling, hands out of our sight, with what I'd assume is his fly. His friends either side of him are watching, sipping beers and laughing.

"Fucking useless, mate," he says and looks up at his friends then back over his shoulder to us, me and Matt, Nick gone to get more piss.

"Don't *even* fucking bother," he says, grinning at Matt and me before he turns back, head bent to his trousers, although we've got no idea what he's talking about.

He straightens, knowing he's being watched, and starts to

pull something out of his fly, his hands moving in front of him, obscured by his rugby-jerseyed back, and he's pulling at something, head down, concentrating.

"More than two's a wank," warns the boy to his right, and he squats a little and hunches his shoulders and I see something dangling between his legs, a black tube, and he shudders and says, "oooh," laughing, as the last of whatever's happening happens, then he straightens, moves his arms and a thin black bicycle tube flops over his left shoulder spraying drips from its jaggedly cut open end that hit Matt in the face who recoils and says, "*Fuck's . . .*" and the three boys turn around.

The blonde boy says, "Shit, sorry, mate, bit of overflow there," laughing, and Matt's wiping his face and the boy's turning away, piss-tube dangling down his back dripping, and his mates are watching Matt and me a second longer, waiting for a response and when there is nothing but Matt's wiping of his face with his sleeve one of them says, "nice haircut, mate," and then they turn away and I'm just glad that none of it hit me.

Nick gets back and points out Marc Ellis to me, and tells me that he's only twenty-three and that he is at university here, that he's doing marketing (like you, Souse, ha ha ha), and that he lives down the road from us on the corner of Leith and Dundas. He tells me this, leaning down beside me, talking into my ear while the people around us drink and shout, and I find myself leaning into him, away from Matt, somehow a little bit reassured and protected, but I carefully make sure that the words I say don't reveal this.

Oh yeah. Yeah right. Fuck off. Oh yeah.

We're standing side by side and his eyes are flicking over the field that I can barely see as he tells me things about some of the players, and about what it's like to play this, how it's strange and exhilarating when it goes well, like being a little part of a huge organism, not a machine, not like that, but an organism, like if you don't do your bit it all fucks up and the thing just stops and falls apart, but if you do your little bit right there's like this momentum generated, bigger than the sum of its parts, the thing's no longer some players but a thing, a thing that can fly, attack, break things, conquer and I'm going yeah, yeah, right, man, and then Marc Ellis gets this ball on the wing directly in front of us and some of the people fall over as the crowd pushes forward and I get a totally clear view as he sprints right along in front of us and I can see his face and I find myself leaning and twisting, urging him on with my body and for a minute I lose myself as I will him on and my heart's beating really fast and I don't think it's the nicotine and but then the crowd closes in again and I lose it as he gets taken over the sideline by three South Africans anyway.

COLLAPSED   2

I've finished five cans and started my sixth and Nick tells me he's bought six more and I've got eight cigarettes left and I still haven't eaten anything today but I feel like I could go on forever or at least until the money runs out.

It's not even half-time yet.

—

And then, on the edge of a little drunken epiphany, I'm leaning over and saying to Nick, "This is a whole world, isn't it? This is everything to these people . . ."

And he turns to me and says "Is this really your first ever rugby game, Souse?"

"Well, apart from school, yeah."

"You're probably right," he says, then, "Oh fuck. . . ." The crowd's gone quiet and surly. There's some booing down toward the west end.

"What's happened?"

"They just scored."

"Oh."

"*Cunts.*"

"But Nick . . ."

". . ."

"Is this . . ."

"What?"

"Do you think you'll ever play again?"

"Probably smoke too much weed and tobacco now. But you never know."

"It's just . . . I can't see you watching like this all your life."

"Look, mate, I love my rugby."

"*Your* rugby?"

". . ."

"Are you being sarcastic?"

"What's your fucking problem, Souse?"

"I just want you to explain. . . . You understand it and. . . . Like, they're strong right? They're respected because they're hard and big and not afraid and stuff. You don't even have to play that fairly or anything. So long as you're a hard cunt and you hammer another guy, people like you and respect you, right?"

"Pretty much."

"But then you've got your whole team. . . . Like, you're strong, you train a whole lot, you fuck the other guy up that you've been watching on videos and stuff, first you intimidate him then you fuck him up, take him out, and your team pats you on the back and you go out and you get drunk. That's about it."

"That's. About. It."

"But what about the band?"

"Oh *fuck* off, Souse, you tosser. At least this. . . ." He's waving a hand. "Is *real*. When your pathetic excuse for a life means something more then you can start preaching. You fucking clown."

I don't say anything, shocked. "And that . . . was a try-saving tackle," he says to the blonde boy with the pisstube who in the flux and jostle of the crowd has moved up alongside him and the blonde boy leans forward past him and sneers at me and then I'm blushing fiercely and looking at the ground because people in front of us have heard too and are smiling knowingly as they turn back away from watching us silently and I can hear a solitary slurred voice, far away, up near the scoreboard end, crying out above the murmuring, "Taaa . . . go . . ." and his cry is greeted with some laughter.

TWISTED 2

"Someone got knifed. Someone got knifed." Whispers are going around. People start moving in different directions. Gaps appear

in the crowd and then things finish really rapidly. After half-time Matt and I go down to the Speight's tent for more beer. We loiter around the tent for a while, neither of us saying much.

Then we're halfway back to where we were and I see the Para boys have set fire to the couch. They're standing behind and above it and watching, entranced. Some of them, the drunker ones, are whooping and dancing around. The flames are low but the smoke is thick as tar and floating over the embankment and it mesmerizes many in the crowd who stand and watch it, transfixed.

Our only path up into the embankment is this expanse of gravel that's opened up in front of the burning couch. We run through the smoke carrying our beers and holding our scarves over our noses and mouths. As we come up alongside the burning couch there are some Hell's Angels standing silently and we slow to walk through them and watch the ground intently. We're halfway through and one of them grabs Matt by the arms and pushes him toward the burning couch, just meters away, and a couple of the others are laughing. There's about thirty Para boys now and they're watching this, and Matt's writhing in this big black guy's hands, his feet sledging up urine-soaked gravel as he twists and he's pushed toward the smoke and the flames. He drops his half-dozen and other Hell's Angels pick them up.

I stand there.

Then a meter from the smoldering couch the guy just lets him go suddenly and the boys watch quietly as the Hell's Angel pushes him away with this look of contempt on his face and says, "nice mohawk, cunt," and Matt—crying now—walks away into the crowd and I lose sight of him.

The whistle blows away somewhere and the crowd starts to disperse straight away and then things just finish really rapidly.

The smoke is everywhere as I'm leaving, letting myself get carried out the gates by the crowd. People are coughing and breathing through scarves and jerseys and beanies and I look up above me for signs of sky but there's nothing but twisting oily clots of darkness. Out in the street and it's very dark now and it must be almost six o'clock. I'm still carrying my six cans of beer so I open one and put the rest in the pockets of my coat. I light a cigarette and wait, looking around for Nick, Matt, anyone I know.

But there's no one, no hope of recognizing anyone in this darkness and smog so I turn away from Carisbrook and follow other staggering figures, down King Edward Street, past the pub, over the Oval, into town.

Alone, walking past a war memorial.

Scattered figures pass me and disappear into the darkness ahead. Now and then I think I see a mohawked scalp amongst them.

On Princes Street there are broken windows, a group of five boys bending a parking meter over, a minitanker outside the LoneStar with a table set up and staff selling beer to passersby. Middle-aged couples tense up when loud boys walk past them. The shouts of "Taaa . . . go . . ." are occasionally heard and answered by boys invisible in the smoke and darkness up ahead. There's the sound of breaking glass and right down Princes

Street I hear voices crying, "waaay. . . ." I'm walking, smoking, drinking, alone, trying not to make eye contact with anyone.

It's then that I see a mohawked head disappearing into the Empire with a small group of people also dressed in black and gray. I follow them inside and hide my beer can up my sleeve.

It's dark inside, The Verlaines on the jukebox singing "The Funniest Thing," and people watch me when I walk into each bar and stand in the doorway looking around.

In the back bar the music is quieter, a couple of guys playing pool, both tall and thin and wearing black. I edge inside the doorway and stand in the dark. One of the guys playing pool tries to make his shot from behind his back but misses the white completely and a girl sitting at one of the tables in here says, "Oh, Graham . . ." and he shrugs and smiles and says, "You know, it's the funniest thing . . ." and a lot of people in the back bar laugh at this, for a long time, for too long it seems, and then I leave because Matt's not here, no one with a mohawk even, and I'm back out on the street, walking again, heading north.

Past the new Hoyts multiplex and past the gluesniffers in the Octagon, along George Street, crowds outside McDonald's, younger kids standing in groups, leaning on cars, McDonald's cups, burger wrappers, french fry boxes all over the road, a lone police car cruising past, and up ahead outside Foxy's there are boys sitting on the footpath by the queue eating McDonald's and leaning against the glass frontage of the shop by the queue for Foxy's.

Sebastian, Mark, Rubes, Dazza, Works, three guys I don't know. From inside, up the stairs, I can hear The Exponents playing "Who Loves Who the Most," and voices in chorus.

They don't say anything as I walk up and stand there, until Mark says, "Souser," in between bites.

"You at the rugby?" I say.

"Yep," says Mark, and Rubes nods. Works and the others don't even look up at me. "Good result for the boys."

"Seen Matt?" I say.

Sebastian's watching the queue, which is five-deep and runs down the footpath past the bank on the other side of Foxy's. In the bank's window is a poster that reads "That's the Spirit of Dunedin." Without looking at me Sebastian says, "Saw Tinny with this blonde cat, said they were going to Gardies."

"Oh," I say, turning my head to look over the street.

"Cat. Hey, cat."

I turn back but he's talking to someone in the queue.

"I seen you, cat," Sebastian says, louder. And I'm thinking, "*seen* you?" You were dux of my primary school. You were a prefect at Boys' High just months ago, months that seem like a generation. He's talking to a boy in the queue who is standing with a girl. They're our age and only two or three away from the bouncer. The boy looks over once and turns away.

Mark, Rubes, Dazza, Works, the other three are all quiet now, eating still, leaning forward, watching.

"Come on, cat," Sebastian says.

The girl leans past this young boy and says, "What the hell is your problem," and Sebastian says quickly, like he was waiting for it, "No one's talking to you, bitch, shut your fucking mouth," and Works laughs out loud at this, through a mouthful of chips.

I'm thinking, you used to like astronomy. I'm thinking, I was runner-up to dux and we were semi-friends and we competed, though even then I didn't trust you. And I remember my father taking me to visit you in hospital when you had a bad asthma attack when you and I were maybe seven. I remember you were tiny, thin, and sick in the bed and when I stood close to you like people do on TV I stood on the platform of your IV, and it swayed, and I thought I'd done something really bad.

"I'll fucking rape you, you bitch," is the last thing I hear Sebastian say as I just turn away and walk past the queue and cross the road, heading toward Gardies.

Down Frederick Street there's a fight going on just outside Likely's and I cross the road to avoid it, and normally I'd walk past the Cook but at the corner looking up King Street I sense bad things so it's past the Bowler I have to go and I'm opening a beer and lighting a cigarette as I get closer to the noise.

And past, not looking back till I'm halfway across the one-way and the queue is just a mass of people smoking and breathing steam and shouting and laughing and a couple of guys climbing the solitary tree and no one's even noticed me. So now up the one-way and past the chippie and my eyes on the queues at the Cook. I stand by some trees there for a while, finishing my beer, listening to the sounds. Then I open a new one and head up Cumberland Street.

Car headlights burst out of the mist toward me, roaring down the one-way. University buildings loom and hem the street in. Running footsteps and a young boy in a white T-shirt comes stamping through the Archway on the other side of the street and runs straight out on to the road, heading toward me here under the trees. He makes it across the first lane then slows, stops, hesitates, looks blankly up the street, then over toward me and past me, to the Cook. And at just the wrong moment he starts to run again, and I'm right there on the footpath watching when he gets clipped by the front right quarter of a car that passes and continues on without slowing, no faces visible in its windows.

He crumples, hits the asphalt and rolls into the piles of dead leaves in the gutter and then gets straight up and stands there in the dirty water, his face ashen white, eyes wide and staring, blood spatters on his jeans and T-shirt.

"Are you alright?" I say, but he doesn't say anything, looks past me, through me, dirty water dripping from his hair, and then he walks unsteadily past me and away into the darkness of the trees by the museum.

I walk on up Cumberland, turn down St. David Street, and then Castle Street stretches way ahead.

Walking down Castle Street seems to take a long, long time. There are voices, far away, echoing cries of people lost in the fog. No lights in any of the houses I pass, the roofs' peaks outlined against the clouds. Trees petrified, fossilized in the orange street-lights; frozen, motionless, like claws, deathly still. The cars look like toys in a diorama and dead black leaves bank up in the gutters. A dead bird in the middle of the road, flattened, a geyser of brain squirted and solidified, pushed up and through a hole in its skull like pink toothpaste. One tattered broken wing pointing up into the shifting clouds. Crossing Dundas for a brief moment I see, far away, up the hill, the silhouette of the castle and its blackness, shades darker than the roiling fog that soon rolls back to obscure it. Streetlights hiss and sputter and go out above my head. The outline of a body painted on the pavement. I smoke in slow motion. Music, getting louder. And I'm drinking the last of the last of my cans when at last I see Gardies, the squat brownness of it, hunched in gnarled black trees, solidifying slowly out of the mist. Lights and sounds. A cluster of boys at the Castle Street door disappears inside. On my side of the road an older guy is standing by Abbey Lodge, staring across. I'm walking toward him as he takes a drink from a hipflask of whisky. He's maybe twenty-five, old, with spiky hair, wearing jeans, a paint-splattered white T-shirt, a plain blue denim jacket. As I approach he turns to look at me briefly and he has very green eyes. I start to cross the road and he mutters something.

I stop, and say, "What?"

"Beware, little man," he says, and takes another drink. "If you're going in there. Be . . . fucking . . . ware."

A girl comes out the swing door as I'm heading toward it and calls across the road, past me, not looking at me, "He's not there, Christian. Satisfied?"

"Of course he's not," he says. "He's *dead*, Kate. He *died*," and she's saying, confused, "Well you just sent me in there," as I'm passing her, through the outer door, and the noise is so, so loud; music, voices, shouts, clinks of glass, and there's a huge Samoan standing at the inner door in a Speight's polarfleece who lifts a massive arm in front of me and grins and says, "You're twenty . . . three, right, mate?" and confused, I say, "Oh yeah," and he holds the door open for me and the lower bar is packed out, so many woollen hats, big men squashed in together from the bar to the pool tables, so many that the guys playing pool are making shots in-between guys having shouted conversations. Some of them just inside the door look at me, some of them laugh.

Heart is beating loud and fast.

Looking for a mohawk or dreads but backing out before I can even be sure neither of them are here.

Back past the smirking bouncer and I head up the stairs, passing a couple of boys helping each other down and at the top bar the music is much, much louder, a live band playing an Australian Crawl song, and with a feeling like falling I pull the heavy door back and step inside and make straight for the bar so maybe it looks like I'm not alone or at least that I don't care.

It takes me a long time to get served and a short time for me to drink half the jug I buy, standing at the bar. If I face the bar, watching the mirrors behind the shelves of spirits, I can watch what's going on around me without risking eye contact. The band is playing "Bliss" now, and the boys in here are singing along loudly.

The bar is crowded and I'm getting jostled often. The staff I'm staring past are wearing blue Speight's polo shirts. I light a cigarette and concentrate hard on smoking it. In the mirrors I can't see any sign of Matt or Nick and I can't picture Matt up here now, anyway, not after today. I finish my jug, drinking quick gulps from a seven-ounce glass, and order another one.

"Jug of Speight's."

And with the jug in my left hand, enough drunk for it not to spill too easily, and the seven-ounce and a cigarette in my right, I can leave the bar and make my way through the crowds of boys, many of them still with blue and yellow faces, searching, maybe for Nick, maybe just for anyone I recognize.

I head toward the door I came in, then shuffle left, searching the crowded tables by the windows onto Castle Street. And round behind the back of the bar I see a face I recognize, flanked by guys in chambray shirts and ties, surrounded by mostly guys but a few girls.

It is Marc Ellis. And he's in a chambray shirt and dark blue tie, tan moleskins, and a natural wool beanie. I see in the crowd back here other Otago players whose names I know through pure osmosis talking, laughing, being listened to, petted, passed drinks and cigarettes. Girls, some of the few that are in here, more though than downstairs, touch their chambray forearms and bump their heads on their shoulders when something funny is said.

I lean against the bar, along from the circle of mostly boys but a few girls, that surrounds Marc Ellis. I carefully move closer. He's talking, telling some story. I strain to hear it over the music.

"... *fucking* funny, mate . . . she'll never live it down ay. She was totally comatose, lying on the bar, she was on antibiotics or something, got really fucking drunk really quickly, and the assistant coach makes this bet, he bets Prong . . ."

And the band's started another song now. It's "April Sun in Cuba" and I'm having trouble hearing so I move a little closer and bump this older boy from behind who turns and looks at me and puts his elbow up on the bar to stop me pushing in and

I take a drink and look over to the toilets but it's just so I can hear better.

Then suddenly the older boy turns back again and looks hard at me. He leans toward me and then he says loudly over the music, "Hey. You know Doozer."

Heart starts beating fast and I shrug and drink more from my jug.

"You're Doozer's little brother," he repeats, nodding at me.

I shrug again, and mouth "no," but he's looking away as he leans forward, down to my ear, and shouts, "I PLAYED WITH HIM FOR SOUTHLAND COLTS." He leans back and looks at me again.

I don't know what to do. I just look back at him.

He mouths, "good cunt," and nods, and then he winks at me, with a totally serious expression on his face.

I nod back, not knowing what else to do.

He turns back to Marc Ellis, who's still talking. On the back of this boy's jersey, above the number 17, is JULES, written in big white letters.

". . . so they strip her and then next thing Prong climbs up there on the bar and he's going for it, and there's piss everywhere so they're sliding around and she almost falls off a couple of times, still really out of it . . . the staff have totally fucked off by this point, by the way, they're hired by the club, anyway . . . so Donk and Muz have to get up and go and hold her arms and her legs for him . . ."—he's shaking his head, laughing, and the other boys are laughing—". . . and the whole time, through however fucking long it takes, we're just sitting there, just watching."

One of the girls says, "You guys are sick fucks," and pushes her way out of the circle, and the boys laugh and make hissing and meowing noises. I lean forward and whisper, "No shame," but no one hears me, and he says, "And this was right in the fucking clubrooms, and the union rep and half the administration are just over there, few beers, acting like nothing's going on. But he won the bet though."

There's a lot of shouting now, on the other side of the bar, and everyone over here turns to see, and as he turns I catch his eye and lift my chin and he just barely lifts his eyebrows and looks where they're all looking.

"It's Willy," someone says, and Marc Ellis turns back and looks at someone in the crowd and rolls his eyes.

There's a few shouts of fag, fag, fag, but they wane quickly and the music takes over again. Marc moves through the circle, which parts for him, and heads toward the toilets carrying a jug. I put down my jug on the bar and follow him, and just outside the toilet door I say, "Marc."

He turns to me and says in a kind of sigh, "Yep?" My heart's beating hard and I try to look him in the eyes.

"I was wondering if I could talk to you," I say.

"Piss, mate," he says, pointing to the toilets. "Piss now, talk later." Then he disappears into the toilets.

I light a cigarette and smoke it hard, wondering what the fuck I'm doing, wondering why I'm here, what I'm looking for, what I'm going to say to him. There are chants of "Taaa . . . go . . ." over the song the band is playing now, "There Is No Depression In New Zealand" and I see Jeff Wilson at the far end of the bar, surrounded mostly by girls, not boys, and it seems as if it's getting darker in here, maybe they're dimming the lights as it gets later, to generate a mood, and I run a little personal inventory that tells me I've drunk eleven or twelve cans and one and a half jugs but toward this figure I can't say what I feel, either way.

Then he's there, in the door to the toilets, and he sees me waiting and walks vaguely in my direction, adjusting his fly with one hand, sipping beer from the jug held in his other hand.

"So what's your pressing problem then, mate?" he says, standing feet wide apart alongside me, scanning the crowd like he owns it. I've got this throbbing in the back of my neck and a terrible urge to tell and tell and tell, to reveal everything, to beg for help, for understanding; a terrible urge now to say things that belie my appearance, my ability to drink, my sex, my age, my friendships, the way I talk, the way I act, all the silent sagas of school, and I'm staring at the sticky carpet in front of his and my brown Last Footwear boots, trying to find what to say, how to say it, and I have to say something quickly because he's seen someone and has raised his chin to them and could be losing any interest or sense of obligation he may have felt to talk to me, so I start to try and talk, to try and tell him something true, but this is all that comes out:

"I . . . like . . . don't know . . . I've never been into rugby much, I . . . never played or anything . . ." he might be listening, I can't tell, he's standing hands in pockets, looking out through his fringe that his woollen hat has pushed down over his eyes.

". . . but like today was the first game I've ever been to since . . . the . . . compulsory ones at school . . ."

"Mate, I can't hear you, you're going to have to speak up," he says, leaning forward a little, sipping his jug, watching the people.

I lean closer and say into his ear, "Well, I . . . like I thought I kind of . . . like felt something when . . . you know when you ran down the . . ."—I'm trying to find the word—". . . wing? Just before you got . . . like taken out . . ." and now he's looking at my face suspiciously as I keep going, ". . . I think I . . . felt something and I was thinking about the . . . you know the statistics they show on the . . . scoreboard . . . ?"

"Speak *up*, mate."

"Well, they say . . . like for what's happened to scrums . . . they say they were col*lapse*d . . . or *twist*ed . . . you know?"—I'm looking for something in his face—"And I was thinking that's what like what . . . a person could be . . . ?" He's looking, I think maybe listening, the roar around us receding, the sense of a moment. "Because like, you can col*lapse* . . . your*self*, through your own, like weakness, or whatever . . . like but if you're *twisted* . . . then doesn't it kind of mean . . . something . . . or someone . . . has done it *to* you?"

I'm looking right into his eyes.

He leans closer, says, "I'm the demon Belial and I am hate."

"What . . . ? What did you say?"

"I said you're seeming pretty riled, mate. Speak *up*."

"Can you . . . help me . . . understand?"

His forehead's furrowed, and he's looking right at me.

There's the moment.

He looks away into the crowds of boys, the whirling smoke, lifts his eyebrows to someone, turns back to me. Then he says, "Look, mate, you're sweating like a rapist and I don't know what you're on but it's worth good money and probably shouldn't be mixed with alcohol" and then he's gone, just turns and walks away and a hand on the back of my head, pulling my hair and pushing my head down, I'm spilling my beer all over the floor and my boots, there's two hands on my head now, twisting my neck, pushing my head down into my chest, bent over double, I drop my jug and I'm reaching down to the floor to hold myself up when the hands let go, suddenly, and I stagger sideways, shaking, turn around.

It's the boy in the black rugby shirt, Jules. He's standing next to another boy and he's squinting down his nose at me, his chin up. People are staring at us, moving away from me.

He lunges forward really fast, and grabs the collars of my coat, pulls me forward, in front of them.

He shakes me and shouts to the boy, "THIS IS FUCKING DOOZER'S LITTLE BROTHER."

The boy nods. He leans forward, looking at me from under his woollen beanie. He smiles. He leans down beside my ear.

"Doozer is a dirty little bitch," is what he says loudly into my ear. He leans back and smiles, waiting for me to react.

He mouths the words again: "A dirty bitch."

Jules straightens my coat. He leans over and says something in the boy's ear, but he's looking at me.

The boy says something back to him and then he turns away.

Jules looks at me. Then he motions with his head for me to follow. They're heading toward the doors. So I follow them.

Outside, it's still and bitterly cold and Castle Street is totally empty apart from two Gold Band maxitaxis parked at the curb with their engines running. The boy by Abbey Lodge is gone. A boy is standing by the open doors to the maxitaxi in front, talking to someone inside. The windows are all fogged up so I can't see who is inside. From inside a voice yells, "Fucking *crank* it."

He gets in and the door slides shut after him.

Through the open door of the second maxitaxi in front of me I can see three boys in the very back seat, three girls in the seats in front of them, wearing different colored Holiday Tee sweatshirts over Aertex shirts, and Jules, sitting at the door. He's looking past me at the outer doors to Gardies. I turn around and look back at the doors too, but no one comes out. I turn back and he's looking at me.

"In or out, Doozer junior," he says, and sits back inside.

I wait for a second. Then I'm getting in, past him, stepping over his feet and he's nodding his head, muttering, "Alright alright alright," and I'm sitting down and not saying anything and my hands in my lap nervously playing with my cigarette lighter and when Jules slides the door shut, hard, we leave, behind the first maxitaxi and heading into town.

Jules is turned in his seat and talking to the three girls in the seats behind us, asking about where people are, people named Shannon, Gretchen, Brooke, Jockstrap, someone he calls the Toilet Girl, someone named Wolf, someone named BJ. The girls tell him places like Abalone's, Foxy's, someone's flat, some motel, the clubrooms. In the backseats the boys are having a playfight. Down George Street it's starting to rain and the streets have emptied out. We're heading into South Dunedin when the maxitaxi in front turns up Maori Hill and our taxi follows it.

The girls behind me are talking about some prorector they

know named Zippy who is supposed to have date-raped a resident of his hall and got kicked out when Jules turns back around to the front, leans forward, and tells the driver an address. He leans back and checks his watch.

Without looking at me, he says, "Your brother's doing Parks and Rec at Lincoln, yeah."

"Yeah," I mutter, looking down at my lighter. "Yeah, I think so."

"Sound bloke, Doozer," he says. "Sound."

I'm just nodding.

"Meaty blindside flanker when he played for Colts."

I don't say anything.

"Played some scorchers. Superb in the maul. Totally uncompromising."

As he's saying this his voice changes. I look up. He's nodding, staring forward blankly, his mouth hanging open. The girls have gone quiet.

"And he goes *off* . . . like a *bomb* . . . when he finds . . . *space*," he says, slowly, with the words all spaced out, his accent really exaggerated. One of the girls is starting to giggle.

I'm realizing he's making fun of me.

There's silence. Just the engine, the rain on the windshield, the boys in the back punching each other, the girl stifling her laughter.

I'm trying to think of something to say when I remember something, know what to say, what I should say, suddenly.

"I think . . . he's just a fat cunt," I mutter.

The boys in the back go quiet. The girl giggling stops.

"Well. That's lovely," one of them says.

I look up at Jules and he's looking at me.

"He *is*, though," Jules says, like he's amazed.

He twists around in his seat, and says to the girls, "He's right, though. Doozer *is* a fat cunt." One of the boys in the back punches another boy who hisses in pain. The girls start talking about someone named Nob.

Jules turns back to the front.

"Your own brother, though," he says. He laughs, without looking at me. Then he says, "What a *wanker*," and laughs again.

I know it worked, some test is passed.

It's raining really hard as the taxi pulls into a driveway somewhere up Maori Hill. We follow the taillights of the other taxi down a steep fenced drive, around a tight corner, into a car park. Through the blur of the rain I can see a ute and a van with Speight's Otago markings parked side by side. The taxi pulls up outside a ground floor motel room with no lights on, a pale shape through the windows.

Jules turns to the backseats and says, "You don't have to pay. They're club taxis." He slides the door open and jumps out into the rain. I follow him and the girls and the boys in the back follow me.

It's raining hard and the first taxi has already left. All these boys are climbing the stairs of the room we're outside. I pull my coat over my head and run after Jules, after the boys, to the stairs.

As we're climbing them the door is opened up above us and music, Beastie Boys, is playing really loudly and there are voices and I'm looking at JULES on his black back and then we're at the door and everything is moving really fast.

Going in, Jules is rubbing his head, shaking the water off, the room is all white, the music's really loud, the lyrics asking, "So whatcha whatcha whatcha want," and the living room of this motel is full of people. There is a white Formica dining table and two huge white leather couches with a coffee table between them and sitting on the couches are all these young girls, none of them that look older than me, and they're sipping beer from plastic Speight's Otago 500ml cups and some of them look nervous and almost all of them have collars that are standing straight up. On the table in front of them are lots of crates of beer and bottles of spirits and opposite me are two doors. The right one is closed and the left one is open to a bedroom and some of the boys are going in there, stepping over the piles of clothes and Adidas sports bags that are strewn all over the floor. The others are going into the kitchen beside me, which has a bar separating it from the living room, and Jules is going in there too so I follow him so it looks like I'm with him, like I'm his friend. There's a keg in the kitchen sitting on stained wet newspaper and maybe fifteen guys standing around it, including the ones from the taxi. Most of them don't have any hair and one of them is only wearing boxer shorts and he's all wet and he's got BLOW ME written on his forehead in black vivid capital letters.

I'm so nervous I'm unsteady, my knees are weak, my stomach sick and aching. Jules pumps the keg and pours a jug. They're all talking but I can't hear anything over the music. None of them are looking at me. None of them seems to find me being here strange. I take off my duffel coat so I look more like them because although they're mostly wearing moleskins and chambray shirts and ties I will look more like them if I'm just wearing my Speight's T-shirt and my jeans.

As I'm doing this some of them start shouting, "Meat, meat, meat," and it's because Marc Ellis from Gardies has arrived. He's smiling and someone passes him a jug and I notice all the girls on the couches are looking over at him.

I pick up a half-full jug from the bar and drink a lot of it. All of them are standing side by side and they've all got their arms folded or their hands on their hips and they're all mostly really big. One of them has RUNT written on his forehead. I'm leaning back on the long white counter and trying to look casual but it's covered in beer and water and empty bottles and the water soaks through the back of my shirt quickly so I stand up straight again, take bigger and bigger drinks from my jug. A Maori guy comes out a door into the kitchen and inside there's the mirror of a bathroom and he's got long hair and he's adjusting his fly and he's wearing an Otago rugby jersey with a huge collar and when he turns around to shut the door BLACK BASTARD in big white letters is written on his back above the number 14. Over by the window is one of the girls from the taxi, the one in the pink Holiday Tee sweatshirt and tan moleskins, and she's talking to a dark-haired girl who looks like she's maybe sixteen and she's wearing dark blue moleskins and a beige sweatshirt with Country Road written on it in pitch black letters and they're sharing a cigarette and laughing about something they know together. On one of the big white leather couches these three really young girls are looking at each other's nails and sometimes they're pointing to different boys in the kitchen and laughing together. The youngest-looking blonde one has a tartan tie holding her hair back in a ponytail and ROOT ME written in big black letters on her forehead.

The song changes to a slow chanting one and the boy in boxer shorts shouts out, "Fuck off," and someone changes it to a hard punky song. He starts jumping around and the others shove him. Next to me a short boy I half recognize says, "There's no better halfback in the first division, but if you can't do hard paddock yards before the season begins you're a weakness," to the boys next to him and next to them Jules is talking to the boy in the beanie again who's just smoking a cigar and watching the living room and next to them is a boy trying to listen and next to him is the boy in the boxer shorts banging his head up and down to the music and crammed in the kitchen there are other boys all standing in groups of three and four and the girls are all in the living room and the boys are all in the kitchen and the more I'm drinking the less nervous I'm feeling and but no one is speaking to me or even looking at me so it doesn't even seem to matter.

At some point I find out the motel room belongs to two boys, one nicknamed Dong, the other named Glen. I find this out because they arrive with a really clean-cut athletic-looking older guy with a moustache. He's wearing a blazer and a tie and Dong and Glen are younger, maybe twenty-two or twenty-three, and they both have really closely shaven heads and when they go straight into the bedroom and shut the door, ignoring the boys chanting "Dong, Dong, Dong," like church bells, I ask Jules, because I'm drunk enough, who they are. He tells me Dong,

Glen, that it's their room, that they were on the bench today, ignores me again.

I watch the door and when they come out they're with another boy and all three of them are really red in the face and the older guy with the moustache leads them out and he throws something to Jules who catches it and puts it in his pocket. The older guy heads to the door where he shouts out, "See you all at the clubrooms, ladies and germs. Have a good one," and the naked boy shouts back, "Murray." The guy, who seems to be some kind of assistant coach or assistant manager, says something to the dark-haired girl in the Country Road sweatshirt by the door. He leans in really close to her ear, and she laughs at what he says. Then he leaves and I see her make a face to the girl from the taxi, and the girl from the taxi puts a finger in her mouth, like she's going to be sick.

Some of the younger girls have come into the kitchen and are standing with the boys now.

The boy named Glen walks around silently pouring Bacardi into everyone's jugs, and he pours some into mine.

What I overhear between two boys whose names I don't know.

"Fucking Pienaar hit his straps."

"I rated him today but I don't rate him for staying power."

"Maybe, but today was a blinder."

"He machined on the wing."

"Superb."

"Yep."

—

At some point a Bruce Springsteen song called "Badlands" gets put on the stereo and all the boys in the kitchen sing along to the chorus really loudly.

At some point a Guns N' Roses song comes on, "Sweet Child o' Mine," and a young girl from the couch starts trying to dance in the middle of the living room. She's got red hair and she's really pretty but she's really drunk and she's dancing with her eyes shut. She keeps losing her balance and they're all watching her and they cheer when she has to grab onto the couch to hold herself up.

At some point a big group of maybe twenty people arrive; the living room fills up and I'm starting to drink the Bacardi straight.

At some point the guy I spoke to at Gardies leaves with Jules.

in the toilets and so fucked, splashing water in my face, leaning over the sink spitting and panting, real bad headspins and the music's too loud and in the mirrors I'm just a shape and I'm nauseous and saliva keeps running into my mouth and boys that come in keep patting me on the back and saying things but I can't make out the words and the music's just a pounding sound and I want to be sick but I can't and the door crashes open and three boys fall in against the wall hugging each other and banging their heads together and I spit in the sink and I can't remember getting in here and I can't be sick and two of the boys go back out the door one of them shouting something and the boy that's in here slides down the wall and lies down on the floor and closes his eyes and I'll go back out there again

—

And wake curled up on the couch, fully clothed, boots on.

It takes me a while to understand where I am but I realize that I'm still in the motel room, that I may have fallen asleep on the couch, but I don't remember doing this. The room is near-dark. My mouth is dry and sticky. I feel sick, weak. My right middle finger hurts and I hold it in my mouth then look at it and the nail has turned black. And there are bottles all over the floor and the coffee table beside me. There are cigarette and cigar butts inside the bottles, floating in beer. Across the coffee table someone has thrown a towel over the crotch of a naked boy who's asleep on the other couch. He looks strange and I realize it's because his left eyebrow has been shaved off.

The bathroom light has been left on and it's shining through into the kitchen. The tap in the kitchen sink is running silently and there's water, cigarette butts, toilet paper, clumps of newspaper, rubbish on the white lino. The keg is gone. Where the kitchen meets the living room there's a half circle of dark wet carpet. The bedroom doors are both shut. There is muffled music coming from one of the rooms; which one, I can't tell. I'm staring at the Otago rugby jersey nailed to the wall above the naked boy when there's a voice in the bathroom.

A voice answers. There is a scuffling sound and the naked boy stirs in his sleep.

I sit up very quietly. My jeans are wet on one side and there's an empty stubbie lying next to my leg. Slowly and carefully I stand up. My knees crack and the stubbie rolls into the hollow where I was sitting. I step around the coffee table, careful not to bump it. The carpet is soggy and stained brown around the table and it makes squelching noises under my boots.

I edge past the sleeping boy and almost fall on him, swaying in the darkness. There is the scraping sound of a cigarette lighter in the bathroom, a smell of smoke. I step over a crate, toward the door.

I'm going to leave. I'm going to get a taxi. It's time to go home now. At the door I stop and listen again. I can hear faint wet scuffling sounds. My hand is on the motel room's door handle.

"That's it," a male voice says, louder, slurred, coming from the bathroom. There is a sound like a moan.

I let go of the door handle and turn back, toward the kitchen, away from the door. Around the corner, past the kitchen cupboards, the light from the bathroom shows the water flooding the kitchen. The water is rippling gently, making the cigarette butts bob and move. There is a grunt, and a choking sound. I step into the kitchen. There is a spoken word. A male voice this time. A different voice grunts. A shadow moves in the light on the water.

I step fully into the kitchen, hold on to the fridge for support. My heart is thumping dully and there is a heavy pulsing feeling in the back of my neck. I shuffle forward, quietly, through the water. A cough, a choking sound, down at floor level.

I'm leaning forward, trying not to breathe, into the bright light coming through the bathroom door, to see.

Through the door, I see the bathroom counter and the sink, littered with bottles and cans, a pair of jeans. Above the sink, in the long bathroom mirror, I'm looking at Dong and another guy. They're naked and kneeling in the water on the bathroom floor facing each other. Between them is the young red-haired girl who was dancing before. She's naked now and on her knees in the water, doggy style. There are red scratches and dark pink marks on her hips and buttocks. Her pale skin is wet and shiny and her small breasts are hanging in the water on the floor. Her wrists are tied together behind her back with a leather belt.

Dong is fucking her from behind. He's holding her hips up with one arm under her stomach. The other boy is holding her head up with bunches of her hair in his hands. He is in her mouth. His head is tilted, a cigarette burning in his lips, and he's looking down to watch.

She keeps sagging to the side.

Dong is holding her up.

Naked next to her limp, pale body they are tanned and muscled and big.

I can't see her face but I can hear her choking when the boy thrusts into her and in the back of Dong's head has been shaved the number 12.

Dong pulls out of her. He spits in his palm and reaches down and rubs the spit on the head of his hardon. He leans back to see what he's doing. He holds his cock in one hand and pushes it back into her. Her right leg has some kind of spasm, the wet pale muscles shivering uncontrollably.

The other boy looks up through the smoke from his cigarette over her body.

"Hold her tighter, man," he says.

Outside the rain has stopped and I walk through the streets of Maori Hill until I don't know where I am but in front of a service station on an empty street I find a taxi waiting and I get in the back so the driver won't try and talk to me, but he's old, maybe fifty, and keeps looking at me in the rearview mirror. After we drive for a while I accidentally meet his eyes, and he says something that sounds like, "Is that so you don't forget, or so other people don't forget."

I don't know if I heard him right or what he means and don't reply anyway, just turn back and stare out the window, at the trees of the Belt, lit up from beneath by the taxi's headlights, the shadows moving, shifting shape like they're alive. It's starting to get light when we get to Strangeways and the fare is almost twenty dollars and I pay him with what must be the last of my student loan. In the mirror in my room, something is wrong with my face. There is backward writing on my forehead and one of my eyebrows has been shaved off.

Written on my forehead in black vivid capital letters is DOOZER II.

It was in August, the dead of winter in Dunedin, that we decided to go on a road trip to Christchurch. The decision was made on a Friday afternoon when Matt came home from the dough shift at Stallones. I was watching TV with Nick, Ursula was out, we were bored out of our minds. Matt came home angry at the George Street supervisor and suggested we get drunk. We agreed and we drove to the bottle store on Cumberland Street, bought dozens of Foster's stubbies each, and went for a drive.

We drove out of Dunedin and the mist and rain lifted by the

time we reached the top of the Kilmog. I saw pylons stretching over the endless, barren and unbroken hills, to the north, into the mountains. We had Matt's stereo. Nick had shotgun, I sat in the back, and Matt drove. Nick and me rested our feet on the boxes of beer. We smoked these long thin brown cigarettes Matt had called Mores.

The stereo played old Stone Roses: "Mersey Paradise," "Where Angels Play," "Elephant Stone." We got to Waikouaiti by two and we stopped for petrol.

"You know we could be in Christchurch by six," Matt said, getting back in the driver's seat.

"Don't tease me," Nick said, and looked at me in the rearview mirror. "Souse."

"Whatever," I said.

So we just kept going.

By the time we passed the sign for Weston there were shafts of sunlight breaking through the clouds. By the time we got to Palmerston me and Nick had drunk four beers each and Matt had one between his legs.

We stopped for pies and left again, eating as we drove through the hills.

I remember Matt told us about a new babe at Stallones, a Maori girl named Amber. Hunched over the wheel, leering, tapping his More out the window, he told us he had visions of what her cunt looks like.

"Sometimes I can just see it, man. It has these purple lips. I can see it totally clearly. Soaking wet. Drops of juice like, glistening on her pubic hair. I have these intense visions of purple cunt lips in pitch black pubic hair."

"Get a grip, Easty," Nick said.

"Oh, I do," Matt said.

Somewhere between Palmerston and Oamaru the road dropped down to the beach and Nick climbed out on the sill of the passenger side window, hanging onto the aerial, to howl at the sea. Passing cars honked their horns at us and Matt honked back, holding the horn down for minutes at a time. The stereo was playing Pixies and Nick climbed out his window and around the window strut legs first into the backseat as Matt swerved all over the road trying to put him off. I climbed between the front seats and took shotgun and Nick was gasping, laughing behind me, saying, "You *cunt*, you absolute *cunt*," to Matt and we were screaming the words to "Bone Machine" and giving *sieg heils* to cars that passed us, Matt with his left arm, me with my right, our arms crossing over in the middle because there's not enough room in the front seat of a Volkswagen to even point at anything.

And we kept going. In Oamaru we shut the windows and did ninety down the main street, the dubbie's engine howling, getting actually lifted out of our seats by the humps in the middle of the roundabouts because we didn't swerve for a single one. Outside Oamaru on the open road Matt said, "Right, give us a fucking beer then," and Nick said, "Here you go, mate," in the same exaggerated accent that he imitates my father with and dropped an open stubbie into his lap so it spilled all over him and Matt said, "Tin, you're a dead man," and we were leaving, leaving and it was so new and so different and I wanted to keep moving, keep leaving like this, and so I tried not to speak so the spell would not be broken and I tried not to think of anything else but what music was playing, how drunk I felt.

Past St. Andrews, and past Pareora, and then we did Timaru in less than ten minutes, because a bypass has been built since we left. When you take the bypass you drive through the city avoiding the main street. You see only the bypass ahead and beside the road McDonald's, Burger King, and KFC, supermarkets and pizza delivery outlets, and you can be in Washdyke in less than ten, with Nick still holding Matt's stereo out the window with German heavy metal playing as loud as his little stereo goes. So that's what we did.

We drove on and on up State Highway One, into the afternoon, toward Ashburton and Christchurch.

We crossed rivers I could not name. I saw farms and fields, the mountains far off across the plains. Sometimes I smelled rotting silage. As the batteries ran down the stereo got more distorted, the songs playing slower. We passed Waihi Boarding School and the silences between us began to get longer. When we reached Ashburton we saw that it had a bypass too. As we drove through the streets were empty. I remember Matt saying, "Teen pregnancy capital of New Zealand," and Nick saying from behind me, "Suicide capital too," before he fell asleep.

Signs at the side of the road told me it was only seventy kilometers to Christchurch.

I stared up unnamed roads that split from the highway, heading straight and empty for miles, to the left into the hills, to the right toward the coast.

The sun moved in and out of shifting clouds as it sank.

Before it got dark I sometimes caught glimpses of my shaved eyebrow in the rearview mirror. It seemed like a gray blur above my eye.

We kept going, on and on up the motorway, into the night, and Christchurch.

Gradually, as it got really dark, partly from the road signs and the service stations we saw by the roadside, partly from the traffic on the motorway and the smaller and smaller gaps between the streetlights, we knew we were coming to the city. Nick woke up in the backseat and opened a beer from Matt's box, because ours were both finished.

We took the bypass out by the airport and stopped for petrol somewhere on a long avenue heading into the city. The stereo was playing The Cure's *The Head on the Door*, the volume down low to save the batteries. The roads were wide, the traffic sparse and slow. Huge black trees rose up between the orange glows of the streetlights.

The avenue turned into Riccarton Road, heading into town. There were more cars, more lights, people on the streets. Riccarton Road stretched for what seemed like miles. Hundreds of anonymous side streets split from it. The city seemed vast and impossible to negotiate and I saw a lesson. In this place you had to stay on the road you were on. If you strayed you would be lost. In this place there is no higher ground, no hills to climb to find out where you are.

Before the park we stopped for batteries and cigarettes, and Nick bought a bottle of whisky from a Liquorland. Driving through the park we sculled nips from the cap, Nick passing it from the backseat. The spirits and the city seemed to make us alert. Matt drove fast and hard, silent and tense at the wheel. I watched the mirrors for police in the traffic behind and Nick was hunched in the back, smoking in sharp, violent movements, drinking whisky from the bottle, watching the footpaths through the dreads hanging down over his face.

The first night in Christchurch we parked the dubbie somewhere by the Avon and walked into town with the whisky in a supermarket bag. For me the night was a series of flashes. We were too drunk too early and no one was around; the shops all closed, the clubs still not open. In the square gluesniffers were huddled on the steps of the cathedral and empty taxis lined all the roads. Above us strange clouds moved through the sky, lit and made purple and yellow like bruises by the lights of the city. We ate souvlaki from a Greek kebab caravan and Nick puked it back up in a rubbish bin. Everywhere I seemed to see boys like us, but boys in long wide jeans, caps, different from the ones they wear in Dunedin, long T-shirts, hoodies, trainers, carrying skateboards, walking in groups of three, like us, and but even when they laughed these boys' eyes seemed to me to be always moving, waiting, watching; watching us, watching me, watching their own reflections in the panes of glass they passed.

Matt found an open club in a side street basement and we led Nick down the stairs and inside. There were only five people inside and they were all men. Nick came awake briefly and hissed, "This is a fucking *gay* bar," too loudly and they stared at us as we left, Nick shouting, "*Faggots*," as we climbed back up the stairs.

Out in the streets we walked for a long time and got lost.

Later we found the river again and followed it back to the car. On the windshield of the car next to us there was a sticker with the number 25 in a circle with a line through it. I asked Matt what it meant and he told me it was for the police. If they saw anyone under twenty-five driving that car, they knew to arrest them.

We slept that night in the Draize Train. Matt behind the wheel, me in the passenger seat, Nick curled up in the back.

Saturday morning, gray, glaring. We woke up early, because of the light, with bad hangovers. Nick in a really bad mood; Matt and me silent. We drove to McDonald's on Riccarton Road for breakfast around ten, and sat at a table by the automatic doors on red plastic chairs attached to the floor by chrome pillars. We were all wearing sunglasses and not talking. We all ordered coffee with our food.

Matt said, "You know apple juice is more thirst-quenching than orange juice. For the dries."

Nick muttered, "Yeah?"

"Yeah."

There was a pause. Nick sighed. "Okay, Matt. What about water then."

"When?"

"*Wa*-ter."

"We're talking about thirst-quenchingness?"

I was rubbing my eyes, red and sore from lack of sleep.

"*Yes*, Matt," Nick hissed. "You *dick*."

"I meant when you want something . . . flavored."

—

Sitting at the table near the automatic doors, after maybe half an hour of silence, Nick finally said, "So Souse, you gonna visit this little pen pal of yours. Or did you make her up."

I said, "She's not made up." I had to try hard to remember her address.

Some little kids at the counter were staring at us as their mother got served. They were standing on either side of her, holding tightly to her hands, twisted round to look at us as they waited for their food.

Maybe it was because we looked cool, sitting there strung out in sunglasses, three thin pale boys, one with a mohawk, one with dreads, one with a missing eyebrow. Maybe we looked mysterious, like we had a story. Maybe they twisted round to stare because we looked cool to them. I couldn't be sure.

I looked up Anna's parents in the phone book and called her from a box outside McDonald's. Over the noise of the traffic the conversation went something like this:

"Hello?"

"Anna."

"Mm hm?"

"Hi. It's Richey."

"Well. Hi. This is a surprise."

"Yeah. So, yeah. What have you been . . . doing?"

"This is you, Richey? Richey Sauer?"

". . . yeah. Souse."

"Oh I'm sorry, man. I know two Richeys now."

". . ."

"Hello?"

"Um, me and my friends are up here. In Christchurch."

"Really. Why's that then?"

". . ."

"Richey?"

"Um, I don't know. I don't think we know."

She said we could come over and visit her if we wanted, gave me her address again, somewhere close, in an area that blurs borders; a place no one can say is Riccarton, Fendalton, Ilam, Merivale, or something else.

We drove there, and her house was difficult to find, lost in the winding streets full of trees near the university. A wealthy area, I could tell, from the cars parked in the driveways: Pathfinders, Range Rovers, Outbacks, Pajeros, Troopers.

"Look at them. Fendalton prams," Matt muttered. We drove slowly through the narrow streets, looking for street signs, numbers on mailboxes, anything I recognized.

Eventually we found it, a street named after a Maori tree, near Deans Bush. Anna's house is an old villa, two-storied, surrounded by trees. Because I have only ever been there drunk it seems to me like a house from a dream.

We parked the car and I made Matt and Nick wait while I smoked a cigarette. Maybe because it was my first cigarette of the day it made my heart begin to beat very fast.

Nick and Matt stood behind me.

When she answered the door she was smaller than I remembered her and she was very pale. Her hair was so short, like a number one, but still dark red. She wore baggy track pants, slippers, a Straitjacket Fits T-shirt I remembered, long and loose on her now.

Seeing her, something in me moved, tipped. I felt something spill and fall.

She didn't see Matt and Nick at first. She smiled at me. She said, *"Rich*ey. What happened to your eyebrow? You big geek." She laughed, moved her hand as if to reach out and touch my face.

I didn't answer.

"He won't tell us, either," Nick said from behind me.

We went inside and she met Matt and Nick for the first time. She had made hummus, she told us, and said we had to try it. We ate it in her parents' kitchen with carrot sticks and pita bread and she said it was made from chickpeas and garlic.

She put a tape in a little stereo on the fridge and played us sad, slow music. "What's this?" Matt asked. "It's Morphine," she said, didn't explain, looked at me, rolled her eyes, smiled.

I couldn't look back at her and I couldn't think of anything to say.

She made us coffee. She asked about bands in Dunedin, what gigs we had seen. We went upstairs to her little room with our cups. Her walls were covered in posters, a ripped tour poster of *Screamadelica*, a signed Billy Bragg CD cover, a poster of the cover of *Coney Island Baby*. She had goldfish in a fishtank. She had the ash from burned incense cones on a plate painted with flowers. She had a hand-knitted purple blanket on the chair in the corner of the room where I sat. On her desk she had a fern in a pot and an ice cream container with a hand-lettered sticker that read, PILLS 'N' THRILLS AND BELLYACHES: ANNA'S MEDICINES. On her bookshelf she had rows of CDs and tapes and books, *Ophelia Thinks Harder, The Odyssey, The Narnia Chronicles, Goddesses in Everywoman, Sixth Form Certificate Mathematics.*

Matt began to look through her music collection.

Nick said, "So, where's the nearest bottlestore."

She said, "You do know it's only twelve o'clock."

He said, "That means less to me than you might think."

She laughed, and told him where to find a Superliquor, a few blocks up Riccarton Road. He said, "Coming for a walk then, Souse," and I said, "Alright."

From the doorway Nick said, "Matt?" and he said, "Dozen of anything."

As we left I looked at Anna sitting cross-legged on her bed, sipping her coffee. She wasn't smiling and she raised her eyebrows to me.

I said, "See ya," tried to smile, but she didn't say anything, just looked at me.

On the way to the bottlestore Nick said, "But isn't your friend sick or something, Souse."

And what I could say to him was, "How should I know."

In the Superliquor chiller it was cold and bright and brewer's dozens of Canterbury Draught were $15.95 a box. We bought three of them and the boy who served us was big and good-looking and wearing a blue Superliquor polo shirt. He smirked when he saw my eyebrow. As he scanned the barcodes he said, "Big night is it then, boys."

Immediately, standing right beside me, Nick said, "We're gonna get his other one."

The boy said, "Should have a twistoff then. Get him rotten enough." He handed Nick the eftpos slip. "You ever finished one?"

Nick said, "Always seem to lose track of time halfway through."

The boy laughed. He said, "Have a good one, boys."

We left.

Halfway back to Anna's, walking past the university carrying two of the boxes, Nick said, "You up for a twistoff, Souse."

I said, "Course."

Because the beer was heavy we stopped in a street a few blocks from her house. We sat on the boxes and smoked a cigarette each. After a while Nick checked his watch and said, "And I think we can safely say Matt is now unemployed."

"Why?"

"Because his pizza shift starts in ten minutes."

When we got back to Anna's house Nick rang the doorbell by leaning on it with his shoulder.

She laughed when she saw how much beer we had, and said we had to drink in the kitchen, and that her parents would be home in an hour.

Nick said, "Wait, wait . . ." and put the beer down on the table. Matt came downstairs, excited about something, but Nick held up a hand, silencing him, and stared down at the top box concentrating, tapping it with his fingers.

We waited, and after a minute of silence he looked up and said, "This means we have time to drink the first four point five something stubbies here. Before we have to get the fuck out."

"What are you on, Tin," Matt said.

"We're having a twistoff, Easty," Nick said. "And right now, you need one more than any of us."

So we sat around the kitchen table and started the first stubbie each, timing it by the kitchen clock—fifteen minutes for the first of fifteen, fourteen for the next, and so on until you finish or you forget.

Anna put more coffee on and changed the tape in the little stereo. She stood by the oven, leaning on the counter, watching us.

Matt offered her one of his beers. She said, "I think that would break your rules, wouldn't it."

Nick said, "She's right, Matthew. Don't try and pussy out."

"I'm being polite, Tin," Matt said.

"You're trying to pussy out."

"Tin, I've done more of these than you ever have."

"You're trying to pussy out of this one."

"Fuck off."

"Feeling guilty?"

"Not one fucking iota, mate."

"Seven minutes," I said.

"You're the one who needs to worry about time, Souse, no one else."

"Do I look worried?"

"You look like a freak at the moment, monobrow."

". . ."

". . ."

"You look like . . . a freak, too."

"Oh. Nice one, Souse."

". . ."

". . ."

"Nice one, Tin."

"Good on ya, mate."

"Good on you, mate."

He sighed. "Christ, Souse. Have an original thought. Read a book."

"Come on, Souse. Who did it? Who shaved your eyebrow off?" Matt said.

"Tell us, Souse. I think you did it yourself," Nick said.

They were all looking at me. I got up and said, "I'm going outside to smoke a cigarette."

"Better take your beer," Nick said from behind me. "Running seriously short of time."

Outside in the winter Christchurch afternoon there was no wind and no sun, just a light mist falling, a heavy cool grayness over the city. The leaves of the trees down Anna's parents' drive were a lush deep green, filling up the sky, closing the house in. There was some kind of silence, some stillness I could not understand, could not feel part of. The doors to the garage at the far end of the driveway were old, wooden, the paint cracked and flaking, hanging open crookedly from rusted hinges, obscuring what was inside. The garage seemed jagged, broken, somehow shaken down. There were holes in the asphalt of the driveway filled with muddied water, and in the porch where I stood was a pair of slippers, some old Nikes, the leather cracked, turned gray, and also, weirdly, a pair of wooden clogs. Her father was a vet, I remembered.

I also thought I remembered them owning a dog but I saw no sign of it, no food or water bowl, no chewed plastic bones, no ruined tennis balls, no dented pieces of wood shiny with saliva. Nothing like the things Snoopy leaves at the doors to my parents' house.

The mist fell lightly and slowly the length of the driveway and I smoked until what had spilled and fallen drained away.

Anna said, "Are you alright," from the doorway behind me.

I snorted, to show I was laughing. "I'm great," I said.

Above the warped iron of the garage roof I could see taller, more full trees beyond, trees clustered together and grown high, somewhere either blocks away or kilometers away. I guessed it might be Deans Bush, or, if I had mistaken the distance, they might mean Hagley Park. I couldn't be sure what they meant.

"How's Dunedin?"

"It's . . . bitching."

"Did you have . . . something you wanted to talk to me about? Is that why you rang?" From beside me.

I flicked my cigarette butt into the drive.

"I suppose I . . ."

". . ."

"You want me to . . ."

". . ."

". . ."

"Richey."

". . ."

"Richey. Do you remember when we were at Tekapo for that first New Year's?" She stepped toward the edge of the porch.

"Yes," I said.

"Well, I remember . . . you arrived a day after us and stuff, and we'd just moved down to the camping ground from Michael's place. Anyway. When you arrived. Your parents had dropped you off. I remember you wearing these 501s. Light blue 501s with the cuffs rolled up. And you were wearing this denim Rodd & Gunn shirt. And you had your Last Footwear boots on. I've still got a photo of you. Do you remember?"

"Kind of."

"Well, I remember thinking you looked so uncomfortable. Thinking you looked so fake. So like you were trying to be someone you weren't. And I've always wanted to say sorry to you for what I thought then. For being cruel to you. But now I think being sorry is the most useless thing. But I was. Sorry, I mean."

I said, "I don't . . . even remember things like that anymore."

She said, "Do you mean you don't remember that way, or you don't remember at all."

I said, "You don't . . . you shouldn't try . . . and get . . . close."

She said, "*Why*, Richey. What's *wrong*."

I said, "I'm . . . not who you think I am."

She said, "I don't even know who you are. Tell me who you are."

I said, "I'm a bad person."

She said, "When you're . . . young, some of the things you do . . . are cruel."

I said, "Some of them are unforgivable."

She will never reply, and I turned to see her. "You're different than you are in writing," I said.

As the mist grew thicker, drops began to fall from leaves into the puddles in the holes in Anna's driveway.

I finished my fourth beer, lit another cigarette. I was smoking Dunhills that day.

Leaving again, piling into the Draize Train, loading the boxes of beer in the backseat, another ritual, another motion gone through, someone singing, someone swearing, a blurred scene repeating itself all over a city. Things are left unfinished, gaps are left unfilled, exits are contrived, moments are lost in a rush to get somewhere. Something is lost, something is gained. A door closes, a door opens. There is a girl standing in a driveway before the garage, holding a raincoat over her head; there are three boys running around a car in the rain. One shouts something about time; one swears; one moves in rain like it is not there.

A window opens, and an engine starts. People leave so quickly and easily because there are rules for leaving, techniques to use, precedents to follow.

Out the wound-down window he says thanks again and she moves the fingers of her right hand holding the raincoat above her head. Open, shut.

The car's engine halts, misfires, tries again. There is a laugh, a wave, things are made simpler. The car jerks, Matt's the driver, Nick's the one who howls in the back, I'm the one who reaches silently for a tape.

We stay this way. This is what it looked like. This is how it is shown and how it is told. But she waved only once and turned back up the drive and disappeared before we could disappear. Like she sensed the contrivance, couldn't look at it for long.

Forgiveness is temporary and time is short and she is dead.

And boom onto the main road as the rain began to pour. For the seventh stubbie we had nine minutes but by then I was missing things, unsure of times, distances, rates of change. Heading into the city again, Matt was jerking back and forth behind the wheel, Nick was crouching on the backseat snarling like an animal, I pounded the babyblue tin dashboard with my fist, threw a bottle at a parked Stallones Honda, trying to make someone laugh. Matt swore, drove faster, shouted, "Dumb *fuck,* Souse." In the back like a mantra Nick's chanting, "Chicks, chicks, we need chicks," and a new song started and the volume goes up and the windows go down and we go into town.

First was Lochinvar's on Colombo Street and it was packed out. Signs on the doors said, LONGEST BAR IN THE WORLD, GUINNESS. The queue was two deep, ten long. We were silent, strangers there, tense, our arms clamped to our sides, my armpits chilled and aching from holding hidden stubbies.

Nick whispered, "We have less than three minutes." Inside there were hundreds of people, boys in rugby jerseys, boys in chambray, boys in moleskin, the bar really was long, and the music playing was not Irish. We moved through the crowd as quickly as we could, around tables, through circles of people, moving stools, pushing some boys, avoiding other boys. Nick flicked his dreads back, stood very erect; Matt held his chin high; I stared the weak down.

In the toilets we opened a stubbie each and sculled until Matt puked in the urinal. My belly was swollen and rolling with beer, my eyes watering. There was urine all over the floor and Matt was good to go within minutes.

"Second wind, second wind," he muttered, bent over the urinal, spitting in the drain.

In the square under the cathedral a man was playing trumpet. There were gluesniffers sitting behind him on the steps and a young girl in big black boots and a skirt made of men's ties was dancing a jig around the pillars. As she danced an older guy watched her, his clothes spotted with paint, deep creases in his face, clapping, singing the words off-key in a croaking broken voice.

"*Dirty old town . . . dirty old town . . .*"

Twenty or thirty people were sitting on the steps down into the square. In front of them an old man, maybe forty, in a stained blue windjacket, was standing on a stepladder reading from a Bible. As he read, he paused between sentences, gestured with his hand, looked up to the sky.

"You must not take for yourself a wife and you must not come to have sons and daughters in this place. With deaths from disease they will die. They will not be bewailed, nor will they be buried. As manure upon the surface of the ground they will become, and by the sword and by famine they will come to an end. And their dead bodies will actually serve as food for the flying creatures of the heavens and for the beasts of the earth.

"For I have taken away my peace from these people, even loving kindness and mercies. Jeremiah. Chapter sixteen."

"Sit down," someone shouted. Someone else laughed.

The rain had stopped again and above him the shapes of cloud moved across the sky toward the Port Hills, lit pink and orange and violet. The concrete in the square was shining and wet, reflecting the street lamps and the traffic lights. Nick and I had one stubbie to go, Matt two; but we had lost track of time.

Nick pointed. "Souse. Flying low."

I zipped it up.

Christchurch, or what I remember of it anyway.

An Indian restaurant with unmatching panes of glass in windows that had been smashed and replaced, the sign reduced to PAL'S INDIAN TAURANT, Y.O. Shining wet concrete, grit under my feet. Peep shows with bad oil paintings of naked girls in the windows, their bodies distorted, out of proportion. Narrow doors opening to narrow stairways, painted bright colors like blue and yellow, leading up to massage parlors. Closed-down shops and twenty-four-hour fish and chip bars run by thin Chinese in stained white aprons. Burger King, McDonald's, and KFC. Fenced-off construction sites and sports bars with men's names. A string of bars near the river with names that were all jokes on the word "bar." Long queues outside; boys all wearing chunky black shoes and dress shirts, their hair slicked back, bracelets and big watches. Girls in moleskins and silky colored shirts and black leather jackets. I couldn't understand them, they seemed different from Dunedin. To me they were confused, unsure of who they were. There were older people in the queues in suits and dresses. Everything random, skewed, *uncool*.

Christian bookshops and chain bookshops; young girls standing around smoking cigarettes, wearing hooded sweatshirts stenciled with the letters U.S.A. I remembered the Last Footwear Company. Action Downunder had moved. Country Road was in the same place and there were other shops, Plume, Workshop, Thornton and Hall.

My eyebrow itching so badly.

Clenching my eye shut, shaking, trying to stop it.

Matt saying, "I feel as if I could drink an ocean. I feel like pure energy."

Nick saying, "Be pure. Be vigilant. *Behave*."

Chairs and tables on the footpaths outside the bars, empty, beaded with water. A fight outside Esprit. Finishing the last stubbie, the twistoff forgotten, looking for somewhere to go. Matt giving Nick a foot up onto the awning above The Body Shop. Some police passing, ordering him down. Me and Matt backing off. Nick shouting, "Kill your teachers," and people applauding; Nick twisting his ankle jumping down.

Matt confiding in me, "You know Christchurch was built on

reclaimed swamp. That's why the mist and the smog, all the little rivers everywhere. People say they see ghosts. Kids who
drowned when we first came here."

"Who's 'we,'" I said.

Nick overhearing and saying, "Boring."

Matt saying, "What?"

Nick saying, "Boring. You're *boring*, Matt."

It all moved very quickly; none of it was important.

All the while, though, above me, even though there seemed
to me to be no wind, there were eerie shifting clouds, the colors
polluted and surreal, orange, purple and blue, colossal and moving slowly, relentlessly over the city, out to sea.

5

Escaping

Hi Richey,

This will probably be the last letter I write to you, since I'm
pretty sure you don't really even want to talk to me any more. I
would say that it was good to see you and your friends up here
the other weekend, but I guess I'm not sure that it was.

You've changed a lot. I guess I could feel the change
happening—and plus I suppose I've hardly seen you enough to
really get to know you as you are now—but I remember what I
thought of you when we met at Tekapo, when you helped me after
I was sick from all that Coruba and Douglas had done that thing.
You looked after me.

I was a little bit in love with you, I think. You seemed like this
sort of lost, bewildered little boy—kind of baffled by all the shit
that was going on around you. You were sweet and you said

things I've never heard a guy say before. I suppose I imagined you staying like that: listening to great music, being in a band, staying sweet, staying like a child, sincere, being creative like a child. Probably my idealism, my dreamworld kicking in I suppose.

You were very quiet when you were here. You seemed really full of anger at something. Was it anything to do with me? I can't see how.

Anyway, you could've stayed at my house if you wanted to. I know I'm not that exciting anymore, don't do the town thing that much now, and I suppose drinking and drugs always call. Bronny said she saw you at the Palladium later that night, looking—her words—"very drunk and very evil." Two things probably necessary to survive an evening there.

Did your friends enjoy it up here? You're a strange crew, the three of you. Matt seems nice. He was so excited when he found out I had that Smiths song, the Draize Train, on my weird double-tape of The World Won't Listen. Is it really that hard to find? He said he'd been looking for an original version of it since he first started listening to them. It's nice to see people genuinely excited about something like that. And weird; this guy all dressed in black, with a mohawk, really scary-looking really, all happy and laughing just over finding I had this song. And it's only an instrumental. This was all when you guys were at the bottlestore, of course. He was quieter when you got back.

Nick seems different to you guys. Really confident, but in a kind of arrogant way, I thought. Kind of like he doesn't give a shit about anything. That can be a strength though, I suppose.

Well, my cancer is still in remission and next year I can probably go back to school. Things will be very different though.

I will be a year behind what few of my friends are still there. This "glue" has failed her appointed task, it seems. Kim's still in England and not writing. Bronny's still at Girls' High but moving in more Merivale/Country Road/Coyote/Plume circles now. Julia's doing broadcasting at Polytech. It doesn't bother me the way it used to though. If they're all doing what they really want, that's all that matters. "I have to look after myself first," is my philosophy.

Although physically I am often very weak, I feel mentally very strong. I can face things now with a sense of proportion, with a sense of what is important.

I think there are two kinds of pain. The first is pain that comes on you from outside. Like cancer, like grief, like loss, like randomness, like the ways people act to each other.

The second is pain that you visit on yourself. Like self-hatred, like depression, stuff like that.

The first is real pain. The second is your own creation. It is not real and not legitimate pain. The second kind is what people feel when they've never tasted the real thing. The kind felt by people who need something to feel, to convince themselves they're real.

I know you've done things to yourself. I know girls at school who used to scratch their arms up, eat one apple a day. I saw the blisters on your hand.

But you can't stay like that forever, Richey. If the pain you feel is your own creation then the thing that will ease that pain will be your own creation as well. It takes a kind of effort, a kind of strength. To save yourself, you have to do it yourself.

That's all the preaching I have to do today. I won't be writing back unless you write first. Please do. I'm thinking about you, believe me.

As for me, I go on. There is pain, but it only goes so far down. So far and no more. I go on, alone if necessary.

You can't die to taste life, and I won't, not the way I see people do.

I'm remembering you, little blonde-haired boy, shy, sweet, with your beautiful eyelashes, the way you were.

With love,

Anna

A knock on my door disturbs me, lying in bed reading Anna's letter, which arrived today with another official-looking letter with a printed letterhead that says UNIVERSITY OF OTAGO and under this a stamped and slightly crooked letterhead that says DISCIPLINARY COMMITTEE in blue and that's lying on my desk unopened, a clear plastic window in the front displaying my name: RICHARD J. SAUER.

Today is November 5th, Guy Fawkes', eight days away from final exams. No one comes into my room anymore—they just knock and shout from the hallway.

"Getting up, Souse? It is now eleven past eleven. We're going with Ursula to get the piss now. Sarah's is at eight or nine and we're going to drink on the garage till then. Get *up*, my son. We're going to have . . . fun."

Strangeways sits on a hill. The garage is at ground level, the level of Dundas Street. The path and the steps that lead up to the front door are next to the garage, parallel to the road. What this means is that the level of the foundations of Strangeways is about the same as the roof of the garage, the back of which is underground, roughly beneath the lawn outside my room. By sidling along the shelf of brick that runs beside the steps under the hedge you can climb onto the top of the garage; a parapet that protrudes a meter from the earth, three meters above the footpath, and the width of a queen-size bed. The parapet overlooks the street and much of student Dunedin: the perfect place to set up armchairs, stack a stack of beer, light a cigarette, and get drunk, watching what passes by, waiting for the time to leave for this party—Sarah's party, a Guy Fawkes' night party—trying to keep the panic attacks at bay by drinking quickly, trying to keep myself under control, not wanting anything bad to happen, *wanting something bad to happen.*

The boy Anna remembered (remembers from three years ago—how horrible to think that I can now measure parts of this existence by *years*) no longer exists. He was a naïve fool, without experience, without volition, without knowledge. I am here, I am now. They shall see all I'm capable of. Everyone: my father, my mother, my sister, Anna, my "friends," these big guys I see standing talking to these girls who listen to them, not noticing these guys are laughing to each other behind their backs, these fucking women that are actually attracted to these massive lumps of meat who sneer and laugh at them, who fuck them on bars, in the bushes behind pubs.

Oh, I know I rant but I get so angry, and frightened at how angry I get. Like I'll maybe get so far into my anger that something will happen that will make it impossible to return. Like I'll really and truly lose control one day and *become*. It's a strange feeling to be frightened of yourself. It's a kind of poise, like an insect on the skin of water; too much of any kind of movement this way or that and you'll just plunge in, lost forever in something that's part of yourself but somehow bigger than yourself. Your *rage*. It's a sense of being frozen, wanting to escape, knowing it's too risky to move just yet; times of tension, times of stress, times of strain. Wanting to and not wanting to. Not being able to act, because there's nothing to do, there's no place to go, just living on so many edges that you're finally left balanced on a point.

According to my reading, I am well aware this rage would make me *a disorganized killer*.

There are things I use to stabilize myself here.

I have tools. You can live on Lucozade, brown rice, and vinegar. Lemon juice is a diuretic. Hunger soon passes into a state very similar to this balancing. I am too weak to act, suspended in my weakness by my own strength; a paradox I could never make my father understand: that to be weak can take awful amounts of strength and willpower. That kind of hunger gives me a terrible sense of now. I can't expend the mental energy to remember the past, or to imagine any future. When I'm hungry enough and weak enough I can suspend myself in the very here and now, and stave off the panic attacks and silence my voice that tells me I'm sinking into ash—that is, my future, the future of my little blonde-haired boy (*shy, sweet, my eyelashes*) is a falling orange ember in a chasm of ash.

Yes, so I am strong. Plus there are excellent spin-offs. I now weigh fifty-eight kilograms. I'm thinking of Kurt near the end. How good he looked, so thin, so beautiful, his clothes so loose.

Sometimes when I walk these streets I feel like I'm barely there, I almost float away and I love that so.

It feels like the first days of summer, though it is spring. Inside this room, in my bed even, I can feel the pressure of the mugginess outside. I roll over in bed and part my curtains a little. Up beyond the castle the clouds are thick and low. I get headaches in northwest winds. My skin prickles and itches with sweat and my teeth feel furry and loose.

Weak with hunger, I fall back and lie here.

Just wait till they get back. Just let them decide how things will go.

After we got back from Christchurch Matt used some of his paint to write the words "The Draize Train" down along both sides of the Volkswagen in foot-high black capitals. On the bonnet, first in thick pencil then painted over, he drew a startlingly good portrait of Johnny Marr from a photo in an old N.M.E. Johnny looks thin, calm and cool, wearing round mirrored sunglasses like the ones he wears in the photo on the inside sleeve of *Rank*. The car gets lots of looks around Dunedin now. Most student cars that are painted are done so as to look like Speight's or Monteith's labels.

Matt has been trying desperately to get a copy of "The Draize Train." He has the live version on *Rank*, the Smiths live album, but for some reason only Anna's copy of *The World Won't Listen* has the studio version. He has been to every record store in Dunedin, looking for it: Echo, Tandy's, Records Records. He says he saw Martin Phillips in Records Records.

But the song eludes him. Anna is the only person I know who has a copy. He knows it is a b-side to one of the singles circa *The World Won't Listen*, but they are only on twelve-inch and they are rare, expensive, and seldom found in New Zealand record stores.

Late at night Matt will disappear into his room and try and work out the guitar parts from the live version, and the keyboard parts from memory. His favorite Smiths songs have no words.

"Just flag it away, Matt," Nick says, laughing at him. And Matt never replies, like it's too serious a business to even attempt to explain. I remember a time when Nick would have got excited about the search as well.

Matt often disappears in the Draize Train for whole days at a time, sometimes leaving in the middle of the night, sometimes really early in the morning. If he says anything, if we're up, it's usually, "Just going for a drive for a while."

He never asks us to come; we never offer.

Nick—when he's there—and Ursula and I get stoned on oil smeared on cigarettes, watching TV. One night Nick and I poked around in Matt's room looking for cigarettes. We found a mound of photographs from sixth and seventh form in a shoebox underneath his bed, alongside all his self-portraits that he has taken down from the walls of his room. The photos were of parties, us, some of the girls, Jane, Megan, some of Sarah. I remember that Matt had a thing for Sarah in seventh form as well.

Almost every photo had been mutilated. A straight cut then a little round jagged hole in every photo that Matt appeared in. He had cut his face out of all of them, including one I used to love: a photo taken in seventh form at the Old Mill, this club in Timaru, when the band was playing. I didn't drum for them at this point, and for some reason that I can't remember Matt wasn't playing either. The band had no name. It was just Nick and three other guys, one who was replacing Matt on rhythm guitar.

The actual photo, though, is of the band that played after our band that night at the Old Mill. They were a metal covers band named Warhammer or Lifeless or something like that. The photographer is looking over the dance floor toward the stage. The dance floor is full of the Timaru rednecks who were booing our band. But they dance in a little circle around Matt and another boy from our school whose nickname was Munga, who are standing directly in front of the stage, staring back at the camera through the dancers. The singer in Warhammer is looking down at the two of them a little uncertainly. Matt and Munga have their hands clasped solemnly before them, standing like mourners at a funeral, with looks of utter disdain on their faces.

It used to make me laugh every time, this minor tribute to the band Matt wasn't even allowed to play in, and I probably would've laughed again that night, but Matt's face was gone, cut out of the picture, a jagged ring of white photographic paper all that was left.

In the bathroom, the dirty bathroom whose window looks up to the gray walls of the castle, I stumble getting into the bath. Days like these, these humid, sultry days, it sometimes feels like daylight will never leave, like nothing will ever end.

I stand beneath the showerhead in the end of the bath and don't look down at my body.

The first time I ever did anything to myself was an accident, when I was fourteen (I'm a late bloomer in all things). I was moving a lit candle for Christmas dinner, raging at my parents, the three of us stuck in the house together for too long over the holidays, and a drop of hot molten wax fell and spattered onto the back of my hand. Amazed at the pain, and amazed at myself for not flinching. I stood there, knowing it would quickly cool, just quietly waiting for the sting to ease of its own accord. I felt very calm, suddenly thoughtless, delight in my surprise.

It only happened very subtly at school. I used pins to prick my forearms or the sides of my knees. Pins don't leave scars but the pain is not as good. At school stuff like that though—a visible burn or cut known to be self-inflicted—would be the instant and permanent status of a freak, so I was careful.

Sometimes when I'm too drunk it can sober me up. And I can do so much worse after drinking than I ever do sober. I hold a cigarette's lit end hard against my skin until it goes out. Five times, once, in the toilets at Foxy's. Five little ashy craters in my arm, the hairs all singed and shortened. The blisters are fat and ugly though. And they infect easily, take weeks to heal, leak red-tinged fluid that stains the sleeves of shirts. When they eventually do heal they become shiny pink circles that no hair ever grows from again.

Sometimes I feel sick and wasted, disappointed in myself, after I've done it drunk. Weak, not strong enough to do it that badly when I'm straight.

But the feeling of calm, stillness, strength, is good. And I'm doing more and more to get there. I am only a freak in other people's terms. My behavior is internally logical, it serves a purpose, accomplishes all I ask of it. People who don't understand assume you're damaged goods. But my scars set me apart. They speak of my strength, and of a past. Because it's the others who are the dishonest ones, the weak ones. They do things to others to feel strong. My goal has been to minimize the evil I bring to this world. The ultimate achievement of this goal will be when I slit my wrists in this bath. When that will occur I am not sure yet. But it lurks in my head every day.

Very calm. Strong, and brave. Thinking about it makes me feel brave. No more to change the world I have crawled through.

Dressing in my room, very slowly, I watch *A Book of Murder* lying by the other books on my bed. It is crumpled and beer-stained, the tacky cover ripped from when I threw it at the wall one angry night.

I've read the thing so many times. Staring at the words, trying to fathom some deeper sense, trying to find the real horror behind words like "detached," "penetrated," "stabbed," "raped," "removed," "eviscerated," "murdered." Through winter I read it again and again, little epiphanies coming to me, tiny moments of insight that stung and calmed. Though it is a scholarly work, it captures nothing, let alone me.

Later I began to get more and more irritated at words like "woman," "she," "her," "the women," "the victim." All were described as "the woman, aged" whatever. It grew frustrating; the epiphanies receded. What did they do? Who were they? Did they get drunk and laugh at the guy? Did they just never even register his existence? The book never told me. I would try to imagine, but my imagination just showed me arrogant girls from Unicol who came down from Auckland; rich, haughty girls in Country Road and Rodd & Gunn sweatshirts, moleskins, only ever talking to the guys from Auckland Grammar and King's who wore those same clothes.

I remember thinking it would be a favor to other girls like Ursula to get rid of them.

Later I just stopped reading it.

Let it sit there, a book of statistics and cognitive theory as useless as Todd Johnson, a book of veiled accusations I could no longer stand hearing, I could no longer pull truth from. I never even finished the last chapter properly. I can't read anymore. No books can help me now; things are too far down. The effort to read and understand just seems too immense, the prospect of finding myself or any opening too elusive. Let it sit there, along with the other books that just sit there, that lie beneath my bed gathering dust, that lie stacked next to the khaki cloth–wrapped shape of my father's rifle and the box of bullets I stole from my parents' house when we stopped by on the way back from Christchurch, all the killer books picked full of holes, and my *Marketing Research Methods 1.3* and my *Oxford Complete Shakespeare* and my *Top 500 Poems*, the covers and the edges of the pages all beer-stained and cigarette-singed, the pages themselves pristine, white and clean, untouched, unread.

Twelve o'clock. Dressed. My ripped jeans and dirty shirt don't look cool on me. They're embarrassing. After twenty minutes with just me and the full-length mirror, the car's pulling up outside.

Nick has distanced himself from us in many ways over the last couple of months. He has been sporadically attending lectures, still maintaining a foothold at university, but more and more he has been going out on his own. He would ask us to come to the pub with him—me and Matt, sometimes Ursula but only when he's really desperate—but we almost always said no. Nick likes to go to Gardies and I haven't been there since July. When Matt drinks he prefers to stay close to the flat; Ursula drinks and smokes in front of the TV; I drink with her or in my room, or out on the porch if it's warm enough.

One night when it was still winter Nick came home and for once didn't roll his eyes and mutter, "Good night then, Souse?" when he found me watching infomercials stoned in the living room at 3 A.M. He sat down and we made fun of "Amazing Discoveries" for a while and it was good, like some of the old times were good.

After being quiet for a while, getting closer to four, he started talking like he'd never done before, telling me about the test he'd just had that evening for LAWS 101, and how he knew as he was sitting there in the gymnasium filled with desks that he'd fucked it up, how it was the second test for LAWS and he'd missed the first one completely and how this one was thus crucial: the missed test was worth 25 percent; that night's fucked-up test: 25 percent; the final exam: 50 percent. To just pass the course now he'd have to cane the exam like no other exam he'd caned before. He estimated that he'd need an A+ to gain a C as a final grade after what he'd done that night.

He told me he worked all this out as he stared at his hopeless answer booklet, and then left the exam early and walked straight over the road to the corner bar at the Cook and drank for hours with these West Coast biker types, and how he'd not once been afraid of them, had bought them beers, had beers bought for him.

"Complete despair gives you this power, Souse. When you just don't care anymore you're not afraid of anything. You can *do* . . . anything."

He seemed happy and a little surprised to have figured this out.

I acted cool, like I'd known all about despair for a long time.

Today's drinking has been arranged by Nick for nostalgic reasons, I believe. One of the first days that can be called summer. Drinking outside. I can tell he's been thinking about last summer and the end of high school and all the kegs and crates we used to get with Mark and Sebastian, Cam, Dan, all the guys we never see anymore. Those crate days: Dan finishing one in just over two hours, the new record, so far unbeaten. Parties that began at 2 P.M. with four boys and a fifty-liter keg and ended at 4 A.M. with loads of people and those same four boys bumming wine cooler and alcoholic lemonade off the girls once the keg died.

Nick wants it all back, and Matt's going along with it because in the last couple of days he's been in a good mood.

Ursula's going along with it because that's what she does.

Car doors slamming. Voices, laughter. Boots tramping up the steps. Bottles clinking. The front door doesn't crash open. They've gone up onto the garage.

I used to think of Ursula as just passive and apathetic, just an alcoholic kid, a dead end. She enrolled in a course at the Poly-tech—not photography, she's given up on that—but she stopped going after a fight with a tutor who, she claimed, after coming home with the news that she was quitting and a dozen cans of Speight's Extra Gold that was selling at the time for $9.95, was "a condescending fucking arsehole," and now she's spending her student loan on bourbon and Benson & Hedges and caps of oil and twenty-dollar foils. But Ursula is generous. Whenever I run out of money—which is often—she buys me cigarettes and alcohol without asking for, without even expecting, any payback. In these last crazy few weeks, as I've tried to block out any reminders of my impending exams, she and I have spent a lot of long evenings watching TV and drinking and smoking, wrapped up in a blanket, together sometimes, on the couch.

Her room is papered in posters of Kurt Cobain now, little else apart from her waterbed and a supermarket trolley full of clothes in there.

We don't talk much when we drink, the both of us being quite businesslike about the whole thing—we finish whole 1.125 liter bottles of bourbon in a night together, nights when the two of us would lurch silently together down to the two-four at 2 A.M. to buy more Coke and Zig-Zags with her money. One time when she did talk she told me that her abortion wasn't really an abortion: she was at school at the time, suspected she was pregnant (she never said why she suspected, what had happened, why she hadn't got a normal one, and I never asked), and so she went on a drinking binge for a month, ate only Farex baby food until she miscarried. She was fifteen at the time, staying in a friend's flat in Holloway Road in Wellington. The father was some older guy she met at a party at this flat. She quit school after this and moved down here to get away from her parents properly, saw Matt and Nick's ad in the *Otago Daily Times* and was the first one to ring— from the Dunedin Railway Station, all her stuff in one big back-pack. She bought her waterbed later that day out of the same newspaper and Matt picked it up in what is now the Draize Train.

This, her immediate past, is all we get out of her. All I get out of her at least: Matt and Nick barely speak to her now apart from when they ask if she wants any gear from Caversham.

Some part of me finds her hard, sordid little life—finds her— compulsive. Some part of me wants to find out why she lives like this and why she does the things she does. Some part of me wants to understand a sixteen-year-old girl who can be like this, drink like this, fuck guys like the way she tells me those drunk-en nights. She laughs when she tells me about the miscarriage, laughs about how much she was drinking:

"All day every day, man."

But sometimes late at night—there were many nights—

when I see the phone cord trailing across the hall and under her door and I hear her crying and murmuring quietly to someone in there I'll find myself standing in the hall, suddenly emptily lonely and alone, wondering if there's more than what she's told me, if there's someone else, if there's not some other awful secret that makes her cry, that makes getting drunk with me not enough for her.

I get jealous.

I haven't touched her. I want to.

No, I don't.

I haven't touched her, no, I have not.

Now I'm opening my door. Now I'm going out there to let today happen.

I pull the front door open and there's the Draize Train and Studholme Hall opposite's catching the sun and the white concrete's glare blinds me, sends further headache pulses back behind my eyes. I stand there in the porch with my eyes closed, fumbling for my cigarettes in my jeans pocket. I can hear them talking quietly—one voice at least—over on the garage. Plus bottles clinking.

I light my cigarette and with squinted eyes edge around the end of the hedge and onto the crumbling brick shelf above the steps. I shuffle along holding the straggly hedge's gnarled branches, my head tilted back to keep my cigarette's end away from what few leaves are left.

"Right, Souse?" Matt's voice along from me. He laughs but not cruelly.

"Yep. Daylight's a bit of a shock that's all," I growl past my cigarette.

I reach the step to the garage roof and Ursula's sitting on the edge looking down over the street. Nick, then Matt, sitting on rusty chrome kitchen chairs that have been up here since Orientation, an empty box at the other end for me, two crates of Speight's, jugs, cigarettes, lighters, et cetera, et cetera.

"Into it, boy," Nick says as I edge past behind them to my box.

"Yeah boy," I say, and take my seat. "Fill us a jug then."

"You *are* going to help pay for this aren't you, Souse," he says as he opens another bottle. Matt's leaning back in his chair, feet on a crate.

"He's good for it, Nick. Don't worry, mate," Matt says and pats Nick on the shoulder. I hide my surprise by exhaling smoke toward Studholme, leaning forward, elbows on knees, supercool.

"Yeah, mate, you know I'm good for it," I say.

Nick passes the jug he's filled to me and says, "Right, charge your glasses, boys. Here's to a . . . let's all make a toast, right?" He looks around us, across to the trees of Studholme, makes a gesture with one hand.

"Here's to getting drunk in the sun, going to this party, scoring free booze, dropping some hallucinogenics, scoring a moisty each, and having sex while tripping." Ursula laughs and we drink. "Matt?"

He pauses, thinks for a while. "Here's to us and to how long we've known each other. To being friends for a long time," he says quietly. I can't tell if he's being sarcastic or not.

"Yep," says Nick. "Cheers," he and I say, and drink. "Souser."

"Here's to . . ." I'm trying to think of something to say, something moving, something real-sounding, " . . . um . . ." something real or something cool, something funny, " . . . here's to . . . like . . . just being . . . young men."

"Yep, cheers," says Nick, and drinks. Matt just drinks. Nick turns to Ursula. He's actually acting like he's MCing something.

"Got one, Ursula?"

She's hunched over, her jug tucked into her lap.

"To the future," she says, definitely sarcastic, then she looks up and smiles. "And to beer."

"Yep, to future beers," says Nick.

We all have another drink and a strained silence descends as Nick sits back down.

It's muggy and humid. The sun occasionally appears as we keep drinking, but mostly there's just a lead-gray brightness glaring through the clouds that makes my head throb. Each of us here, including Ursula, has at least five thousand dollars' worth of student loan. Sometimes I hear firecrackers going off somewhere down in the city.

"Nick. Hey, um, Nick," I say, after the silence goes on a little too long.

He doesn't answer, just drinks from his jug, looking down the hill at some girls walking up the other side of Dundas from Leith Street.

"Nick."

Ursula raises her eyes from her jug and looks at Nick, then looks back down at her jug. Nick sits forward on his chair, looking down the street, past me as I stare at him.

"Nick?"

Between us Matt sighs, stares at the ground.

"Nick?"

He drinks from his jug.

The glare seems to brighten with the afternoon and the mugginess gets more intense. I'm sweating, can feel the sweat rolling down my ribs, tickling the folds of fat above the belt on my jeans. Earlier, as the girls passed on the other side of the hill, Nick said, "I sense moisture," and Ursula had sniggered.

"We should have some music," Matt says.

"Did you recognize any of those chicks?" Nick says, brightening.

"Might be . . . Salmond maybe?" Matt says.

"You'll be in then, Souse," Nick says, looking at me for a quick second.

"Oh, I think they're more like rugbyhead types," Matt says, and Nick looks away.

"So?"

"So they probably wouldn't go for guys like us," I venture.

Nick snorts. "Speak for yourself, Souse. And if the rumors are correct, isn't it *you* . . . that goes for *them*?"

"Nick," Matt says, looking at him.

"What?"

"Just . . ."

"What?" He starts to laugh, glances at me. *"Matt?"*

"What did you mean when you said hallucinogenics before?" I say quickly.

Nick sighs, looks away. "If you must know, ask the drug baroness there," he says tiredly, pointing his jug at Ursula.

She looks up and smiles at me. "I scored some microdots, man, off the guys at Caversham."

"Oh."

I wait.

"What're . . . microdots?"

Nick sighs.

"LSD, man. Four microdots for a hundred and twenty bucks," she says, and Nick's nodding his head looking at no one and then she laughs, looking at us, and Matt laughs too, looking back at her, then Nick laughs loudly and jumps to his feet and crouches down, fists balled, and shouts, "We're gonna have a *good* time . . ." in this American accent, and then I start laughing too, trying to catch up.

I have no sense of the time. The beer is making me less hungry but I feel weak and I've smoked too many cigarettes because they calm hunger pangs. The heat's everywhere, rising up from the concrete of the garage, hovering around us like a cloud. I try to just not move, to stay cool. Matt moves the crates into the shade of the hedge but there's really no sun, just this dead glow from the sky like the afterimage of a flashbulb.

Someone lets off a skyrocket down on Forth Street but there are no flashes or lights, just a whistle and a bang and a few small puffs of smoke.

To wait and drink here until nine o'clock seems just too impossible an ordeal, but really, there's nothing else to do.

"I know man, let's shave our heads," Nick says.

He's leaning back in his chair with his shirt off, and he's not as thin as he used to be but he's still got a good body.

"I'll be in for that," says Matt seriously, which shouldn't surprise me but does, for some reason.

"Ursula?" says Nick, grinning this bright, famous grin.

She shakes her head, smiling back at him, and I can definitely sense something between them, though Nick would never touch her, he's said.

"No way, man."

"Souse? You up for it?"

"Yeah, I suppose."

"*Right.*" He's up, jumps down off the side of the garage instead of negotiating the shelf, runs up the stairs and his boots clump on the porch.

Ursula gets up too and clings to the hedge unsteadily, peering down through her hair at the crumbling brick shelf as she steps down.

"Where are *you* going?" I say.

"Toilet."

There's a silence for a while as she finds her way inside. Then Matt turns to me and says, "Do you like her, Souse?"

"No *way*, man."

"It's just, like you've been spending a bit of time with her, I thought maybe something was going on."

"Fuck *off*. No way, man. She's damaged goods," I say, shaking my head.

"Okay, man, just asking." He sips his beer. A silence.

"Nick's fucking loving this isn't he?" I say almost bitterly.

"He's just trying to have some fun, Souse, that's all. It's just fun. Don't let him get to you. He doesn't mean anything, it's just that he gets bored easily."

"Yeah, right," I say.

Matt smiles at me but his eyes look glassy. "Don't worry, man. Everything will turn out fine."

And now I'm getting up, muttering something about a piss and climbing down to the steps and as I get to the front door I hear the living room door slam at the end of the hall.

I hesitate outside the door to my room.

Looking at the closed living room door, hearing laughter behind, a girl's, a deeper voice, and looking at the bathroom door and looking into the darkness of my room.

Then I'm walking quickly into my room and shutting the door behind me, lighting a cigarette and smoking it furiously, walking back and forth across my room for a while, then sitting down and leaning against the side of my bed, my head resting against the mattress, my hand reaching under the bed to touch the fabric that covers the butt of the rifle.

And but I have to put a bullet in my pocket so I can calm down enough to go back out there before my absence gets noticed though.

Nick shaves Matt's mohawk off, which doesn't take long.

Matt shaves Nick's dreads off, which takes longer.

Nick shaves me.

All done with Matt's electric razor and two extension cords while we kneel, leaning our heads over the edge of the garage so the hair falls down to the footpath. A couple of people passing whistle and cheer.

And it feels good when Ursula looks at the three of us sitting back down drinking again and shakes her head and says, "Man, you guys look real scary."

The first crate's finished and we've just opened the fourth bottle in the second when it starts to get darker. We only notice because now we can see the flashes of skyrockets down over Forth and Clyde. Nick's changed clothes. Ursula's slumped over, still sitting in the same position on the edge of the roof. Matt's gone a little quieter, his mood darker with the alcohol.

I'm drinking steadily, more than the others though no one's noticed.

There are more people passing in the street as it gets darker, more people letting off fireworks down around Castle Street. Sometimes the crackles and bangs sound close to us, echoing back off Studholme and the castle.

Nick takes every opportunity to speak to girls over the edge of the garage, invites them up to touch his head. I'm mostly silent now, the beer flattening things out.

Nick suggests we walk down and get some fish and chips. I tell him I'll wait here, I don't want anything. He and Matt leave.

While they're gone Ursula only lifts her head four times, to drink from her jug. Four times, I count them, watching her. She doesn't speak once. I spill some beer down my shirt when I tip the jug before it reaches my mouth. Four times, saying nothing, while I watch her sitting there in her jersey and her black jeans and the little skirt over the top, picturing her body, her small breasts, how white her skin is.

Four times and she doesn't speak to me once.

They're back.

I can hear them talking and laughing just down the street. The streetlights are on. There are more firecrackers going off now. Ursula is still silent and slumped.

"What's going on here?" Nick says, climbing up the shelf.

". . ."

"We have food." Matt throws the package up to Nick and climbs up after him.

"Still awake, Souse?" he says when he sees me slumped on my box.

"Yup."

"Gonna eat?"

"Nup."

"Fair enough."

He and Nick open up the paper and start eating and the smell sickens me and wakes up my stomach at the same time and I'm suddenly really hungry, but not wanting to eat because I haven't all day and it seems like purity to hold back and watch while they stuff their mouths with potato and batter, it feels like strength as I light another cigarette and look away over the city but the cigarette tastes like shit and I'm suddenly weak with hunger, my vision blurring and I don't think it's the beer and my eyes are filled with water and my stomach's making sounds weakly and so I throw my cigarette over the side and mutter, "Can I have a chip?" and Nick grunts.

I eat one and it tastes so good I can't stand it so I grab a couple in my hand and sit back, trying to eat them slowly but I don't and so I get some more and eat them and eat more, taking a big handful and sitting back and I'm eating all that until I'm licking the salt off my palms and fingers and grabbing some more and they don't even notice or care when I'm leaning over the package eating more and more chips until I suddenly feel this weight in my stomach, the brute fullness of it, and I can picture the mashed up mound of fat and potato just sitting in there, a ball of it, leaking fat onto my body, giving me energy to be stupider than I already am and I'm so angry at myself I sit back on my box bolt upright and drink half a jug in one long drink and light a cigarette immediately but it does no good because I can still taste the salt on my lips.

—

It's completely dark but light up here on the garage because the streetlight outside Strangeways is on. We all look pale and white and my eyes feel wide. The shadows are harsh and Nick's eyes look scarily green, almost alien, the pupils just pinpoints as he hands out the microdots.

Mine is a tiny black tablet like plastic, the size and shape of a lower-case u. I put it in my jeans pocket.

Nick lights the empty fish and chip paper with his cigarette lighter, throws it flaming out onto the street and gets an idea.

The four of us, me, Matt, Ursula, swaying, still sipping from the foam in the bottom of her jug, and Nick, in the little courtyard in the back of Strangeways, standing in front of the mound of fat black plastic D.C.C. rubbish bags that fills half of it, that's stacked up to the level of the grass around the castle, which looms blackly above us, the windows deeper shades of dark. Crackles and bangs away somewhere. I'm so close to Ursula I could touch her. I'm shaking with tension.

"Alright. Let's do it," Nick says and picks up a plastic supermarket bag and lights it with his cigarette lighter. It catches and shrivels, smokes a thin trail of thick black smoke from tiny blue flames, and he drops it into the rubbish quickly.

A full, swollen rubbish bag instantly pops open and horrible stuff bursts out that I stare at closely and we step back. Things hiss and fizzle and smoke, then flames start to catch hold and we step back further, sip our jugs, entranced.

As the flames grow bigger and hotter the sounds become more alien and ominous, pops, muffled, deep within the rubbish, hissing wet stuff, scrabbling, like something alive deep inside this mound that's as big as a car.

The castle starts to look orange and strange as the flames grow higher, running over the bags that burst and settle, and we step further back. The heat gets quickly intense.

"Fucking hell," Nick says.

"Better be careful of the house," Matt says.

"*Fuck*, man," Nick says, excitedly, as the fire becomes suddenly huge.

"And now we should each burn a book," Nick says, and I'm snapped out of a dream. He's looking from Matt to me, back to Matt.

"Each one of us has to choose a book of our own to burn. One with like symbolic value. Or sentimental value. Alright?"

He doesn't look at Ursula because he knows she's got no books.

"Okay," I say, slowly, before anyone else, which turns Nick's attention to me.

"Alright. Matt?"

"Yeah. Yeah, okay," Matt sighs, standing stock still, like me, staring into the fire, like me, orange light playing over his face and shaven head. He looks stoned, his eyes bloodshot and desperate.

"Right. Let's do it. Get your books."

We go inside and separate into our different rooms and a few seconds later I hear Ursula's uneven footsteps come down the hall and into her room.

I pick up *A Book of Murder*.

Nick brings back sunglasses and hands a pair each to me and Matt, puts his on then burns his Heinemann's Legal Dictionary. Throws it into the middle of the smoldering mass and shouts, "Fuck you."

Matt steps up and throws in *Morrissey and Marr: The Severed Alliance*.

"Matt," I say and Nick says, "No, no, let him. This is great."

Ursula steps forward clutching a thick pad of brown jotter paper. As she throws it in it flutters open and there's tiny black spidery handwriting all over every page. She doesn't say anything. The fire is reflected in the boys' sunglasses as they stand side by side staring into it.

"Souse," Nick says, "It's your turn, man."

I step forward and rip off the cover with the clown and flick it into the flames. Then I carefully rip out a handful of pages that approximates the introduction. A handful of pages for chapter one, fluttering, rising over the heat, bursting into flame in midair, casting strange shadows like ghosts on the walls of the castle.

A handful for chapter two and I screw them up and throw them hard into the fire.

Chapter three. Chapter four and I'm tearing at the pages angrily, ripping the spine in half, wrenching it apart with both hands, papercuts slicing through the soft flesh on the insides of my index fingers, chapter five I tear out page by page by page, crumpling each one and throwing it in hard without looking at any of them, and there's blood all over my fingers again.

And I'm holding the thick back page of the book, I realize, and I look down and see a picture of the author on the inside back page that I never saw before because I never read the final chapter, never found out the conclusions, and I've flicked the rectangle of cardboard into the fire before it processes that the photograph was of a red- and short-haired woman in her thirties in a black turtleneck, sitting in front of a high bookshelf full of old books, staring downward just like Anna did, a sad-eyed woman, with sad eyes, Dr. S. J. Johansson is Dr. Simone J. Johansson is a woman, and the possibility that I may have been wrong, horribly, fatally wrong for so long, for a year, for forever, occurs to me and my stomach drops for all the things I miss, for my fucking dumb poverty, for what I won't believe and can't comprehend, what happens without my knowledge and all I cannot imagine outside me but then the page is gone, vaporized in an instant in the intense heat.

"Souse? What the fuck was that?"

"Leave . . . me . . . alone."

". . ."

"Let's finish the beer and go to this fucking party."

"Gosh, Souse. You're so . . . *force*ful."

Reeling down the steps, when we finish the beer and throw the bottles in the fire, after we've burnt one of the armchairs and the kitchen table, drunk, a blur, slipping down the steps we are, the four—three?—of us are, leaving for the party, and we're on Dundas heading down the hill not saying anything and Nick whoops sometimes and there's people coming toward us so he gets quiet and he watches them.

It's a big group of nine or ten boys in rugby jerseys and jeans and we're passing through them silently and they're parting just a little and Matt gets jostled but Nick and I don't because we've got a look in our eyes, and we get past the last two boys just as I hear a voice say, "Souser."

Turning back, ready for anything, and the other boys keep walking, leaving this boy, and it's Henry, ex-head boy of our school.

"Lads," he says past me, to Nick a few steps ahead and Matt away down the hill.

"Waddaya up to," I slur. He looks at me.

"Just been down at Sarah Hills' party," he says. "What about you boys?"

"Sright, mate. Cruising down there too." I mumble.

"Yeah, yeah."

"Hey, Henners," Nick says from beside me.

"Tinny. Long time."

"Yeah, mate, yeah, mate," Nick growls, taking the piss, which Henry doesn't notice. I sway backward and have to step back with one foot.

"Getting smashed tonight?" he says, grinning at Nick.

"Mother*fucked*," Nick says. "Later."

"Yep," Henry says, and Nick walks off.

"What's it . . . like?" I mutter at Henry, at his chest.

"Not bad ay, few familiar faces."

"Yeah."

"Sure you'll recognize a few people."

"Like . . . ?"

"Oh, Sarah, Sebastian's there, few of us Salmond types, oh

yeah, Rebecca Gilbert's there. . . ." I look up into his eyes and he's looking down at me and they're full of kindness. "So you might be in tonight hey, Souse?"

"I don't . . . know what you're talking about," I say, and my eyes might close for a while.

"Yeah you do."

"The fuck are you talking about."

"Seriously man. I understand. You can talk to me. Just the boys here."

I'm shaking my head, back and forth.

"Alls I'm saying, Souse, you're a figure of legend."

Shaking my head, back and forth, staring at the concrete.

"Have a good one, mate," he makes a clicking sound with his mouth and then he's gone and I turn slowly and Matt and Nick are gone and the street's empty and all I can hear is music from Sarah's house at the foot of the hill and I'm scraping through the pockets of my jeans and peering down at the stuff I find, sand, fluff, a tag from a beer can, a bullet, tobacco and there it is, a little black bit of plastic, and I eat it quickly, licking my palm then examining it in the harsh light from the street-light, staring down at my hand with one eye closed because it was so small I couldn't even feel it in my mouth.

Out the front of Sarah's house everything is dead and gray in the bitter, bright light and there's music from beyond the house, round in back, and it's Nirvana again, plus voices, lots of voices, murmurs, loud laughs, shouts, squeals, and the roaring of fire. There are firecrackers going off in the darkness all around me, each way down Dundas, ahead up in the trees of the Botanic Gardens, back behind me beyond Studholme and Arana.

The streetlight above me flickers and hisses and goes out and I sway there, in the warm dark and the sounds of explosions, the music, the voices. And I realize I've come to a point where maybe a decision can be made, where maybe I can choose to walk back up the hill and get into bed and sleep and get up early to study for exams or maybe just go back up to bed and sleep and then buy a newspaper in the morning and look for a job or maybe just go back up to bed and turn out the lights and go to sleep.

The options pass before me, but in them I realize I am picturing myself maybe twelve years old, in blue sweatshirt and gray shorts, an image from a school photo in form one, the last photo of myself I can remember looking at and thinking I was good-looking; I realize that I am standing here slumped, not twelve, not young, drunk, ugly, alone, and I remember that the LSD will kick in, that I have a letter on my desk and a gun under my bed and that no one knows and no one cares and the inertia is suddenly too great, it crushes the options and carries me through the tiny gate and along a dark concrete corridor formed by the wall of the house and a fence, a corridor red and flickering at the far end that this bitter determination carries me to— to see this out, to find out conclusions, to take this to its logical end.

A huge bonfire at the end of the section, burning under a tree that's partly on fire also. Three smaller fires scattered around the backyard that's just a big expanse of gravel. Dark figures, forty, fifty, silhouetted by the flames, standing, sitting in groups, some in armchairs, some on the ground. Smoke and ash whirl away over the rooftops. Nirvana playing louder now from a stereo in the window of a room facing the backyard. Laughing and murmuring, shouting, the roaring of the fires, someone shouts "*Bazza*," and it sounds like they're facing me and I move along the back of the house past the stereo room and there's a lit window and inside there are more people in a kitchen and beyond in the living room another thirty people at least, three guys spotting up on the oven, people sitting on a mattress drinking port, a keg on newspaper, two plastic bowls of orange liquid with lemon slices floating in it on the kitchen bar, strangers everywhere and I know none of these people.

Turning away from the window I can see no faces, just shapes against flames, and I take a step toward it all and slip on the gravel, which covers the whole backyard, just gravel and a thin concrete path that leads only to a washing line, a garage and the tree that's withered and smoldering all over one side where the bonfire is.

With all the fire the dark is darker.

I badly want a drink but going in to that keg is not an option. Light a cigarette and walk around to the fence so I can see light on faces to find Nick or Matt or just anyone. The song playing is now "In Bloom."

Passing three girls leaning against the fence talking, drinking from wine bottles. The girl that's speaking sees the other two look at me and turns, still speaking, sees me, turns back to them and they exaggeratedly focus their attention on her and I pass them and try to snort but nothing comes out.

Passing one of the smaller fires and I glance at the faces to see anyone but they're passing around a joint and their faces are flickering and a guy with dreads stares back at me for a second after he sucks on it and passes it on and I try to pretend I'm just casually glancing and he says, "Take . . . a fucking . . . *pic*ture," and the others turn to look and I look away quickly and move toward another fire.

Turning the bullet round and round in my pocket, glancing at faces, not long enough to catch anyone's eye and not long enough to recognize anyone. A big group of boys in black standing near the garage with their feet on brewer's dozens of Speight's laugh loudly at something and I veer left, away from them, eventually toward the big bonfire and the tree and a circle of people, of black figures, surround it at a distance, all their backs to me. I stop a meter behind them and someone turns a black shadowed face to me, forcing me to look at the ground until they turn away. The people around the fire are mostly silent, just staring into the flames, drinking from beer cans, bottles, cups.

I stand there for minutes, looking at the fire in the gaps between people.

"Repent Satan," the voice behind me says, and I turn quickly and there's a guy standing next to a girl watching the fire past me and he stops talking when I turn and looks vaguely at me, without seeing me because I am just a shadow to him. The girl laughs, and says, "Lust hard by hate, from Aroer to Nebo," and he, still looking at me, says, "Na, just a rink, last weekend," and then, "Can we help you?" and I mutter "fuck you" and the girl crinkles her forehead and says "arsehole" and the guy says "fuck *you*" and I turn back and walk away around the circle of people and the flames but there's no one, no one, and so I have to get a drink at last and maybe Sarah's in there and maybe she'll walk up to me again like she did and so I veer away from the fire and back toward the house.

"Souse, you sick fuck," a voice says from the darkness by the garage.

And it's Sebastian.

"Sebastian. What are you doing," I say.

"Drinking all the pitchers, cruising all the bitches," he says.

"Oh."

His hair has been dyed pitch black and it's all slicked back and there are other boys standing around him and I don't know any of them. They're all drinking Speight's Old Dark from bottles and they're all wearing black rugby jerseys. Sebastian is too and he introduces me by pointing to each one without looking at them.

"This is Death. This is Ibex. This is Howitzer, this is Toad, Pan, Simon, and this is Pazuzu, of the rotting genitals. This is Souse. Another madman from Boys' High."

One of the boys, Death maybe, has high, spiky black hair and it's got something on it that makes it shine and his eyes are really black and he watches me.

"Hi," I say.

"Soon," he whispers to me and smiles and the others ignore me and then he turns away too. Sebastian's lit a cigarette, blows smoke up to the black sky.

"So what's going on in the world of Souse," he says and doesn't look at me, scans the crowd.

"Nothing much," I say.

"Nothing much, he says."

Some boy bumps Sebastian from behind and he turns really quickly, like he was waiting for it to happen, and hisses, "Come on, fuckboy," with his cigarette clamped between his teeth, and he grabs this boy who looks only fifteen or sixteen and pulls him close and jabs the cigarette's end at the boy's face. The boy's freaking out, recoils away from Sebastian, mutters, "fuck you," but a little high-pitched and walks away, looks back over his shoulder. Sebastian spits the cigarette after him.

"I'll see you later, Sebastian," I say.

"Hey, whatever, Souse," he says and he puts one hand on my shoulder and with the other points away somewhere and without looking at me he pushes me into the crowd.

Walking in the door into the kitchen squinting my eyes against the light and the music's louder in here because one of the stereo's speakers points from the door of a bedroom into the living room and "In Bloom" is just ending.

One of the guys spotting up turns around, bent over the oven, and he's wearing swimming goggles and holding a table knife in each hand and he exaggeratedly looks me up and down and then he says, "Self-destruction therefore sought implies not thy contempt but anguish and regret."

I stare into his blank glassy goggles.

"What did you say," I mutter in a monotone.

"Bitch, pick a heart full of holes, like you did your pet's."

"*What.*"

"Hello? Dude. Wake the fuck up. Because you can have a spot if you've got a cigarette."

So I can tell him "alright," and give him a cigarette and another guy gives me a two liter Coke bottle cut in half while the boy with the goggles holds the knives down on a glowing red element and as the first distorted echoing bass notes of "Come As You Are" start rumbling from the speaker he dabs the left-hand knife on the end ball of a line of little balls of marijuana on the oven, turns quickly, the knife smoking already, and I put my mouth over the bottle opening and he rubs the ends of the knives together under the bottle and I suck in hard. But half the spot falls off the knife and I only get a little smoke and I step out of their way as they hurriedly crouch on the floor to find what they've dropped.

There are four girls and two boys sitting on the mattress in the living room passing around a big bottle of port. I pour a glass of punch and step over and between their feet, heading toward the door to the hallway, which is full of people. In the corner of the living room is a rusty logburner with no door and ash has spilt on the floor and been tramped into the carpet.

I lean in the door to the hallway and there's twenty people at least, sitting and standing in the corridor and walking through them all seems just too much.

I ask a boy next to me where Sarah is and he says, "fuck's Sarah?" so I have to go down there, have to find a familiar face to ask.

It's hard but I take strength from a lyric I can hear playing back in the living room behind me, a lyric that helps me almost smile as I pick my way between feet and legs and people moan and laugh and mutter, their bodies and limbs a tangle down the hallway, and he swears that he doesn't have a gun, and I pass a door to a bathroom where someone's being sick in the toilet and a door to a darkened room where there is muttering and shifting sounds on a bed and small slapping noises and then another door and it's a bedroom dimly lit by a cluster of candles in the fireplace and there's Sarah sitting in front of it between two other girls and they're waving incense sticks. She's changed. She has a nose-ring and small round blonde ponytails all over her head and a silver spot on her forehead.

"Sarah," I say and all three of them turn to me at once and I blush.

"Hey man," she says, smiling lazily, her eyes bloodshot.

"Can I come in?" I say.

"Of *course* you can. Of *course* you can come in," she says nodding at me while the other two girls turn back to the fireplace. I step behind them, past the door and there's a futon that I sit on the edge of.

"It's a good party," I say to the backs of their heads and there's a brief silence and all three of them laugh at once but when Sarah and the girl to her left stop laughing the other one doesn't and rolls over the floor laughing, her dreads draped over her face. Sarah swings around to sit cross-legged facing me.

"Shut up, Lynn," she says smiling at me and the girl says, "I can't," between laughs, which I think get more strained and fake-sounding.

"So you think it's a good party," Sarah says, nodding at me with a fake-serious expression.

"Yeah, I . . . think."

Don't you dare make fun of me

"Nick's here."

"I was looking for him outside."

"So . . . I hear you've been scoring your little flatmate up there. Is it . . . Ursula?" She tries to wink when she says Ursula but she can't wink and just blinks both eyes.

"No, no, that's bullshit," I say.

Don't you dare, don't you

"Come on, it's alright. They *do* say don't screw the crew but *I* say give me convenience or give me death," she turns and says this to the other girl who says, "mmm," as she blows on an incense stick.

"*It's not true,*" I hiss and she looks back at me suddenly serious.

"I wouldn't get so worried. It's better than your regular pick-up lines."

I'm silent, looking for my cigarettes.

"Rebecca Gilbert's somewhere here tonight, did you know that?" She's looking at me and I'm looking at my cigarettes and the other two girls are silent.

"So?"

"So how do you think she's going to feel when she sees you?"

"You're full of shit."

"*Am* I."

"No shame."

"You guys have just got no idea how warped that saying is, have you?"

"No . . ."

"Get a fucking life, Souse. It's not an affirmation. It's a pity."

Don't you dare

"Fuck . . . you."

"Fuck *you*," the other girl says and they've all turned on me and I stand up and kick my cup of punch over and then I suck on my cigarette and drop it casually on the futon and I'm walking out the door as Sarah shouts *"arsehole,"* and one of the girls screams and I think of anything, of Sebastian, and I mutter, trying it out for the first time, "I'll fucking rape you, you bitches," but it sounds half-hearted and a boy standing in the hallway hears me and laughs out loud and says, "Man, that's cool, don't take any shit" and then he looks hard at my hair and then my face and then he says, "Man, you look like a prisoner of war"

and standing at the kitchen bar smoking a cigarette I drink cup after cup of the sickly punch that tastes more strongly of vodka only at the bottom and speak to and look at no one until Sarah comes out really drunk and screaming and hits me in the chest screaming, "you burnt my duvet, you really burnt it you fucker," until three rugbyhead boys standing over the keg pull her off me and one of them says to me, "Mate, she's fucked, maybe you'd just better leave," earnestly, almost apologetically, and adrenaline is pulsing through me as I watch her being held by these guys, screaming at me, her eyes never more full of drunken hate, and he's holding her with one hand on her arm and the other hand over her shoulder on her breast and I don't answer him, just finish my drink and ladle another one into my cup and then I stagger as I step out the kitchen door and hear her voice cry out, "fucking sick *arsehole*" and I stagger around the house in the flickering firelight and people's stares, holding the walls for support, and I see the first girl I saw when I arrived and I look her straight in the eye and say, "nice tits"

up Dundas I punch concrete walls until my knuckles bleed and then sobbing and growling I head-butt a garage door for a while

slip on the mossy steps up to Strangeways and don't try to save myself as I fall against the steps with my arms held to my sides and slide to the bottom and rip my jeans and then I do it again

kick in the front door and a splinter of wood a meter long falls into the hallway and the darkness and the silence and a note I try to read with one eye shut is blue-tacked to the door of my room and says *Dick! lost you came back then gone to town Matt's gone for a drive somewhere Nick*

kick my door in and pull the gun out from under my bed and I scream with frustration when the cloth cover catches on the trigger guard and smash the stereo with the butt I swing the gun over my head the cover still half on and smash the light hanging above me and bash my stereo again and again and then the speakers too punch holes through the wall and through Lou's face on the *Coney Island Baby* poster and plaster dust and then the window through the curtains and swinging the big heavy rifle around and around above me and it hits me in the head and barely noticing and sobbing and grunting and growling and glass and plaster and plastic and blood

a second's pause in noise I can hear the telephone ringing and thumping on the front door and I'm able to stand the rifle behind the bedroom door

into the darkened hallway where a thin sliver of bright white light lies the length of the corridor from the front door crooked and ajar to the back door wide open to a faint red flickering glow and the phone's shrieking

knock the phone off the table then pick the handset up as I'm staring into the gap between the front door and the splintered doorframe and a shape moves into it and out again as I hold the handset to my ear and a voice says "Richey? Richey?" and I say nothing, motionless, watching the gap where the shape appears again and the voice in the phone says "Is Richey there? It's his mother? For Richey? It's Mum" a girl's voice from the front door saying "Hello? Is someone here?" another harder knocking and the front door creaking and scraping slowly open and the shape of a short girl is silhouetted against the streetlight with one hand in the air and one hand holding a bag and she says "Hello? Is that Richey?" and dropping the phone with a clatter that makes her jump and she says "I can't see anything. Am I at the right house? Is Richard here? I'm looking for Richard Sauer" and growling terrible "No fuck off Anna just fuck off" she stops silent for a moment neither of us able to see the other and says "Do you know my name" and tensing all my muscles and screaming *"Fuck off"* and running down the hallway and she disappears into the porch and scream-ing "it's not my fault you're dead" and smashing the front door shut in her face and turning back to my room but the door creaks open again because the lock's smashed so holding it shut scream-ing "fuck off leave me alone fuck off fuck off"

and it's after she goes that I wedge the door shut with the piece of wood and go back to my room and shut the door and sit among the plaster and broken plastic and wires that I try to set fire to and but soon I'm loading the gun's magazine with drunken shaking fingers that stop shak-ing after a while

"Ursula?" Knock, knock. "Ursula? You home?"

A mutter. A moan. Shifting, bubbling sound of thewaterbed.

" . . . who is it?" A slurred sigh.

"It's me."

"Who?"

"Can I come in?"

"Fuck *off*, James."

"It's . . . Richey."

" . . ."

I turn the knob slowly until the door loosens in the door-frame and swings open a few inches. It's black, utter darkness in there.

"You asleep?" I ask in monotone.

Shifting sounds again and her voice a few feet away just inside the door.

"Na, man. Come in." A sigh.

I push the door open further and step inside, facing the bed with my hand behind me. I push the door shut until it latches. The room is deep in darkness, thin lines of light outline the curtains of the window that overlooks the street. The bed and her, invisible. I pad slowly round to the foot of the bed and lay what I've brought down on the ground out of sight.

"What's going on, man," from the head of the bed by the door. I sit on the foot of the bed and face away from her.

"I just . . ."

" . . ."

"I went . . . to the party . . ."

"..."

A thought occurs to me. "Were you there?"

"Na, just went to bed ay."

"..."

"Are you alright, man? I heard all this shit going on. You sound like you're crying . . ."

And suddenly I am, uncontrollably, hunched over hugging my knees, crying properly. In between hitching sobs there's the thought that this is just because I'm drunk and that crying in front of her is pathetic and weak, and that crying at all means there's something wrong maybe, and at this I jerk upright and wipe my face roughly with my sleeve and sniff hard and the waterbed shifts behind me. I can tell she's sitting up now.

"What's wrong man?" Her voice level with me, behind.

"Fucking rude party. Should be glad you missed it."

"..."

"Usual fucking pretentious people."

"Yeah."

"I just . . ."

"..."

"I feel like . . . I'm going insane sometimes, like . . ."

"Man . . ."

"Like there's nothing for me, you know? I feel like I'm going fucking insane."

"Man, tell me about it."

This is not what I thought was going to happen, this is getting out of control

"Like, I feel like I'm losing it. I just can't go on with this all the time, on and on . . ."

"This what?"

"What?"

"Go on with *what,* man?"

" . . ."

" . . ."

"Just like, everything."

"But every what thing?"

"Like I've got all these expectations, you know? From my parents, and . . . because when you're a guy you're supposed to be . . . all these things . . ."

" . . ."

"But if you're not, you know, you get picked on and you can't afford to make any mistakes because you're supposed to have all your shit together aren't you? If you're a guy you're supposed to know, to be . . ."

" . . ."

"All these things I know I'm not." It sounds so dramatic, it sounds right.

"There's an open bottle of piss down there, man. Can you pass it to me?"

A sudden wave of anger that she could say this. I reach down in the darkness and my fingers touch metal and then along a bit and there's glass and it clinks on something as I pick it up. It gurgles behind me. Angry at her, I say, "You should've seen this fucking party. Just so many fake people."

"Mmm."

"Everyone standing around like they're waiting for someone to take a photo. It's like, look at me, I'm having a good time at my party."

"Yeah, I know."

"Why didn't you go?"

"I was too smashed ay. Wouldn't know anyone anyway."

"There was free piss."

"Yeah? Maybe I should've." She sniggers and I shake my head and sneer, hidden there in the dark, and then I remember what I've just confessed, how vulnerable I've made myself to this dumb, alcoholic bitch and I curse myself, and then I remember what I've said, that it was in fact true and it gets too complex suddenly trying to figure out what to feel and I slump forward.

"I just . . ."

". . ."

". . ."

"Man, sometimes you just sound so unhappy."

"No, no, it's not . . ."

". . ."

"It's not as . . . *simple* as that, anyway."

We sit this way for long minutes. A liquid sound behind me. I light a cigarette and smoke it in the dark. I light a cigarette for her. We don't talk for a long time and I'm thinking about the words, *it's not as simple as that.*

And I'm thinking about the very real possibility that because she is who she is I can tell her what I've told her and she will forget it all, or at least never bring it up again. Realizing that what I have confessed I have confessed into a self-made void, called Ursula, and but that confession itself is a dangerous game because it can mean that change is obliged.

And out of nowhere, because I can't stop myself, comes a test of this axiom, because I can't stop myself.

"When I was at Unicol, me and the boys . . . this was after Orientation . . . we went to this party at the Polytech ballroom that Salmond Hall had organized. . . . And we were so drunk on all this homebrew, and then we were doing all these bongs in the toilets with Mark and the others. . . . And I . . . slipped over . . . into a urinal, and all of them were laughing at me. And later on we did more bongs and we went out into the party and we were cruising around and the others were getting sleazy and stuff . . ."

I think I hear her snigger.

" . . . and one ends up scoring some girl and one disappears as usual and I was left there on my own . . . and I'd just never felt so . . . and I was still trying to pretend that this was all fun and stuff and I was used to it, but I could feel people looking at me, and I've heard all the stories boys tell you about this shit and they all tell you how funny it is and stuff, but when you're actually the one, the one getting chosen and *looked* at and you can't control any of it because you're so drunk it's just . . . so . . . like and what really happened is that . . . like what really happened is there was a girl with blonde hair and she was wearing pink silk summer pajamas, pink summer pajamas because it was a P party and I just saw her and she was like, just . . . so perfect . . . like a summer in a person, I thought of that when I was looking at her and I thought that if she was next to me I could just sleep it off with my head in her lap, you know, nothing . . . bad, or . . . I could just be better if someone like that thought I was alright. If she thought I could be . . . good . . ."

I've lit a cigarette without knowing it.

"And I was so . . . like . . . brave. I've never done anything like this before. I just went straight up to her and stood there in front of her until she noticed me, and I decided I'd say what I really thought. I'd be totally honest. So I tried to say it—'You are like summer in a person'—right to her while she looked at me and everything. Just to say something like that once."

I take a drag, my elbows on my knees. All is silence and I can't stop it now.

"And then she looked at me. She turned away from this other girl to see, and she sees me and she looks me up and down and the look she gives me is . . . was . . . pure contempt. Pure revulsion, just by looking at me she could have this . . . look . . . on her face."

A long drag.

"And the way I felt I just wanted to give her back with so much more, I just wanted to . . . grind her up that she could make me feel that way."

There's a long silence. It's completely pitch black in here. Part of me wants to say, "Do you know what I mean?" Part of me wants to say, "I'm very sick." But I don't. I wait. And then she speaks from behind me.

"What did you do, man?"

There's another long silence. I'm not sure what to do.

"What?" I finally say.

"What did you do to her?"

"What do you mean?"

"What . . . did you . . . do . . . to that girl?" the girl's saying. "*Nick.*"

I'm suddenly aware of the faint light in this room, a faint flicker from the streetlight, and my posture, sitting on the frame of the waterbed. Her voice behind me, trembling slightly, a hint, maybe, of excitement, the smell of smoke, the high ceiling, the thousands of men like me in rooms like this all over the country, adamantine chains, the blinding glare of the fact that *no one understands*, she doesn't understand, *no one understands, or even knows*, a surge of bright white light through me, I'm suddenly aware of my body, power and purpose, right and wrong are just feelings and there are stronger feelings, things move in the void, defend yourself, people are alone and do not comprehend one another, *defend yourself*

"I'm not Nick," I'm saying, standing, grinding my cigarette out on the carpet, reaching down to the ground.

"*What*, man," she says and there's a trace of fear there now.

"No," I'm saying, and laughing, standing up, holding what I have brought with me.

"What do you mean. James?"

"Nup," I'm saying, giddy now.

"Who is it? Matt. Sean? *James* . . . don't fuck around . . ." she's saying

"No no no," I'm saying, shaking my head and trying not to laugh and then I'm holding the gun up in the dark, waving it around, shaking it, pointing it at her as I loom over the bed but she can't see and then suddenly now there's me touching her with it and now there's me explaining quietly, my hand over her mouth and she's jerking and now there's me sitting astride her in the dark pushing my hand on her mouth harder as she struggles and listening hard my head cocked to the window and now there's me stripping the bed with one hand and now there's the rifle my grandfather's rifle from the war the only relic from my parents' home lying along the pillows to her temple and there's my cock hard and the tip hot touching the inside of my thigh and my rage and there's me stripping her and raping her and holding her thighs back against her wide and hitting her hard in her jaw and her nose to stop the cries and things going on too long and tying her up with her pantyhose now and hitting her more for a while and she's shutting up and then

there's a feeling, a feeling like a big long sigh and darkness closing in and swelling up and time slowing down and a big relaxed feeling coming down and I'm moving through the darkness thick like syrup listening for the crying from the bed the sounds become visible things floating in the darkness small red roses dropping petals to the floor that splash on the carpet and turn it all deep red close to black and as I walk slowly to the door leaving her leaving her through the passing of years my feet sink deeper into the liquid with every step and I'm slowed, slowed by its pull, swaying in the dark with my arms waving, the gun abandoned, groping my way through thick red clouds of the petals of her cries that hum and vibrate softly and I know, I know I have to get out, a terrible sense of time running out, the final stretch begun, a last huge exertion, a great imperative roars slowly, far away, *do it*, the door takes a mighty pull to open and red roses spill into the silvered hallway as I stagger through and down and out the back door and stars in a clear sky skewer me with splinters of shivered glass that I snap to free myself and shivering I wade over the embers of the bonfire, a soft reassuring warmth rising around my arms and I'm climbing the wall and crawling through the smoldering grass that warms my blackened hands and rising toward a great darkness, a near abstract black monolith that looms and fills my sight and there's one tiny wooden door with a tiny window at the foot of all this that I hammer at with all certainty but remains shut, no handle just an empty keyhole, hammering, hammering, a glimpse of my face reflected in the window and they say when you're tripping you should never look in the mirror because you might see the devil but what I see is no devil just a pallid oval with no eyes and a gaping maw for a mouth.

Carl Shuker was born in 1974 and is a graduate of the University of Canterbury in Christchurch, and the Victoria University of Wellington, New Zealand. He won the 2006 Prize in Modern Letters for his first novel, *The Method Actors,* the only debut to have ever been so honored. He lives in London.